a place between dreams

A Novel

jess munday

Cover design by Luísa Dias
Edited by Halley Sutton
Interior design and formatting by Lebanon Raingam

ISBN: 979-8-9999601-0-8 (Hardcover)
ISBN: 979-8-9999601-1-5 (Paperback)
ISBN: 979-8-9999601-2-2 (eBook)

Sutro Ink Press, San Francisco, CA

First Edition

For more information, visit: jessmunday.substack.com

a place between dreams

A Note for Readers

This novel contains depictions of domestic violence, substance abuse, mental health crises, and psychological trauma that some readers may find triggering. The story is told from the perspective of someone who commits acts of violence, and while it explores the psychological factors that contribute to abusive behavior, it does not excuse or justify such actions.

A Place Between Dreams examines the devastating cycle of trauma and how untreated wounds can perpetuate violence across generations. Millions of people experience childhood trauma without becoming abusers themselves. This story follows one individual's failure to break that cycle, serving as a cautionary tale about the critical importance of seeking help, taking accountability, and addressing mental health before it's too late.

If you are easy triggered by fiction scenarios involving drug use and addiction, domestic violence, suicidal ideation, or murder, consider if this book is appropriate for you.

Below are some resources for those in need of support:

National Domestic Violence Hotline:
1-800-799-7233 | thehotline.org

National Suicide Prevention Lifeline: 988

SAMHSA National Helpline (Substance Abuse):
1-800-662-4357

Crisis Text Line: Text HOME to 741741

For my mom, Sherry, and my sister, Brianna—
who believed in this story and me, even at times
when I didn't.

Prologue

"911, what's your emergency?" the operator said steadily, with practiced calmness.

There was shouting on the other end of the phone. Voices carried from a distance—a muffled commotion that was just too far away from the receiver to make out any of the words.

"Hello?"

A shrill scream pierced through the muffled sounds. The operator sat up straighter, her head jolting slightly as she listened intently.

"Hello? Is anyone there?"

"Oh my god—hello?" a woman's voice came over the line in a panic.

"Hello, ma'am. What's your emergency?"

"It's my ex-boyfriend," she whispered. Her loud exhales crackled in the operator's headset. "He's at my house. I think he just did something *really* bad. I think—I think he's going to do the same to me."

"I understand you're afraid. I'm going to help you. First, I need your address so I can send officers there right away. You said you're at home?"

"Yes, it's my apartment. I'm at 596 Irving St." Her whispers echoed slightly, suggesting she was hiding in an enclosed space.

"596 Irving Street in San Francisco, correct? I'm sending officers to you right now."

"Mhm. His name is Alexander Tennessee Walker, but he goes by his middle name. Apartment 505. Please hurry." Her voice cracked. She sounded absolutely terrified.

"I just dispatched the officers. They're already on their way. Can you tell me if you're physically hurt? You said he did something bad? What did he do?"

There was some banging, and she could hear a man's voice now in the background.

"Oh god, he found me," she whispered. "Please send someone here, quick."

"They'll be there soon. Can you give me a physical description of him?"

There was more pounding in the background. The woman's breath was growing more strained, and the man's voice was growing louder.

"Please, Tenny," she begged. "I know somewhere deep down you still care. Just please try to remember that. You don't have to hurt me."

"I'm staying on the line with you until help arrives. The officers are just minutes away. If you can, try to keep talking to me. I'm right here with you."

Then there was a series of loud bangs, followed by more

distant shouting.

"Please, just go!" the woman shouted.

"I know this is difficult, but is there anything you can tell me that will help the officers when they arrive? Is your ex-boyfriend armed? Have you seen any weapons?"

The banging got louder and more rhythmic. Then the distinct sound of splintering wood tore through the receiver, followed by a hollow thud.

"Oh my god, he broke the door down," she squeaked into the phone. A sharp intake of breath, followed by silence.

"I understand. What door? What part of the home are you in?"

"Don't touch me." The woman's words came out like a growl.

"Like I said, I just wanna talk." The man sounded like he was right above the receiver now. His voice was eerily calm—a sharp contrast to the panic in hers—making his presence all the more threatening.

"Ma'am, are you still there? Officers are now just four minutes out."

"Yes, I'm here," the woman peeped.

"Does he have a weapon?"

"Lucy, we don't have time for this!" the man's voice boomed. "I just need to get something off my chest and then we can both wake up from this awful nightmare that's gone on for far too long!"

There was shouting on the other end, punctuated by the crash of something shattering against a wall. Both voices were now muffled again, though it was clear some sort of altercation was happening on the other side of the phone.

"The officers are approaching your building now. They'll be at apartment 505 in just a few moments. Can you make any sound to let me know you're still there?"

Then her voice came back just as distinctly as before, as she released a loud and blood-curdling cry for help: "Help! Help! Someone help me!"

Chapter 1

Tennessee blinked his eyes open and realized he was standing with his hands deep in a stainless-steel sink. Hot water poured out of the faucet and scalded his skin—a hiss escaped his mouth, and he pulled his hands away. Suds of Dawn dish soap lined the gaps between his fingers and the bowl of the sink—its artificial clean scent wafting up with the steam from the water like a thin veil over something more metallic. There was a particularly harsh burning sensation across his knuckles.

He squinted down into the sink—for some reason he was having a hard time getting his vision to come into focus. There was a red-tinted ring of liquid that spun in a cyclone above the drain before escaping down into the pipes.

"Is that...blood?"

It sure was. He turned his red, blotchy hands over in front of his face to see they were covered in dry and flaky blood. It was even caked deep into the crevices under his fingernails. As he bent his fingers, a wet, fleshy crack revealed itself across his knuckle. The cut spit dark, fat droplets down into the silver sink. A chunk of skin at the base of his index finger stuck out to the side. He tugged at it and winced. It was very much still attached, even though the skin itself felt more like hard plastic than a piece of flesh. He grazed over his palm and was met with a stinging that he could feel deep under his skin.

"Splinters?"

He turned off the faucet and grabbed a paper towel, pressing it into the open cut on his fist. On the counter surrounding the sink, there were at least a dozen crumbled paper towels, their pristine white print stained with crimson red.

"Lucy?" he shouted into the dark apartment. "How'd we get here?"

Just moments ago, they'd been at her place on the other side of the city. But now, for some reason, they were here at his apartment.

"Lucy?" he yelled again. A few moments passed and only silence answered back.

He tried to piece together the last thing he could remember prior to finding himself standing at the sink. None of it felt real, like he was waking up from a dream where the most important scenes had been redacted. There were patches of darkness between moments of clarity— gaps that his mind couldn't fill.

"Babe, we're okay, right?" His voice cracked.

Maybe she was sleeping in his bed. Maybe there was a reason she wasn't answering him.

He headed down the hall toward his bedroom. It was a small room with little in it. There was a twin-sized mattress with no bed frame, a small desk with piles of used books stacked on top of it, and an upside-down milk crate that he used as a nightstand.

"Luce?" he said as he cracked open the door.

But Lucy was nowhere to be found. His eyes were drawn to the holes in the wall that hadn't been there before. When did that happen? And why? His gaze fell to a picture frame that was now on the ground. Usually, it sat atop one of the piles of books, but now it was shattered glass in a cracked wooden frame. The photo of him and Lucy that was once inside now lay in shreds across the floor, their tiny bodies ripped apart.

"No, no, no. This can't be right." Tennessee's heart started to pound wildly in his chest.

He squeezed his eyes closed and tried to conjure up the most recent memory he had of her.

"I can't do this anymore." The veins in his forehead bulged.

"This time I'm serious. It's really over." His stomach dropped.

"You're just like your father." His fingers twisted up into fists.

This was just too much. He waved his hands out in front of him, trying to physically shoo away the bad thoughts. Before he knew it, he was pulling off his clothes.

Naked, Tennessee stomped out of his room and into the bathroom he shared with his roommate. He turned on the shower and slumped his body down into the basin, curling in upon himself. He placed his head down on the tile, finding a bit of relief from the pulsing behind his temples. The bones in his knees and back pressed up against the hard walls and his thick, brown curls cascaded down into the drain. After a few minutes, the water rose to meet the corner of his mouth. Pressure began to build in his ear. He inhaled and exhaled in staggered, choppy breaths.

This was something he'd been doing since he was a little kid. Sitting underneath the water gave him a moment of peace that was hard to come by in his childhood home—it offered a brief escape from the chaos. This habit of sitting in the shower followed him into adulthood. He kept it harbored away like a dark little secret. In here, he could let the warm water wash all his problems away.

But as it turns out, Lucy liked sitting in the shower, too. His bond to her became all that much stronger when he found that out. This piece of him that was hiding in the shadows could finally come out. If she was here now, she'd probably be sitting down there with him.

Lucy was the life of the party. She spent every weekend in a different neighborhood of the city, dancing on bar stools, ordering rounds of tequila shots for her friends—whether or not her friends wanted them—and wearing colorful, gaudy outfits inspired by whatever HBO show she was watching at the time.

More often than not, she'd take it one or two drinks too

far and the spins would take over. She would stagger home, rip off her crop top and pants, and curl up in the corner of her shower. She claimed that the steam sobered her up, but Tennessee learned that part of it was so she could cry in the shower after the party was over.

On one particular night, she was more anxious than usual—she'd dropped out of college without telling her parents. With each round of shots, it became more obvious to Tennessee she was trying to numb her discomfort.

Later that night—in Lucy's shower—they sat with their legs entangled as black mascara ran down her face, the strong scent of agave and lime on her breath.

"What if they make me move back to Portland? They were paying for my rent, tuition, everything," she said.

He nodded. He wasn't sure what to say. As much as he wanted to give her some advice, Tennessee couldn't relate. He could barely afford to pay his own rent, let alone afford to go to college.

"What if this was a big mistake? What if the band never takes off? What if no one listens to us? This will have all been for nothing." She put her face into her hands and continued to sob. "They're going to think I'm a failure… maybe I should just go try to re-enroll."

"You're following your dreams—that doesn't make you a failure," Tennessee finally said, trying to comfort her.

"You don't know them," she shook her head. "They wouldn't understand."

"Yeah, but I know enough." He reached for her chin and lifted her face. "I know your dad got you that Fender you love so much. I know your mom forces all the nurses at the hospital to listen to your demo tracks. Why do you think that is?"

Her tears slowed as she nodded.

"They are proud of you," he continued. "Whether or not you finish college, and regardless of how successful your band is. They might be mad for a little while, but so what? They'll get over it eventually."

She rubbed her eyes, spreading more dark lines in horizontal streaks across her face. "I'm just scared."

"That's good. You should be a little scared, you're taking a leap of faith. But are you really going to let fear stop you?" He stroked her wet shoulder. "And you need to stop with the whole *nobody's-gonna-listen* shtick. You're way too talented to be worried about that shit. Like, shut up already," he teased.

A smile returned to her face as she splashed water at him.

"I love you," she said, leaning over to kiss him, "in this lifetime and the next."

She was sweet. It was one of the things he loved most about her.

But something about her changed when they would fight. It was like she became an entirely different person. She knew just what to say to push his buttons. She'd twist his words to give them new meaning. She cut him open with the precision of a surgeon. If he didn't know any better, he would've thought that she actually enjoyed hurting him.

Today wasn't the first time she'd threatened to leave. She always seemed to be halfway out the door. But after the first six or seven times, he began to think these were empty threats.

So, what was so different about today?

It was just a normal Sunday. They went to the farmer's market, got pho, and went back to her place. Everything was going just fine. But maybe she'd gotten bored with just fine.

Like a gust of wind, the tone in her voice shifted the energy in the room, transforming the space between them into something charged and dangerous. Her words were like a thousand tiny paper cuts, slicing him open slowly until they made an open wound that bled memories of his childhood. He thought it was just another fight. He assumed that she was just threatening to leave like she always did, a well-rehearsed line in their cyclical script. He didn't really think this time was any different than all those times before. Until it was.

"I can't do this anymore."

"This time I'm serious."

Then, at some point, the fire was lit.

"You're just like your father."

And the next thing he knew, he was washing the blood off his hands in the kitchen sink.

As the water in the shower rose to meet his nostrils, he pulled himself up from his prone position and pulled his knees into his chest. He put his hands out, so they were under the water. Blood ran down his forearm from the gashes on his fist. His fingers were growing swollen and red. Tomorrow they would be purple and blue.

But the water couldn't wash away the swirl of his thoughts.

What did I do? Was that just my blood? Or could it be…

Is Lucy okay? Is she…

Chapter 2

"That'll be $4.80," the chipper barista said as she handed him a plastic cup with a white paper straw that would be mushy and broken down in a matter of minutes.

Tennessee was already running late—just like most mornings—but he stopped for iced coffee anyway. He needed the caffeine even more than usual. As he tapped the back of his phone against the payment reader, the sharp squeal of brakes cut through the coffee shop. Outside, a bus barreled down the hill, preparing to stop at the next corner.

Shit. He needed to get on that bus. The moment the green checkmark flashed on the screen, he snatched the drink from the barista and ran through the glass doors of the café.

Outside, the crisp air bit at his nose and ears. His hand, wrapped around the icy drink, tingled with a prickly numbness as he ran awkwardly through the cold, foggy morning.

The big gray and red bus already had its doors open, the pixelated screen on its side flashing "38" in bright yellow lights. Through its steamy windows, he could see passengers crammed inside, packed like sardines, filling every possible inch of space.

"Goddamn it," he growled, joining the crowd attempting to get inside.

Moving as a silent mob, the crowd on the sidewalk surged forward, cramming the already-packed bus even tighter. Tennessee could feel the tension before he was even part of it—a visible resistance, a battle between those forcing their way on and those inside, who couldn't possibly squeeze another inch.

In the end, only a handful of people waiting at Geary and 25th managed to make it onboard. Tennessee had somehow edged his way to the front of the crowd, only for the doors to shut in his face, leaving him and at least a dozen others in a cloud of black exhaust.

For reasons he never quite understood, San Franciscans always referred to bus lines with a "the" before the route number—so this was *the* 38. It ran down Geary from the quiet, residential Richmond District all the way to the Financial District—better known as FiDi.

The Richmond was divided into four parts. The Outer Richmond was home to the surfers, while the Inner Richmond held all the shops and restaurants, offering just about every kind of Asian cuisine—Korean, Chinese, Burmese, and several more. It was also where the ever-popular Sunday farmers' market was held. To the north was Lake Street, home to the ultra-wealthy—tech CEOs, high-level financial executives, even members of Metallica lived there—each with stunning views of the Golden Gate Bridge. Stretching across the neighborhood's southern border was the lush, sprawling green of Golden Gate Park.

Tennessee lived in the often-forgotten Central Richmond—a middle ground between the beach and the farmers' market, rarely recognized by name. It was sometimes called Little Russia, as it was home to one of the largest Russian Orthodox churches outside of Russia. The Holy Virgin Cathedral's golden domes were a sight to behold, standing proudly against the gray morning sky just across the street from the coffee shop he'd stepped out of.

In recent years, yuccies had started taking over the Richmond—especially the Inner Richmond. Tennessee didn't know this term—Lucy corrected him once when he called them hipsters.

"Come on, Tenny. Only millennials call them that. It stands for *young urban creatives*—a mix of yuppies and hipsters." Apparently, she'd seen a TikTok about it.

This part of the city was full of them—handlebar mustaches, rolled-up beanies, obscure eyewear, platform boots and loafers, shaggy haircuts. On weekends, they flaunted their vintage finds and curated aesthetics, but on weekdays, you could spot them by their Patagonias. Every day, it seemed like a new trendy coffee shop, wine bar, or plant store popped up, catering to this privileged millennial

flock. They thought they were better than everyone else—
different because of their rare vinyl collection or their
taste in natural orange wine. But they wouldn't hesitate to
throw a hissy fit if their morning latte came with dairy milk
instead of oat.

Tennessee pulled his phone from the pocket of his
black denim jacket and checked the time—nine minutes
until eight. Stepping off the curb, he leaned into the street,
craning his neck as far as he could without getting in the
way of traffic. But as far as he could see, there were no
buses on the horizon. A sigh came rattling out from deep
within his chest.

Stepping back onto the sidewalk, he opened up Google
Maps, checking when the next bus was expected to arrive.

"Come on," he muttered at the screen, waiting for it to
load.

A notification box popped up: YOU'VE RUN OUT OF
DATA ON YOUR 5MG PLAN. VISIT OUR WEBSITE
WHEN ON WIFI TO BUY ADDITIONAL GIGS.

"Ugh, useless," he groaned, swiping up to exit the app.
This was a recurring problem he had with his fifteen-dollar
phone plan—especially as it neared the end of the month.

He cycled between checking the time and stepping
into the street, tapping the soles of his Vans against the
pavement as the minutes slipped by. The longer he waited,
the bigger the crowd at the bus stop grew.

First, his phone read 7:55. Then 7:58. And finally, 8:00.

"Great. Just fucking great," he muttered. He was officially late for work and there was no bus in sight.

Clenching his jaw, he ground his back molars together and sucked down more coffee through the disintegrating paper straw. The caffeine brought a buzz to his head.

At 8:02, a bus finally crested the top of the hill.

The horde of would-be passengers stirred, readying their plastic transit cards and digital wallets, inching as close to the curb as possible. A quick scan of the crowd made it easy to spot the ones Lucy would've called yuccies. They wore their Patagonia vests and jackets like uniforms, their chrome over-the-ear headphones perched atop mullets and micro-bangs. Corporate-branded backpacks and faux leather messenger bags slung over their shoulders made sure everyone knew exactly which tech or finance job they were heading to. Tennessee hated their smugness—the way self-importance oozed from them. They carried themselves like they deserved a spot on that bus more than he did.

He shoved his way to the front, cutting ahead of those who'd been waiting longer. As the bus came to a stop, the back doors opened just a few feet away. He trampled over shoes, shoved his elbows against the branded bags, and pushed up against the shoulders of anyone in his way. Whatever was necessary to secure a spot on the bus.

After some shuffling here and shoving there, he took one big step onto the vessel. He'd made it. He'd beaten those entitled jerks. As the doors sealed shut and the brakes released, he grabbed hold of an overhead loop and braced himself as the bus lurched forward.

Inside, the air was thick and humid—a sharp contrast to the crisp cold outside. The breath and body heat of the passengers fogged up the windows. There had to be at least sixty or seventy people crammed inside. He could smell the deodorant of those around him and the pungent odor of those who'd gone without.

Tall enough to see over most heads, Tennessee adjusted his stance, angling his arm just right so he could lift his drink to his mouth while looking out the window. The ride went by like a blur. Tennessee stared blankly out the window, eyes glazed over, barely registering the world outside. Eventually, the automated voice announced *6th Avenue*—his cue to snap back to reality and get off the bus.

By the time he walked into Pink Peach Bookstore, he was more than fifteen minutes late.

"Good morning, Tennessee," Mr. Green greeted him, hands buried in a crate of used books. He was already sorting through the weekend's new arrivals, marking tiny prices inside their covers with a yellow pencil.

"Another late night, I presume?" He glanced down at Tennessee over the brim of his thin metal frames.

Tennessee was late more often than not. But today was different. He wasn't dragging himself in after oversleeping or because he was too lazy to get out of bed. He hadn't slept at all—despite his best efforts. Honestly, Mr. Green should be glad he showed up at all.

Besides, was fifteen minutes *really* that late?

"Yep. Very late night, to say the least." A loud, obnoxious slurp filled the bookstore as Tennessee sucked up the last bit of his drink. "Sorry."

"I'm sorry to hear that, son," Mr. Green said sympathetically as his calloused thumb flipped through the pages of a thick used autobiography.

Tennessee rounded the counter, tossing his empty cup into the trash bin at Mr. Green's feet before dropping his backpack behind the register. Mr. Green's eyes flicked to the bin, a knowing smile spreading across his wrinkled face.

"Maybe after those late nights, you can skip making a coffee stop on the way in?" He nodded toward the trash can before turning back to the book in his hands.

A knot tightened between Tennessee's shoulder blades. A scolding was the last thing he needed right now.

"No! It was the bus—it wasn't my fault!" Tennessee blurted out, now totally flustered. "There were too many people, so I couldn't get on. It had nothing to do with the coffee!"

"Ah, those dang unpredictable buses." Mr. Green pushed his glasses up the bridge of his nose. "Maybe try catching an earlier one, then."

He wouldn't understand. Mr. Green's commute was a simple walk downstairs—he lived above the bookstore. Must be nice to own the whole damn building.

"But you don't get it. Last night, I—" Tennessee bit his tongue. A pit formed in his stomach. He had no idea what had happened last night, but he knew it was something awful. Something he shouldn't talk about.

"Last night, what?" Mr. Green asked.

"Never mind." Tennessee yanked off his jacket and tossed it behind the counter. He grabbed a milk crate of used books that Mr. Green had already priced and turned toward the back of the store.

"Are you alright?" Mr. Green asked as Tennessee started to walk off.

"Yep. Just fine," Tennessee said coolly. "No more coffee. Don't be late. I got it."

Tennessee walked through the aisles at the front of the store, where featured books and new arrivals sat stacked with fresh offerings. He winced, shifting his grip on the crate, trying to hold it in a way that wouldn't reopen the cut on his hand.

He passed through the small section that held the staff favorites—one modest slot for him and each of his co-workers to display. While the others seemed to swap theirs out only once a year, if at all, Tennessee rotated his monthly. He didn't gravitate toward any particular genre, but he was drawn to literature of the past. Currently in his backpack was a novel from 1926 called *One, No One and One Hundred Thousand,* translated from an Italian writer, that was about the thousands of identities a single person possesses in the perception of others and oneself. Some of his·favorite authors included Hunter S. Thompson and George Orwell—he'd read *1984* at least four times. Right now, though, the shelf above his name displayed *The Eye* by Vladimir Nabokov—a Russian novel originally written in 1930 that captured the morbid post-suicidal experience of the book's main character.

As he ascended the wooden staircase, the steps creaked under his weight. The floors across the entire store ached and moaned after years of holding the place up.

A while back, he'd found a black book in the reference section called *The Dictionary of Obscure Sorrows* where he discovered a new word: *vellichor*. He'd memorized the definition because it so perfectly described the Peach.

vellichor [noun]: the strange wistfulness of used bookstores, which are somehow infused with the passage of time—filled with thousands of old books you'll never have time to read, each of which is itself locked in its own era, bound and dated and papered over like an old room the author abandoned years ago, a hidden annex littered with thoughts left just as they were on the day they were captured.

The Pink Peach had been in the Richmond for more than fifty-five years, though the building was even older than that. Mr. Green loved to tell the yuccies who would wander in about how the store's foundation was actually an old Victorian home that was built in the last years of the 1800s.

There'd been dozens of remodels and makeovers in the hundred-plus years since its construction. Layers remained that only a knowing eye could see. Once aware of the building's history, you could discern pieces of its past. The Peach as it stood today was a labyrinth with alcoves and nooks that had no purpose, doors that led to different rooms, narrow staircases that connected all three levels of the store. Customers often emerged from the depths laughing about how they'd gotten lost within its walls.

Hand-written signs made of faded construction paper hung from the ceiling, labeling each of the different sections of literature. Some of the center shelves had index cards taped to them that highlighted the book that sat above— whether praise for the author or a call-out for readers about what made that particular book special. Tennessee no longer needed the guidance of these signs to find his way around the maze-like store. He knew how to navigate the different rooms, sections, and shelves better than anyone.

Turning into the anthropology section, Tennessee dropped the heavy crate at his feet and pulled a pair of knotted wired headphones and his keys from his pocket. He took a few moments to untangle the knots where he could but left the ones that he could tolerate. Eventually, he plugged them into his phone and played "Icky Thump" by The White Stripes, turning the volume up as loud as it would go.

With music blasting in his ears, he finally found enough privacy between the shelves to pull out the tiny Ziploc bag he kept in his front pocket. He held it up to the fluorescent light between his index finger and thumb.

"Just enough for one bump."

Using the largest key on the ring to scoop up all the powder inside the baggie, Tennessee filled its grooves and raised it to meet his left nostril, inhaling sharply through his nose.

The crystal substance burned through his nasal cavity with a familiar intensity, sending a rush to his brain. The pupils of his brown eyes dilated, his heart stuttered then accelerated. Reality gained a sudden, crystalized clarity. Seconds later, the drip began its descent at the back of his throat, coating his mouth with that unmistakable chemical bitterness— it tasted like gasoline. As the cocaine-laced mucus scorched a path down his esophagus to his stomach, he longed for the remnants of his morning coffee to wash away the taste.

As the dopamine flooded his system, the world gained edges and momentum. Now he could truly begin his day.

Even after two years of working at the Peach, the morning shift still hadn't grown on him. When Tennessee was desperately looking for a job when he first moved to the city, he was willing to do just about anything to avoid having to move back home. Mr. Green only agreed to hire him if he would work the mornings—which Tennessee begrudgingly agreed to.

But even with the early hours, he'd found an unexpected sanctuary in shelving books. One after another, Tennessee pulled the books out of the crate and guided it into its designated new home. It gave him first dibs on the new arrivals, he could hide between the shelves to sneak key bumps, and he could avoid talking to people, at least for a little while.

As Tennessee slid a thin poetry book into one of the upper shelves, he caught a glimpse of his knuckles, and something constricted in his chest—a tightness that had nothing to do with the drugs.

The skin at the base of his fingers had darkened, now covered in a mass of splotchy bruises that transformed his pale hands into a landscape of purple and blue. The cut that crossed his knuckle was now dry and lifted—brownish blood congealing along its edges, the surrounding skin pulling away in dry, papery flakes. His hands looked like that of a stranger's.

Her voice broke through the rhythm of the bassline pulsing in his headphones.

You're just like your father.

The drip at the back of his throat inflamed, creating a hard knot beneath his Adam's apple. His mouth turned to sandpaper, a metallic flavor coating his tongue. Each breath became shallower than the last, as though the air in the store itself had thickened.

What little fragments of memory he possessed haunted him—shards of broken glass that reflected distorted images he couldn't fully comprehend.

This time I'm serious. It's really over.

Part of him so badly wanted to figure it out. Part of him desperately wanted to arrange the puzzle fragments into a coherent image. He had only scattered pieces, edges without centers, but nothing that revealed the complete picture. Yet beneath this urge to know lurked a deeper fear.

He pulled the sleeves of his shirt down over his wounded hands. A new anxiety bloomed—had others noticed the evidence on his skin? Mr. Green? The overly friendly barista? The people on the bus? His heart accelerated to match the thundering drums in his ears.

"What did I do?" he whispered into the narrow space between shelves. The wood seemed to whisper back with subtle creaks.

He uncurled his fingers to examine his nails—dried brown flakes still clung beneath several of them. Flashbacks of Dawn dish soap and blood flooded his memory. The shredded photo scattered across his bedroom floor like confetti. Plaster dust from the punctured wall. The hollow absence in his chest when he realized Lucy wasn't there.

He had no idea where she was. He hadn't heard from her at all.

"What the fuck is wrong with me," he punched his bruised fist into the shelf. "Remember, goddamn it! What did you do?"

The lump in his throat pulsed like a second heart. His skin began to crawl. He could feel his heartbeat in his wrists and in his neck, and eventually across his whole body. The bitter taste intensified, flooding his mouth. Tears gathered at the corners of his vision. His shoulders rounded inward as he gripped the shelf in front of him, knuckles whitening around the bruises. He closed his eyes and saw only her face.

"You're just like your father," he pictured her pink lips forming the words again, each syllable a tiny dagger.

His torso suddenly felt like it weighed a thousand pounds—the simple act of lifting a book from the crate now seemed impossible. Sweat droplets formed on the back of his neck and chest, his face turning a bright red. Every breath became more difficult; each inhale grew more irregular and fractured until it felt like there was no air left in his lungs. Silver constellations danced across his vision as the room tilted.

His body folded inward as he surrendered his weight to the bookshelf. Tears splashed onto the hardwood floor. The store began to revolve around him, the knot in his stomach twisting tighter. The music in his headphones became background noise, becoming distant and irrelevant beneath the deafening sound of his own heartbeat.

"I don't even want to know. I can't—I can't know," he said into the wooden shelf. "I can't know what I did to her."

The bookshelf rattled beneath his hands and his knees trembled. He punched the shelf again—harder this time— sending several books cascading to the floor. Snot and tears fell in streams out of his face. He'd lost all control, trapped in a battle between his brain and body that felt like it would never end.

His vision eventually faded to black.

"Fuck!" his legs gave out beneath him. He collapsed to the floor on hands and knees with a loud thud. A sharp pain shot up his arm and he felt heat rush back into his wounds.

He laid there for several long moments, weeping onto the splayed pages of fallen books. As tears flowed, his breath shuddered. He fought to capture a few deep inhales, struggling to reestablish a rhythm in his lungs. Gradually, the tightness in his chest loosened and air flowed more freely again.

"Get it together," he muttered and wiped his nose with his sleeve, leaving a damp streak across the fabric.

He squinted against the harsh fluorescent lights of the Peach, carefully avoiding the sight of his bruised hand. After several stabilizing breaths, he grasped the bookshelf and pulled himself upright. Though able to support his weight, he was still shaking. He felt as fragile as a rag doll.

Eventually, he was able to get his weight back underneath him and release his death grip on the shelf. He pulled the headphones out of his ears and came back to reality.

When silence fell, goosebumps rose up on the back of his neck. A strange, eerie feeling came over him. It was that spine-crawling sensation that came only from knowing you were being watched.

He glanced over his shoulder to find a woman with micro-bangs and thick-rimmed glasses staring at him. A look of concern and confusion washed over her yuccie face, a memoir clutched in her hand.

His face flushed pink. He struggled to collect his scattered thoughts as the woman's judging gaze pierced through him. Behind her glasses, he watched her eyes travel from his face to his trembling hands, then to the literary debris scattered across the floor. She stood with her head tilted slightly, as though awaiting an explanation for the scene she'd just witnessed.

He needed to speak. But he had no words to explain what just happened.

"Can I help you find anything?" he eventually squeaked out.

Chapter 3

While the drip was still raging in the back of his throat, his high had quickly worn off. The cocaine's effects were long gone, leaving only the chemical aftertaste and a hollow feeling in his body. Before the clock hands hit noon, he was already on the move to replenish his fix. On his lunch break, he jaywalked toward the neon emblems hanging in the dark windows of the bar across the street.

The smell of stale beer and lemon-scented cleaner washed over him as he walked through the lower half of the bar's Dutch door. The dark walls and tinted windows made it feel like nighttime even though it was midday. A handful of the other regulars had already started downing the first of many afternoon beers, hunched figures scattered around the bar nursing their pint glasses with care. He paid them no mind as he made his way to his usual barstool furthest from the door.

Vera hadn't noticed him yet. All he could see of her was the top of her platinum blonde head and her dark brown roots. She was tucked underneath the bar, struggling to tap a keg, muttering unintelligibly. Since getting the job at the

Pink Peach two years ago, Tennessee stopped into the bar on his breaks at least once a week. In that time, he'd gotten close with the daytime bartender, who eventually turned into his coke dealer. Somewhere along the way, their relationship blurred the line between that of friendship and one that was purely transactional.

Defeated and fatigued from the panic attack earlier that morning, he crossed his arms over the tin-topped bar. He put his head down on his wrists and waited for Vera to come over to him. The metal was cool against his skin. The world narrowed to the smell of spilled liquor, distant conversations, and the memory of Lucy's face—which he so desperately wished he could shake.

After a few minutes, Vera gave a little cheer, having successfully reconnected the line. He heard the clinking of glass cups and a rush of foam coming out of the tap.

"Ten! Is that you down there?" she shouted at him as she waited for the pint glass to fill up.

Tennessee kept his forehead glued to the counter. She seemed to be in rather good spirits today, which was too much for him to handle in his current state—even though she was the very person he'd come to see.

She slid the drink to the customer in front of her and bounced over to his end of the bar.

"How you doing, babe?" she said, looking down at the back of his neck, her breath a cloud of menthol that she attempted to mask behind peppermint gum.

He was at a loss for words. He didn't know how to describe how he was. He hadn't felt this low in such a long time, as if he'd been hollowed out and left with only a dull ache.

Part of him wanted to talk about it so badly. To have someone help him make sense of all the little fragments of memory he had so that he could put the pieces together. He trusted Vera with this kind of stuff. He talked to her about the fights he and Lucy had gotten in before. And just a month and a half ago, he'd talked Vera through a breakup with her now ex-girlfriend.

But this felt different. He was afraid to give away too many details, even though he had very little to begin with. He really didn't know what happened. But he knew it was probably better that few people found out.

Without lifting his head, he extended an arm toward her and unfolded his fingers to reveal a wrinkled hundred-dollar bill that he'd been nervously folding in his pocket on the walk over.

"Oh, I'm sorry," Vera scoffed, "I only take orders from people who can look me in the eye."

A sigh came out of his body, but he still didn't move, anchored by the weight of his misery.

She swatted at his hand and began tapping her short, chewed-up fingernails against the bar. The tiny impacts created a metallic rhythm, counting out the seconds. Vera was stubborn; she could wait there all day if she had to. He once watched her stare down a customer who tried to pay with a credit card until they eventually left the bar—there were signs everywhere that said the establishment was cash-only—all without her having to say a word. If the tattoos and facial piercings weren't enough to intimidate you, her threatening stare was.

She waited and methodically tapped against the metal bar top, each ping making him more agitated, the sound reverberating inside his skull until it was almost unbearable. Eventually, he lifted his head to meet Vera's gaze, revealing a scowl and a pair of dark circles underneath his eyes.

"You look terrible." Brutal honesty was part of her charm. "You okay?"

"I'm fine," he shrugged. The lie felt so transparent it was barely worth voicing. "Can I get a whiskey ginger?"

Vera leaned over the bar to get closer to him, the smell of menthol cigarettes coming off her even stronger now. "Not until I get an explanation from you."

"I just didn't sleep last night, okay?" It wasn't exactly a lie. He didn't sleep. Any rest was replaced by an image of blood circling before it escaped down the drain.

"Mmhm, sure," her skepticism hung in the air between them.

"Can I just get my drink? I really don't have time for a therapy session." His words came out sharp.

"Oh, so it's *bad*-bad." Vera's eyes got wide. "Did you and Lucy have another fight?"

He winced at the sound of her name. "Please," he begged, "I just need to take the edge off."

She begrudgingly pulled out a bucket glass and filled it with ice, each cube clinking as it fell into the cup. Without even looking, she grabbed the soda gun with one hand and the well whiskey in the other. Even at just twenty-three years old, it was as though she'd been pouring drinks her whole life.

Vera had worked at the bar since she was seventeen. Her fake ID got her in the door, but her persistence got her behind the bar. She started out washing dishes and cleaning up after closing each night. But having spent all those years watching the bartenders, she'd memorized every cocktail and mixed drink there was before she could even legally touch the bottles. By the time she was actually twenty-one, it didn't take too long for her to convince the owners to move her from busser to bartender. Now, she didn't even need a jigger to pour the perfectly sized shot.

"Thank you," he said remorsefully as she put the drink down in front of him, the outside of the glass sweating in the bar's musky air.

"Come on, you've gotta tell me what's up. I'm dying to know." She leaned against the back counter with her arms crossed. This pose put the tattoo on the back of her forearm in perfect view—a heart with a dagger through it, the black and red ink slightly blurring at the edges. "This doesn't seem like a typical Tennessee temper tantrum."

He shook his head. He really didn't need her pestering him today. But as much as he didn't want to admit it, she was right. Things were far worse than they'd ever been before, beyond their usual arguments and fake breakups.

He grabbed the glass and gulped it down until the drink was halfway gone, the cheap whiskey burning a trail down his throat that briefly relieved him from the drip of the cocaine. He exhaled and let the few innocent details he could share fall out of his mouth.

"Lucy broke up with me, okay?" It was the first time he'd said it aloud. The lump in his throat came back, swelling until he had to force himself to swallow past it. The words hung in the air, making the situation all the more real now that he'd spoken it.

With this news, he noticed Vera's demeanor dramatically shifted. Her eyebrows lifted behind her razor-cut bangs— she cut them herself. Her cheeks began to flush with a heat that seemed to emanate from within. Her lips pursed together like she was trying to hold back a smile, the corners twitching upward despite her best attempt at control.

"I'm so sorry to hear that," her tone shifted. In an instant she became softer, her voice taking on a velvet-like quality. "What happened?"

He took another gulp of his drink and forcefully swallowed.

"I don't know. I have no idea what happened. She just said… she said that I was like my dad." His thumbs traced circles around the outside of the glass in his hands, leaving trails in the condensation.

"What? What does that mean?" she asked.

He exhaled and took a sip of his drink, doing his best to fight off the memories. Behind the blinking of his eyelids, images flashed back—the ripped-up photograph, the holes in the wall, the heat of the water when he came to. His jaw clenched and unclenched rhythmically as he weighed how much to reveal. The urge to confide in someone collided with his instinct to bottle it all up. He'd already said more than he should've about the whole thing, but the words spilled out like water through a cracked dam.

"I—I don't really know what she meant," he paused. "My dad was a drunk. He was mean, especially to my mom. But I'm nothing like my dad. I would never do anything to hurt her."

The cuts on his hands burned beneath his sleeve.

"I love her so much." Tennessee's eyes started to well up, the world going watery around the edges. "It kills me to know she thought of me that way."

Vera paused and chose her next words carefully. "I know how much you cared about her. Some days you wouldn't shut up about her," she laughed. "I know it's tough, but if she can't see how great you are, then good riddance."

A single tear rolled down his cheek that he quickly wiped away. "I just wish I could show her that."

"Eventually she'll see it," Vera reassured him, her hand briefly touching his arm. The contact sent a jolt through his system. "And she'll realize just how wrong she was."

He lifted his head to meet the warm look in her green eyes. His shoulders softened and the lump in the back of his throat loosened until it dulled away. Her words felt like a beam of light in the darkness that had been encapsulating him.

"The drink's on the house."

"Thanks," he said, and a small smile crept across his face, the first one since everything fell apart.

A familiar itch crept up the back of his throat, yanking him back to reality, reminding him why he'd come into the bar in the first place.

"Wait, can I get a gram?" He extended the hundred-dollar bill to her again, the paper now damp from his palm.

A twinkle came to her eye and the smile she'd been trying to hide showed itself fully now, spreading across her face. "You know, hun, I'm actually out right now." She waved her palms out in a shrug.

He let out a loud groan and his head fell back down onto the counter, his forehead connecting with the tin with a dull thud.

"But I should be getting some more tomorrow," the tone of her voice shifted, taking on that fake sweet quality that surfaced when she was lying. Her words came out too measured, almost deliberate. "You can come by my place and pick it up then? It might be nice to hang out outside of the bar for once."

He groaned loudly again. He wasn't sure if he could wait until tomorrow—but he had no other choice.

"Fine, I'll stop by after work," he said with a sigh.

She plucked the—now damp—bill from his hands.

"Great, see you then," she beamed as she walked away, her steps seeming lighter than before.

As she went, he could see some clear plastic poking out of her vest pocket, the unmistakable glint catching the bar light. It was too late for him to change his mind or argue with her now; he had to get back to work. He downed the rest of the drink, ice cubes clacking against his teeth. Then he dragged his feet back across the street to finish his shift, each step heavier than the last.

Chapter 4

The loud grinding of skateboard wheels against pavement filled the store. Then a massive crack as a foot slammed down on the board's tail. A few seconds later, Tennessee's roommate Tanner came bobbing into the doorway of the bookstore. For the last two years, the pair shared the bottom unit of a duplex that Tanner's parents rented out.

"Yo, Ten! Whatcha reading there, bud?" Tanner had on the same black oversized hoodie he always wore, and a backpack covered with spray paint strapped to his shoulders, his skateboard tucked under his arm. As he got closer to the counter, Tanner reached his closed hand in Tennessee's direction for a fist bump.

Tennessee instinctively reached his hand over to meet Tanner's. Just as their fists touched, a jolt of pain shot up his arm. He quickly pulled his hand back into his lap, tugging the sleeves of his shirt down past his knuckles while mentally counting his breaths to keep his expression from faltering.

"Nothing really, just a literary piece about a depressed girl in Ireland." His voice came out steadier than he expected, a forced casualness that hid the chaos beneath the surface.

He forced himself to meet Tanner's eyes briefly—not too long, not too short—while silently praying the fist bump had been quick enough that Tanner hadn't noticed the bruises across his knuckles.

To call them roommates was an understatement. Even friendship felt like too small of a word. The two of them grew up in the same small country town outside of Fresno and had been friends since they were twelve. After all these years, they were brothers in every way that mattered—not by blood, but by choice and the shared history between them.

"Aren't all books literary?" Tanner didn't read much— that was always Tennessee's thing. Though his parents had sent him to school for graphic design, Tanner spent most of his free time skating around the city with a backpack full of spray paint, in a never-ending search for his next canvas.

"No, not all books are literary, you idiot. It's a genre." Tennessee rolled his eyes, grateful for the familiar rhythm of their banter. It was like muscle memory, a back-and-forth they'd perfected since middle school. "Did you just stop by to say hi?"

"Oh, no. My mom wants me to pick up some cookbook Mr. G special-ordered for her." The Coopers were family friends of the Greens, which was how Tennessee landed the job at the bookstore with such little work experience. "She texted to remind me to grab it, like, three times since I'm headed back home tonight."

"That's right, you're going back to the Valley. How long are you gonna be gone for?"

"Probably about a week or so. They want me to spend some time with them before school starts back up again for the spring semester. You know how they are."

"Nice. Well, let 'em know I say hi." Tennessee's lips curved into what he hoped was a convincing smile. Inside, his mind raced, realizing that he'd be alone with his thoughts—and what he'd done, whatever that was—for a full week.

Tennessee wasn't sure how to tell Tanner about what happened with Lucy. A wave of shame rose in his chest, followed quickly by a flicker of anger—the same toxic mix that showed itself last night. Their friendship had survived everything from childhood bullying in gym class to Tennessee following Tanner to the city after his dad started preaching the gospel of his twelve-step program. But this? This might be the thing that finally broke what their teachers had called "the inseparable Ten and Tan."

"You're still totally welcome to come with, if you want," Tanner said. "My mom offered to set you up in the guest room, so...you know, you don't have to stay with your folks. She even said she'd make the lambchops you like. Totally up to you, though."

Tennessee had many good memories at the Coopers' dinner table. It was a place of laughter and shared stories. An intentional moment for the family to come together. At Tennessee's house, meals were eaten separately, or sometimes not at all. The warmth of the Cooper household was both a sanctuary and a painful contrast—each time he would return to his own family, the differences felt sharper, more impossible to ignore.

"Nah, I'm good. I can't afford to lose the hours." Though his words said one thing, the look on his face said another. The two of them both knew that Tennessee hadn't gone back home to see his family since the day he moved out.

Tanner nodded knowingly. "Totally get it, maybe next time."

Tennessee let his gaze fall back down to the book that lay open on the counter in front of him. The two of them could say so much with so few words. They could talk about almost anything—except for Tennessee's home life. Tanner and his family knew things were rough for Tennessee, but they never asked for any details and Tennessee never gave them any.

But what they didn't say in words, Tanner's parents said with their actions. They treated Tennessee like he was part of their family. When they were kids, Tanner's parents would let Tennessee stay the night as many nights as he was allowed to, always handled pick-up and drop-off for their hangouts whenever needed, and would even occasionally send Tanner to school with an extra lunch if they noticed Tennessee was looking extra bony. Even now, the Coopers were a lifeline to him. Without them giving him a place to live and helping him find a job, Tennessee would be left with nothing but his hand-me-down 2007 GMC Sierra.

Nobody really knew what went on behind the closed doors of his family home. Even when things were at their worst, Tennessee's mother made sure they kept up the appearance of a normal family to the outside world. Tennessee refused to talk about what was really going on with anyone. Whether it was the pressure to fit the façade his mom created or that it really was just too painful to deal with, he wasn't sure. Regardless, he did his best to block out those memories from his mind. And the further he got away from them, the less heavy they felt.

The only person who could break down the walls Tennessee had built up was Lucy. She was the first person he confided in about any of it. He'd trusted her with the most vulnerable pieces of himself—the dark memories he'd spent years burying, the fears that kept him awake at night. That's what made her words all the more hurtful. A strange emptiness filled him now—not just guilt, but grief for the safe space that now seemed destroyed.

"By the way, bud, what were you up to last night?" Tanner asked. "I heard some banging, and I found a ton of bloody paper towels all over the kitchen this morning."

"Oh, you were home?" At the mention of blood, Tennessee felt a cold wave wash through him. The store's fluorescent lights suddenly seemed too bright, too exposing. He fought to keep his expression neutral while his pulse hammered in his ears. The skin around his knuckles felt tight and hot, a persistent reminder of what he'd done but couldn't remember.

"Yeah! Seemed like you were pretty fired up about something," Tanner continued. "And those weren't just a few drops of blood, man. It looked like you tried to clean up a crime scene or something." He said it with a half-laugh.

Tennessee resisted the urge to flex his throbbing hand beneath the counter and forced himself to swallow. Could Tanner know what happened?

"What did you hear?"

"Well, it sounded like you were definitely punching some holes in the walls." Tanner shrugged. "Don't worry, I won't tell my parents. Just patch them up before I get back."

"Yeah, sorry. I'll fix those." His mind raced through potential explanations—punctures from the drywall, a nosebleed, a cut from a steak knife, anything.

"You were screaming some weird shit, too. In the kitchen."

"Screaming?" A single word, barely pushed past his lips. "Saying what?"

"You don't remember?" Tanner's eyebrows lifted.

Tennessee felt sweat beading at his hairline. He quickly tried to spin up a lie, his eyes fixed on a spot just over Tanner's left shoulder as he forced a sheepish laugh. "Ya know, I was just a little drunk and yakked out is all." He rubbed the back of his neck, his attempt at a casual gesture. "Things got a little blurry when I got home."

"Ahhh, for sure. I'm not really sure. I couldn't make sense of it. You kept saying the same few phrases: 'nothing like him' and 'she deserved it.'" He said the last part almost like a question.

Tennessee felt his chest cave in. Horror at his own words collided with a sickening flash of whatever rage had possessed him last night. And the fact that it was all gone from his memory terrified him more than anything.

"Did you hear Lucy at all?"

"No, I don't think so. You guys in a fight or something?"

"Mmhm. You know how it goes with us," Tennessee pulled his eyes away from Tanner's gaze, looking past him at the bookshelves. His eyes glazed over, unable to focus on anything. Their arguments had never gone this far before—nothing like whatever happened last night. But he and Lucy had always been volatile, something Tanner had witnessed enough times to brush this off as just another one of their spats.

"Okay, well, I'm gonna go back to Mr. G's office to grab that book for my mom. I'll catch ya later."

"Sounds good," Tennessee nodded.

Tanner took a few steps toward the back of the store, then stopped and pivoted. "Are you good, Ten?"

Tennessee's eyes snapped back to Tanner's face. Damn him. He knew. He always knew.

"Never better. Why?" Tennessee said shortly. He couldn't tell Tanner the truth. He couldn't tell anyone the truth.

"Just checking. You just seem a little... Ehh, forget it," Tanner waved his hand through the air dismissively. "See you in like a week."

"I'm fine." The same words he'd said a thousand times in their friendship, through black eyes he claimed were from basketball and bruised ribs he attributed to skateboarding accidents.

Tanner's eyes told Tennessee that he knew this wasn't the truth but that he wouldn't be pressing him any further—which Tennessee was grateful for.

As soon as Tanner's head disappeared behind the bookshelves on his way toward the back office, the mask crumbled. Tennessee's carefully maintained expression collapsed, his face falling into his throbbing hands. The breath he'd been holding in escaped in ragged gasps.

"What did you fucking do?" he whispered to himself, his voice breaking. The question echoed in the empty space of the bookstore, leaving only silence in response.

Chapter 5

The next day, Tennessee awkwardly hung around the Peach after his shift, sifting through the philosophy nook that was tucked in a separate room upstairs. Vera's house was just a few blocks from the store, so he thought it best to wait until they were supposed to meet up and he would head home after he got his drugs.

By the time he left the store, it was golden hour—the sun was saying its goodbyes for the day, casting long shadows across Clement Street. He took his time strolling past the neighboring grocery stores and local shops, admiring the bright, fresh produce that lined the sidewalk. Piles of glossy red apples stood next to mountains of plump oranges. The leaves from the bundles of forest-green bok choy waved up from wooden crates. A bin of honey-yellow Asian pears caught the last rays of sunlight.

The trendy coffee shops in the area had already flipped over the signs on their doors—their metal gates shuttered and locked. The fluorescent lights of the record store across the street remained on, a few meandering beanie-wearing customers inside digging through the crates. He passed a vintage clothing shop where mannequins dressed in worn denim jackets and faded band t-shirts watched him through dark windows.

At the corner, he took the pack of Marlboro Reds out of his jacket pocket, pulling out two cigarettes and the black lighter he'd left in the box. He put one of the cigarettes behind his ear and the other between his lips. The breeze coming off the ocean combined the smell of tobacco with those of the neighborhood—the rich aroma of Burmese coconut curry and lemongrass, the bready scent of BBQ pork buns, and the smoky tang of bulgogi beef and short ribs.

As he crossed the intersection, heading south toward the park, there was a break in the buildings that allowed him to see off into the distance. Perfectly placed in the clearing, past the telephone poles and power lines, was a big red structure atop a hill that stuck up toward the sky.

He wasn't surprised to see it. He couldn't have avoided it for much longer; it was bound to happen sooner or later. But it still felt too soon. He stopped walking for a moment and took several drags as he stared up at the tower.

On a clear day like this one, with no buildings obstructing the view, Sutro Tower was visible from nearly every corner of the bay, standing atop the highest peak in San Francisco. To some, it was a historic landmark. To others, it was a glorified radio antenna.

But to Tennessee and Lucy, it was so much more.

He sighed as he exhaled another cloud of smoke. There was a twisted satisfaction that came with seeing it—like the painful pleasure of picking a scab. No matter how bad it hurt, he just couldn't stop himself. The bittersweet ache of remembering their time together was somehow both a torture and a comfort. Memories were all he had now to feel connected to her, even if those memories were tainted.

He and Lucy met at a house party that Tanner dragged him to shortly after Tennessee moved to the city. Lucy and Tanner ran in the same social circles at school, and Tennessee fell for her the moment they met. The cramped apartment was packed wall-to-wall with students—bodies pressed together in the mood lighting that cast everyone in a soft purple glow. Tennessee had been nursing the same lukewarm beer for over an hour, feeling out of place in a sea of strangers—when she emerged through the crowd and reached her hand out.

"Hi, I'm Lucy."

She was brilliant and far more extroverted than anyone he'd ever met. One of the first things he noticed about her was how beautiful her eyes were—a bright blue, full of wonder and life. The delicate silver septum piercing that adorned her nose caught the light when she moved. The whole room lit up when she laughed, her head tilting back to reveal a cluster of freckles along her neck. She took up all the air in the room when she spoke, somehow making herself heard perfectly despite loud music. There was something magnetic about her that just made people gravitate toward her.

By midnight, they'd found their way to a quieter corner of the kitchen, perched on the countertops away from the chaos, sharing a bottle of tequila even though he hated it. She asked Tennessee questions that he'd never been asked before, like she was trying to break down his walls. And for some reason, he let her. Slowly but surely, she got through his guarded exterior.

They'd been practically inseparable since that night.

Those first few months went by like a whirlwind. They spent every night they could together—sometimes dozens in a row. They would only leave each other's side if they had to—like if he needed to go to work or if she had class or band practice.

It didn't matter if they didn't have anything to do; they just wanted to be near each other. Many of their nights together were spent driving around in Tennessee's truck, with no particular destination in mind. Often at two or three in the morning, they'd sneak away from their apartments. She would crawl into the passenger seat, only to push up the center console so she could sit as close to him as she could. He drove in whatever direction she told him to. Many of those times would lead them up to Twin Peaks, with Sutro Tower standing on the next hill over.

As he drove up the winding, dark hill toward the lookout, she would turn on her favorite songs and belt the lyrics out the window, singing until her voice cracked. If she was even a little drunk, she would sit on the window with her hands out wide and the wind in her red-tinted curls—only satisfied when she had become one with the trees and star-speckled night sky. Every so often, he'd steal glances at her. If he was lucky, her freckled face would be perfectly angled in the side-view mirror. It was worth the risk—taking his eyes off the treacherous roads—to see her like that.

During the day, Twin Peaks was usually overrun by tourists, which made finding a parking spot up on the hilltop nearly impossible. But in the middle of the night, they had their own private view of the city.

Sutro Tower stood on the hill just to the west of Twin Peaks. As they wound up the curved road, Sutro would greet them with bright red flashing lights dancing along its body. It stood at their sides as they looked out over the sea of lights coming from the buildings and streetlights downtown. Sutro was awake with them as the rest of the city slept. The tower heard all their whispers, kept all of their secrets, and became the embodiment of their favorite memories.

She was the one to give Sutro Tower its significance one night in the pouring rain when she said: "No matter where we are, no matter how much time has passed. Just look up to the tower and know that I'll always love you."

And that's exactly what he did. Whenever the tower would show up in his day, poking its head out of the skyline or up over the fog, he would think of her, in hopes that she was off in a different part of the city doing the same. On days when he missed her a little more than usual, he'd take a detour on the way home just to see it and remember what she said that night.

He'd walked all the way to Geary with the tower in his view, now only a few blocks from Vera's place. The sun was sinking lower into the sea with each passing minute, painting the sky with deep pink and orange hues. The rustic red color of the tower was washed away with the dimming daylight, leaving a dark, shadow-like silhouette in its place against the colors in the sky. The beady red lights that lined the tower had just come on and were blinking intermittently.

"Just look up to the tower and know that I'll always love you."

His brow furrowed and his chest became heavy. This promise of unconditional love had become a lie. She wouldn't always love him. She wouldn't have said what she did the other night if she did.

The tower's metal prongs caught the dark clouds that started to creep in from the Pacific Ocean. His romanticized version of the tower crumbled under the weight of reality. Every flash of the tower's red lights felt like reopening a wound. Before his eyes, it transformed into a relic of the past and now reminded him of everything he was trying to forget.

Tennessee checked his phone—twenty minutes had slipped away while he was caught up in the past. He pulled himself back to the present and why he was here tonight. He needed the drugs from Vera to dull the sharp edges of these memories. He couldn't wait another second. He needed to be high right now.

He threw the first cigarette to his feet and ground it into the pavement with his shoe and lit the second one he'd stashed behind his ear as he crossed the intersection at Balboa Street, finally at Vera's.

"Hey Ten!" Vera shouted down from her apartment window before he could even text her that he'd arrived.

Her face was sticking out of a third-floor window of the rundown apartment complex. The front of the building had an overhang with green fabric that was waving in the wind and a black metal gate beneath it that kept him out.

"Be right down," she yelled. He gave a thumbs up and continued smoking as he waited for her to bring down his drugs.

A few minutes later, behind the black bars of the gate, Vera bounced down the steps. She wore a thick fleece-lined jacket, something she didn't have on when she stuck her head out of the window.

She smiled wide as she pushed open the gate. "So glad you came!"

He shrugged. "Sure, no prob. Just doing what I gotta do." He held his hand out, waiting for the fresh bag.

To his surprise, she grabbed his hand and began swiftly

walking away from her apartment building into the cold January night.

"Uh…" he stammered and fumbled behind her, his lit cigarette falling to the ground as she dragged him away. "Where are we going?"

"It's a surprise," she said mysteriously, turning back to give him a wink.

He gulped. He was never too keen on surprises.

Nerves took over. He began to question everything, recalling every conversation they'd ever had. Did she always drag her customers somewhere else for the deals she did at home? Did her apartment complex have cameras or something? It was hard to tell, given this was the first time he'd picked up from her outside of the bar.

Tennessee knew better than to ask for too many details from a drug dealer—even one to whom he'd gotten close— but his anxiety just wouldn't let up.

Did he owe her money? Had he done something to piss her off?

He looked down to see she was wearing scuffed-up black combat boots with metal chains and buckles that clanked against each other as she walked. He realized this was the first time he'd ever seen her shoes. He thought about pulling his wrist out of her grip and heading home without the drugs or his money to avoid whatever was at the end of this trek.

"Hey…uh… Did I do something?"

"Do something?" She released his hand, pulling out a metal flask from her jacket pocket. She took the first swig and then handed it to him. "Like what?"

"Uh, I dunno…" He took a sip. Whiskey. It burned his mouth and sent a river of warmth down into his stomach. The alcohol only moderately soothed his growing fears.

They walked farther and farther, away from any recognizable buildings or streets. He began to wonder how much cash was in his wallet.

Suddenly, she stopped walking and declared, "We're here!"

He looked up to see a large cement parking structure. The entrance gaped like the opening of a mouth. There were hardly any lights on in the interior, and those that were on flickered sporadically, illuminating just enough to make the darkness feel even more daunting. The wind whistled through the concrete levels, creating an eerie, hollow moan.

She began walking toward its bleak opening. What could they possibly be doing here? Whatever it was, it certainly couldn't be good.

Perhaps he should've just gone home, after all.

Chapter 6

"Uh…here where?" His eyes scanned the graffiti tags crawling up the wall of the intimidating parking structure.

Vera didn't waste any time answering his question. Instead, she made her way toward the entrance of the garage, her attention set on some unknown destination within. Something about the way she was walking into the building told him that she'd clearly been there before.

"Hurry up! Let's go!" She waved back at him before she ducked under the plastic barricade, the sound of her footsteps echoing as she made her way into the abyss. Within just a few steps, her silhouette disappeared into the darkness, leaving him alone on the sidewalk.

This was his chance. He could run away and avoid whatever surprise was waiting for him inside. But where were they? He'd been too in his head to remember what streets they'd turned down or even pay attention to which direction they'd walked.

The surrounding streets were dead quiet, which was unusual to find in the middle of the city. There were no car engines or human voices echoing across the avenues.

The only sound he could hear was the wind rustling through the branches of nearby trees and whistling against his ears.

And what about the coke he'd already paid for? He felt a craving bubble up inside him as he thought of it. He needed those drugs.

Against his better judgment, he charged into the darkness after her, into the unknown. Each step felt heavier than the last as the ominous garage enveloped him.

"Vera, what are we doing?" His voice bounced off the concrete walls and returned to his ears sounding like a stranger's. "This is just a weird, empty parking garage."

She turned on her heels sharply. "Shhhh!" She brought her index finger to her lips. "We gotta sneak past the night guard."

"To do what?" he whisper-screamed.

She ignored him once again and continued to creep deeper into the empty garage until they came to a cement stairwell at the back corner of the building. The metal soles of her boots made far more noise than any words they could have said, a loud clacking sound that echoed throughout the building with every step she took, a metallic percussion that marked their ascent. They both remained quiet nonetheless as they wound up each floor.

His mind prepared for the worst. Would he be jumped once he got to the top of the stairwell? Mugged for whatever cash he had? Did Vera know something that he didn't? Could she have known what happened to Lucy?

The questions multiplied the farther they climbed, feeding off one another. He was quickly starting to regret agreeing to meet her outside of the bar.

After seven floors, they approached the top level, and a rush of cool air swept across his face, a stark contrast to the stale atmosphere of the stairwell. As they stepped onto the rooftop, he could see it was marked up by the white lines of empty parking spaces.

He walked slowly into the opening, scanning the lot diligently, examining every inch of space, squinting to inspect each dark corner for signs of danger. There were no cars or people to be found, just concrete and shadows. He looked back into the stairwell and tried to listen for the sounds of footsteps following behind them—the silence was almost more unnerving than any sounds would've been.

But there was nothing. There seemed to be no danger of any kind. None that he could see, anyway.

Relieved, at least for now, he took a moment to catch his breath, letting the brisk night air refresh his lungs after their climb. A gust of wind came over the cement ledge that was a few feet from where he stood, carrying the smell of the sea, prompting him to walk over to it. As he did, he was greeted by a new view of the city—one of his own backyard. As he looked out, his fears fell away, and a feeling of wonder took its place.

The skyscrapers that usually took center stage at Twin Peaks were nowhere to be seen. Sutro Tower and San

Francisco's iconic skyline were out of sight and out of mind. It was a far more serene view that showed off the west side of the city and the Richmond neighborhood. The streetlights that lined the residential blocks went on for miles until they dropped off where they met the coastline—their white lights danced and twinkled back at him. From this height, the city seemed both familiar and new, a different perspective of the streets he'd been down countless times.

"Almost there," she said behind him.

"There's more?" He turned around to see her halfway up a rickety metal ladder with a cigarette between her lips.

She was making her way up to a thin platform at the base of a big wooden billboard that was located just above the rooftop lot. Its canvas was stripped and covered in various spray-painted tags—it clearly hadn't been updated in months. The ladder that she was climbing was in even worse shape. It jolted under the weight of her body and had large patches of brown and orange rust in the places where its white paint was chipped.

She was unfazed by the ladder's wobbly nature. In less than thirty seconds, she reached the grated platform which creaked under her boots. She pulled the cigarette from her lips and lit it before sitting on the ledge of the platform with her feet dangling off. Seemingly fearless, she sat there, unbothered by the height.

Back on the ground, Tennessee's feet were frozen in place. He needed to tilt his head as far back as it would go to see her up on the platform above him. The catwalk was no wider than one of the shelves at work. Could it even hold the weight of two people? It rattled as she swung her legs out like pendulums off the grated platform. He could hear the sound of his heartbeat again.

He looked back over at the stairwell they'd just come from. He could make a break for it before she even noticed. He would be long gone before she could make it back down the ladder.

"What are you waiting for?" she called down.

He didn't want to admit it, but he felt he had no choice.

"I'm afraid of heights."

"Oh, come on! It's fine." She took another swig from her flask. "I've done this like a million times, it's totally safe."

Goosebumps rose on the back of his neck. His palms grew moist and clammy. The color drained from his face. His arms stuck at his sides and his boots were glued to the cement beneath him. Beads of sweat formed on his forehead as his eyes darted back and forth between her and the stairwell as he contemplated making a run for it. The wind picked up and filled the silence as he weighed his options.

She must have noticed just how paralyzed he was. The playful swing of her legs slowed, then stopped as she studied his face from above. Their eyes met briefly, and something in her expression softened. Without a word, she put down the flask, stubbed out her cigarette, and tucked what remained of it behind her ear.

"Hold on." She pulled herself up by the handrail and began her descent back down the ladder.

When her boots touched the cement again, she came up to him and stood closer than before, close enough that he could smell the whiskey and the faint trace of menthol smoke on her breath.

"You don't have to," she lightly touched his shoulder, sending a jolt of warmth down his arm, "but I'm here to help, if you want to give it a try."

His stomach twisted tighter as he considered his next move. Was his fear stronger than his pride? Vera had so effortlessly made it up and down the ladder without even a second thought. How could he ever hold his head up high at the bar again if he didn't at least try? He would have to get a new drug dealer purely out of embarrassment.

"I guess I have no choice," he grumbled under his breath as he stepped over to the base of the ladder.

"Yay!" She stood just a few steps behind him. "It'll be worth it, I swear."

At this point, he didn't care what was at the top. This was for his ego. He wiped his sweaty hands down the front of his jeans before wrapping his fingers around the sides of the ladder. Hard flakes of crusted metal paint dug into his palms and crunched under his tight grip. He set his right foot up onto the first step. Though he hadn't even put a fraction of his body weight on it, it had already started to give. As he lifted his other foot off the cement and onto the ladder—now being fully supported by it—his shoulders grew tense, and the ladder let out a low creak.

"Just hold on and keep your weight in the middle," Vera said as he lifted his knee to get up to the next beam.

He climbed at a snail's pace, taking his time to breathe and contemplate between steps. The ladder shook as the muscles in his arms trembled. The longer he was up there, the sweatier his hands got, making it harder for him to keep his grip. He couldn't risk looking down; his eyes were laser-focused on his hands. The skin on his fingers was now completely white. The scab that was starting to form on his fist pulsed.

"Honestly, I don't know about this, man," he yelled down to Vera, who was just a few feet below him. He'd only climbed up four or five steps and had no reason to be yelling as loud as he was.

She giggled quietly to herself. "No, you got it!"

There was a hurricane spinning in his gut. He breathed in sharply and pushed through to climb another two steps. He missed the stability of the ground, but he'd gone too far to turn back now. He'd spent too much of his life feeling small and weak. If he couldn't even make it up this ladder while Vera had done it without even breaking a sweat, what did that say about him? Stepping down at this point wasn't an option.

"You're so close!" she kept on.

He had no idea if her words were true, but he needed to be done with this mortifying display. He needed to get it over with. Exhaling all the air from his lungs, he climbed up the remaining beams quickly and stepped onto the awning. There was a brief sense of relief to finally be off the ladder, but the platform provided him with a new source of anxiety.

He swiped his hands down his clothes again and quickly crouched down, grabbing the grates for support. The platform felt even less stable than it looked from below. His knees shook as he adjusted his body, unwilling to commit to any position that wasn't pressed firmly against the billboard's base. The world seemed to tilt beneath him as his eyes darted between his grip on the grate and the distant ground. He inched backward, pressing his spine against the cool metal of the billboard frame, finding small comfort in anything solid.

In a matter of seconds, Vera was back on the ledge with her feet dangling casually, as though she was sitting on a park bench. She relit the cigarette she'd left behind her ear, the brief flare of her lighter illuminating her face in the darkness.

"You made it!" Her voice carried a hint of genuine enthusiasm. "Not a bad view, huh?"

He'd been far too focused on soothing the sinking pit in his stomach and his death grip on the cold steel grates to look out at the view. From up here, he could see the entirety of the Richmond neighborhood and beyond. Victorian-style cottage homes and low- to mid-rise apartment buildings lined the avenues—no two buildings were exactly alike. Many of the windows that looked back at him were black, but a few of them let out fragments of white and yellow light, letting him know which apartments and homes had people inside. In between the buildings, trees peeked their heads out and let their leaves dance in the breeze. In a city that had been taken up by so much cement, he was surprised to see so much greenery.

From this height, the city's soundtrack transformed— the sound of car engines blended into a distant hush like ocean waves, broken only by the occasional siren in the distance.

Among the residencies and treetops, there were some recognizable landmarks that helped him figure out where exactly they were. The Star of the Sea, which was a prominent Catholic church in the Inner Richmond, stood angelically in white not too far from where they sat. The ever-familiar golden plumes of the Russian Orthodox Church were farther off in the distance, giving him some sense of how far he was from home. Even farther, peeking up over the tree-lined hills of the Presidio, he could see the two red towers of the Golden Gate Bridge that lit up the surrounding mist with a hazy orange glow.

The streetlights were far more mesmerizing from up here. The stagnant beams took turns flickering against the night sky, going on and on for miles in all directions. They lit up the forty-block grid until they dropped off into the Pacific Ocean—where the land ended and total darkness began. From up here, the ocean looked like a void with no end, with a rolling fog floating above it that was slowly creeping further inland.

The knot in his stomach released and he unlaced his fingers from the metal grates of the platform. He uncrossed his legs and inched closer to the ledge until he eventually let his feet hang free, like Vera. All the worries and fears he'd come into the garage with all felt so distant now.

Vera tapped his forearm, pulling him out of his trance. In her outstretched hand was his bag of cocaine. He looked up to see her cheesy smile again, swinging her feet in glee. His cheeks turned pink as he took the bag from her palm, stuffing it into his jacket pocket.

"Thanks," he said softly.

He finally got what he needed, but something was still keeping him there. As their eyes met again, Vera's expression shifted to something more probing, as if the cocaine was just the bait for the real reason why she brought him up here tonight.

"So, how are you feeling?" she fidgeted her fingers awkwardly around the flask. "You know, after the breakup?"

The sinking feeling in his stomach came back, but for a different reason this time. For a moment, he'd been able to forget about that—or rather, forget that he couldn't remember.

"Oh, uh." His eyes fell and he grazed his fingers over the raised skin on his knuckles. The dull throbbing returned behind his temples, as fragments of memories flashed in his mind's eye. But he couldn't tell Vera about any of that.

"I'm okay, I guess." The lie felt hollow in his mouth.

"How long has it been now?"

"Two days." It didn't even feel like the truth even though it was. It could have been two years or two minutes—time hadn't felt real since that night. The hours blurred together in his mind. He let a slow, calculated exhale out of his mouth, trying to disconnect from his thoughts as much as he could.

"Oh, ouch—so it's still really fresh." She reached her hand out and lightly touched his knee. "Don't worry, it'll hurt less with some time."

While he wasn't so sure about that, he nodded anyway.

"Can I ask you something?" She handed him the whiskey again.

"Sure." He took the canteen and downed a big gulp.

She paused as though she was searching for the right words. "Why did Lucy say that? What did you do to make her say you were like your dad? It seemed like she knew that would really get to you."

The question took him by surprise. His eyes got wide, and he blinked a few times. His brows furrowed and his smile fell into an offended scowl.

Why would Vera think he'd done something wrong, bad enough that it could justify Lucy saying something so vile— to compare him to his shitty dad?

"I'm sorry, I really don't mean to pry," she attempted to backpedal. "I guess I just feel like there's gotta be more to the story, you know?"

"It's not really any of your business."

"Sure, I know it's not. I just mean that…" she pushed her bangs out of her eyes. "I feel like you and I have similar stories. You know, broken homes, broken people. At least based on the little you've already told me about your family."

He scoffed at her assumption. The word "broken" landed like a slap—casual and stinging. Broken. As if his life were just some object that fell off a shelf. His jaw tightened as he ground his teeth against each other.

And yet, beneath his anger was a flicker of recognition. There was truth in what she'd said, even if he didn't want to admit it. The word itself wasn't wrong—it was hearing someone else say it out loud. There was something too intimate about it, too close to the truth he worked so hard to conceal, even from himself.

"Well, what makes you so broken, then?" he spoke with continued coldness, handing her back the flask.

She took a big drink, bringing one of her knees up to her chest. "I guess it probably all started with my dad leaving."

"Oh." Tennessee started to feel guilty. "Sorry. What happened?"

She sighed. Her demeanor changed as she looked off into the distance. Her eyes glazed over as she focused on nothing in particular and she turned her attention inward.

"Well, my sister and I grew up watching my parents nearly kill each other. There were a few times I had to call the cops when it got really bad."

She was now avoiding eye contact with him altogether. She took another sip of whiskey and put the flask down on the platform between them.

"One day my dad just left. I must have been like twelve or something, which would have made my sister like four or five. No note, no phone call, no explanation. After that, my mom started rotating through random boyfriends. Every other month, there was some new guy hanging around our little two-bedroom apartment. Eventually, she had one that turned her on to heroin and she became more preoccupied with that than feeding her kids—or herself, for that matter."

She transformed right before his eyes. Like watching a time-lapse in reverse—the confident woman beside him was now someone smaller, younger, more vulnerable. The sharp edges of her usual self blurred and softened, revealing the frightened teenager that lived beneath her tough exterior. Maybe they weren't so different, after all.

"There would be days at a time when we'd go without a meal at home. When I got a little older, I would steal whatever drugs they left out and start selling them to make sure my sister and I had what we needed to get by. When my mom found out, she kicked me out of the house. So, I packed up my shit and found the cheapest little studio I could find."

Tennessee shook his head in disbelief. "How old were you?"

"Sixteen." She looked down at her hands.

"And your sister?"

"She's still at home." She wiped the tears from her eyes before they fell down her cheek. "They live in the east bay, so I stop by to make sure she's okay from time to time when I know my mom's not home. Make sure she's got enough to eat and that she's okay. When I save up the cash, I'll get an apartment big enough for us to share."

"Is that why you started dealing?"

She looked up to meet his eyes. "Yeah, I guess so. It's the only thing I've ever really known how to do. Before I started making drinks, that is."

She was even stronger than he initially thought, especially now knowing her past. She was dealing drugs at sixteen to feed her sister when her mother couldn't. It was beyond a form of survival or self-preservation—it was something else entirely.

He felt connected to her in a new way. Not the surface-level connection of sharing stories and drinks at the bar, but something deeper. The kind where you don't need to explain how you've been hurt, because the other person just gets it.

Now "broken" just felt like the truth. Not some generic label applied from the outside, but a reality they both lived with and understood in ways other people couldn't. Broken didn't mean weak—certainly not for her. The same fractures that left scars had somehow made her stronger.

He could see now what she meant when she said they were the same. They were just two people doing their best with the shitty situations they were born into. Two people who could recognize the cracks in each other.

"I'm so sorry, Vera." The words felt small against the weight of what she'd shared, but he had nothing better to offer.

She chuckled, "No, no, don't worry about me. It's really not a big deal."

The cheery façade returned quickly, as she fanned her flushed cheeks. She'd had years of practice, putting on a brave face when there was no one else there to comfort her. She extinguished her emotions like blowing out the flame of a candle and immediately returned to her usual self, the armor sliding back into place.

"Well, thanks for sharing that." He reached out and gently placed his hand over hers, her skin warm and soft. Goosebumps rose on the back of his neck again.

"Alright, then. Now it's time for you to spill your guts."

He didn't really want to get into it. It all felt so fresh after what just happened with Lucy. But Vera had just shared so much of herself and her past, he felt like he had to tell her something, like he needed to repay her vulnerability with his own.

"Well, I already told you my dad was a drunk and that he was fucked up to my mom," he started, unsure how deep into the story he would go. "To cut to the chase, he regularly cheated on her. A lot of the time, he would forget to pick me up from school or force me out of the house because of it."

"Oh god. I'm so sorry."

"When my mom found out, she tried to leave. But my dad sorta…" Tennessee paused, "flipped out."

"What do you mean flipped out?"

"I—I mean," he stuttered, his voice catching in his throat. "He, uh…hit her."

His eyes fixed on a point in the distance. "I don't really remember a whole lot from that time, honestly, just the aftermath. Lucy used to watch some TikTok therapist who called it dissociative amnesia." His mouth twisted with sudden bitterness. "I wouldn't go all that far—I just think it was a memory my mind didn't need."

His fist curled up, a flash of heat came to the base of his fingers. "I hated when she would try to pathologize me with weird bullshit like that."

Vera was only the second person who'd ever heard this story, even if it was only a portion of it. Lucy was the first, and she'd been given every excruciating detail he could remember. Both times he'd told it, all the same feelings came back up. His chest tightened and his insides felt tender, as if it had happened just yesterday. The distance he'd carefully built over years collapsed in seconds—time folding in on itself—bringing him right back to that doorway, to those strange shadows, to the moment his life changed.

"I totally get it. I would hate that, too. So when did your folks split up?"

"That's the thing—they didn't."

"Oh." She sounded surprised. "Well, that's good, right? They must have worked it out?"

"I mean, it depends on who you ask. My sister's still in middle school and needs a dad."

"And what about you?"

He let out a big sigh. He was just drunk enough to let his walls come down a little. He hoped that he wouldn't regret it in the same way he regretted telling Lucy.

"My mom forgave him, but I never did," he shook his head with disgust. "I was the one who watched her cry herself to sleep on the nights when he didn't come home. I was the one who was changing my sister's diapers when she couldn't get out of bed. I was the one who had to bandage her up and help her hide her bruises before she went to work. When my dad was god knows where, with god knows who."

"I can't imagine," she gripped his hand a little tighter. "Do you talk to them much these days?"

"I haven't talked to my dad in years. But that doesn't stop my mom from trying to hand the phone over to him every time she calls. A lot of the time, I just hang up before he even has the chance to say hello. I can't stand the sound of his voice."

He paused to collect himself. He was starting to feel lightheaded—both from the alcohol and the intensity of the conversation. The world beneath the metal grates seemed to tilt slightly beneath them, the edges of his vision softening. The night air suddenly felt thin, like he was at a much higher altitude.

"But what's worse is that he never even apologized—or admitted that he did anything wrong. One day, he started going to church and claiming that he was a changed man. He got on some pills that made him not want to drink and went to some meetings. Then we were all supposed to act like none of it ever happened."

He paused and looked over at Vera. She looked like she was clinging to his every word. His thoughts were swimming in alcohol now, each sentence requiring more concentration than the last, making the rawness of his emotions impossible to filter behind his usual defenses.

"I just always wondered why she didn't actually leave. Did she really love him despite all of his mistakes? Or was she just too afraid to be alone?"

He retracted his hand from hers and rubbed his eyes before any tears managed to escape. A familiar shame washed over him—that same suffocating feeling that always came when he let someone see the cracks. He immediately regretted letting himself go this far, revealing pieces of himself that he didn't let anyone see.

A beam of light briefly swept across the lower level

of the garage, visible in the distance beyond the edge of the platform they were sitting on. Vera took a drag of her cigarette and held the silence between them until the light disappeared around a corner.

"And Lucy?" She ashed her cigarette over the ledge. "What did she see in you that made her say that? Especially since she knew just how much that would piss you off."

Tennessee's chest tightened, a hot pressure building beneath his ribs. The question drove into him like a knife—especially after all he'd just shared with her. His jaw clenched so hard he could hear it click. Something primal and defensive uncurled inside him.

He grabbed the flask and chugged what was left in it, the liquor burning a path down his throat that matched the fire rising in his blood.

"I'm nothing like him!" he said, his voice erupting from somewhere deep and raw. "I don't get why the fuck she wou—"

"Hey! You can't be up there!" a deep voice said from down below. The security guard had found them.

"Alright, alright." Vera stood up fast. "We're coming down right now."

The rage drained from him like air from a punctured tire. His unfinished sentence hung in the night air, the words he'd been about to hurl still burning the back of his throat. He swallowed the anger and buried it back deep down, locking it back inside the vault.

Chapter 7

Nightfall consumed the day's blue sky. Tennessee found his feet at the edge of a dark and raging sea with waves that crashed and beat against the cliffside. The wind lashed out in gusts across the shore, which sprinkled sand into both his and Lucy's hair. Atop the weathered wooden steps, their faces grew damp in the misty air. They sat in silence, but the surf was roaring so loud that they hardly noticed.

Neither the wind nor the water was powerful enough to move them from their statue-like positions. He sat a step above her with a fleece blanket wrapped around both of their bodies, as she wept, her body trembling in his arms.

West Cliff Drive was somewhat of a special place to the two of them. It was out of the city, in the beach town of Santa Cruz about two hours south. The first time he'd ever picked her up for a late-night drive, this was where they went—they later considered this night their first date. Every now and then, they would find their way back here when they felt like leaving the city.

Tonight, however, they returned on a much less joyous occasion.

Lucy's grandfather had passed away that morning. For the last six months, he'd been battling a brain tumor that eventually wore his body down. First, it affected his memory, then his ability to speak, and, eventually, shut down his organs and forced him to be hospitalized. All her family could do was watch idly by and hope that the doctors could reverse the clock. The last time Lucy had gone back to Portland to visit, he was frail and growing weaker with each passing day. His eyes had sunk far back into his skull and his skin hung off his bones. He likely weighed less than the blankets he was wrapped in. Each of her family members rotated sleeping at the hospital for months, with uncertainty as the only constant. He had become a hollow shell of the man he once was. One day, the doctors said there was nothing more they could do for him and sent him home with a hospice nurse to make the most of his remaining weeks.

Today, those weeks ran out.

The rest of her family was at his side—able to hold his hand as they said their farewells and sending him out of this world with their love. She couldn't be there in his final moments. So instead, she sat at the shore and allowed the salt from the sea air to mix with her tears.

Plagued with guilt, anger, and everything in between, she scolded herself for not being able to say goodbye. Those feelings were amplified when she thought about her nana, which made her broken heart sink into her stomach.

Tennessee was there to support her through all of it. He listened to her unfiltered thoughts and wiped away all of her tears. He could only observe the storm of emotions raging inside her and see how the waves within her matched those of the sea. He didn't know what to do, what to say, or how to help. All he could do was hold her tightly.

"It's just fucked up," she said, the wind tossing around her hair.

"What is?"

"That this is how true love ends," she wiped her cheek with her sleeve. "You know what you're getting into from the very beginning—'til death do you part'—but no one ever considers what that really means. One person is always alone in the end, having to watch the love of their life die right before their eyes. After you've built a whole life together, one day that person is just gone…forever. And then what? You're supposed to pick up the pieces and just keep going after the 'life-long contract' you agreed to has been nulled? How is that fair?"

He nodded in agreement—still speechless. He couldn't deny the devastating realities of life and death. She brought light to the harsh truths about the world, but nothing he said would be able to change them.

"It was the closest thing to a true love story I'd ever known. After everything—fifty years of marriage and an entire life that they'd built together, brick-by-brick—she just had to slowly watch him slip away. He couldn't even speak to say goodbye!"

She let out a big exhale and paused her rant. She'd exhausted herself with this rollercoaster of emotions. She looked out over the sea as if she was contemplating not only the fate of her grandparents, but her own happy ending, as well.

He stared out at the dark, rolling waves, collecting his thoughts before speaking.

"That's what real love is, Luce." He dropped his eyes to meet hers. "An unconditional love like that goes through all the good and bad life has to offer. True love isn't that bullshit from the movies. Love is pain, it's resilience, and, ultimately, it's suffering. Those who love each other most, watch each other die."

The water in her eyes dried up and she turned away from him. Her mind chewed on his words with intense deliberation.

She nodded slowly. "You're right," she turned back toward him and tightly gripped his hand. "I want to watch you die."

His heart dropped and shattered like a dish on a tile floor.

"Ouch," he leaned away from her.

She shook her head and grabbed his hand even tighter. "I want to be at your side through the good, the bad, and all the messiness in between. I want to watch you get old and wrinkly, see the world with you, and become grumpy old people together. And selfishly, when you're on your last breath, I want to send you off with a kiss. I love you so much that I want to watch you die."

His heart began to beat again, and a soft smile came to his lips as he realized what she meant.

"You see us spending our whole lives together?"

"Of course," she turned completely around to face him. "It'll hurt like hell, but a lifetime with you is worth it."

He never thought of himself as the marriage type. But despite his own hang-ups, he couldn't help but want to give her the world. As he thought about it more, he couldn't imagine a life without her. If there was such a thing as a soulmate, he figured this was what it must be like to find them.

"Well, in that case, I hope you go first." A soft smile spread across his face as he looked down at her.

The wind calmed for a moment, and the crash of the waves seemed to hush, as if the world itself was pausing around them. He studied her face in the dim light of the moon—awestruck by the way her eyes sparkled behind her tears, how her cheeks flushed in the cool air. He never thought he'd find himself here, making what felt like unspoken promises on a cliff's edge. Yet somehow, it felt inevitable, like the tide returning to shore, like two long-lost lovers meeting for the first time again in this lifetime.

He reached up to brush a strand of hair from her face, tucking it gently behind her ear. His fingertips lingered against her cheek as he slowly leaned forward, closing his eyes and shifting his head down to kiss her.

A few moments went by, but her lips never met his. Behind the darkness of his eyelids, he felt a cold draft washing over his face where her warm breath should be.

He heard her spit out a familiar phrase: *"You're just like your father."*

The words sliced through him like a razor blade, sharp and precise, carving into a wound he'd almost been able to forget was there. His eyes shot open.

He was back in her apartment. The soft morning light coming through her bay windows had once cast a romantic glow but now felt harsh and clinical. Her blue eyes had gone dark. They were now beady and black as she stared down at him. She tilted her head in a way that reminded him of something deranged. Any feelings of blissful, young love had completely fallen away, evaporating in the bright light. The words ignited his rage all over again, a familiar heat rising from deep within.

There was resentment in her voice and in her body language—shoulders rigid, jaw set, fingers curled into half-fists at her sides. She said the words again, this time even more coldly, each syllable enunciated with deliberate precision, like she was possessed by something beyond herself. "You're. Just. Like. Your. Father."

His jaw clicked as he clenched his teeth, the sound audible in the sudden silence between them. The muscles in his neck strained against his skin. He stood up quickly as he drove his heels into the ground. The sound of his weight hitting the floor sent a boom across the apartment.

"Don't fucking say that." His tone was deep and disturbed, vibrating from some dark place within his chest.

"You're. Just. Lik—"

Before she could finish her sentence, he grabbed her by the shoulders and shook her violently. Under the weight of his hands, her skin darkened with bruises that bloomed like time-lapse flowers, purple and blue spreading outward across her entire body from where his fingertips dug in. Blood came rushing out of her nostrils, bright crimson against her pale face, dripping onto her lips and chin. After a few seconds of rattling, her body began to crumble into sand, making a soft hissing sound like an hourglass being overturned. Her shoulders caved into her arms starting from where his hands made contact, disintegrating grain by grain. Her head fell into the hollow of her torso, her expression fixed in that final accusation. Eventually, he was left with only fistfuls of dust in his hands, slipping between his fingers no matter how tightly he tried to hold on.

In a matter of grueling seconds, she was reduced to almost nothing. All that remained was a small molehill where she once stood. A gust of wind rushed through her apartment and blew her away, the particles catching the light for a brief moment before disappearing completely out her windows.

He grasped at the passing sands in the wind—unable to catch them once they were gone. Falling to his knees, his hands moved frantically, desperately trying to gather what couldn't be contained. Panic took over and a scream exited his body, ripping his throat as it escaped.

The sound jolted him awake, still echoing in his ears. He opened his eyes to see the dark ceiling of a bedroom. His tongue felt like sandpaper against the roof of his mouth, and for several disorienting seconds, he couldn't immediately tell if he was in his apartment or hers. A mixture of terror and relief washed over him as he caught his breath and saw the familiar plaid pattern of his comforter. His heart hammered against his ribs, sweat cooling rapidly on his skin as reality slowly settled back in the quiet darkness.

Chapter **8**

Even in his dreams, he couldn't escape her.

His tired eyes looked up at the ceiling fan, dust particles lining its blades as it spun and creaked from the thin cable it hung from. The nightmare still clung to him. When he closed his eyes, he could only see her black, beady ones and the blood as it dripped down her face. He heard her voice say the phrase again and again, like nails on a chalkboard. He could still feel the sand between his fingers, and the feeling in his chest as she so quickly slipped away.

His memories of her were like Polaroids—captured moments frozen in time, grainy snapshots of what once was. These fragmented frames were all he had left of her now. In his dream, it was like he could almost step back into them.

But even those good memories had burnt edges, crisped and black. He wondered how much of his nightmare matched the reality of that day. Could he really have done something to her? Something so violent?

He tossed and turned the rest of the night, contorting his body in every possible position. When on his back, he could feel each of his vertebrae press into the hardwood beneath the mattress. His bony hip dug into the floor when he was on either of his sides. He couldn't get comfortable no matter what he did.

He rolled over to check the time on his phone, its blue light illuminating the small room. It was almost 4 a.m. Letting out a loud groan, he pulled the pillow over the top of his face.

"Just go to sleep," he whispered, taking in a few deep breaths. "Just stop thinking about it."

Her voice spoke to him again from inside his mind: You're just like your father.

Instinctively, his hands curled into fists, and he released an agonizing scream into the pillow before pulling it off his face. He swung his legs out from the blankets and moved to a seated position with his back against the wall and his calves against the cold hardwood. His stiff bones ached even more in their new position, his lower back popped and cracked as he straightened out.

His room was small, more like a large walk-in closet. Its only window opened to another wall. Dark, damp, and depressing, it matched his mental state. The space confined him like his thoughts.

As he grabbed his phone and switched it off Do Not Disturb, he noticed several notifications from Tanner—a few missed calls that were timestamped for just past midnight:

Yo.

Call me. Now.

Urgent.

"Oh fuck."

Tennessee's heart started to thump louder inside his chest. This was far from normal. Tanner and Tennessee almost never talked on the phone during their ten years of friendship. The extent of their digital conversations were dumb memes and brief logistical messages about where they were meeting up or whose turn it was to take the trash out.

Tennessee anxiously ran his fingers through his hair. It wasn't just his relationship with Lucy that was on the line. Tanner still didn't know that he and Lucy had broken up. On top of that, Tanner was expected to come back in just a few days and Tennessee still hadn't thought of a way to explain himself.

"What the fuck am I gonna tell him?"

Tennessee knew he needed to be the one to tell Tanner. He needed to give his side of the story before she did. But he couldn't piece together what that truth was. His lack of memory from that night would only make him look more guilty.

Tennessee didn't know what to do. His thumb hovered over Tanner's messages, the light from the screen casting harsh shadows across his face. Part of him knew he should respond. But what would he even say?

He lowered the phone to his lap. It was four in the morning, which meant that Tanner was probably asleep by now, anyway. Whatever emergency that was happening in their hometown could wait until later—and hopefully it had nothing to do with him and Lucy. At least that's what he told himself as he set the phone face-down on the bed, leaving Tanner's texts and missed calls unanswered.

What remained of the dime bag he bought from Vera gleamed from the milk crate next to him in the dim light. Grabbing it, along with his truck keys, he brought his knees and shoulders closer together until his nose was directly above the open bag. Using the key to scoop the substance into the grooves, he took a bump.

One big inhale, followed by a slow exhale. The coke burned the inside of his nostrils. Each pulse suddenly louder in his ears, a rapid drumming that matched the jittery energy flooding his limbs. The room seemed sharper somehow, every edge more defined even in darkness. The heaviness in his bones vanished, replaced by a hollow lightness that made sitting still impossible. He waited just a few moments and went in for another. His heartbeat started to pick up even more. One more bump. And another. And another. Until all the thoughts were gone.

There was no chance he was going back to sleep now. He got up early and went about his morning—showering and picking up some of the clothes piled up around his room—doing several more bumps along the way. The drugs pushed away his exhaustion, replacing it with a restless sensation that kept his hands in constant motion and his eyes darting from one thing to the next, never settling long enough for his thoughts to catch up.

He arrived at work early with a coffee in hand, as he fought the drip at the back of his throat. While Mr. Green was polite, he made no mention of Tennessee's punctuality—which made the sour taste in Tennessee's mouth even worse. He spent the morning sneaking off to do more bumps in dark corners and in between tall bookshelves.

Two more calls from Tanner lit up his phone throughout the morning. Each time, Tennessee stared at the screen as it vibrated, his heart pounding harder than the cocaine could explain. His finger hovered over the answer button for a few seconds before he finally hit decline, sending each call to voicemail.

The momentary relief was immediately replaced by a heavier guilt. With each ignored call, the inevitable conversation grew more difficult, the explanation for why he'd been avoiding the calls even more impossible to explain. He wasn't ready to deal with whatever was on the other side of the line, but he knew he couldn't stay silent forever.

He finished what was left of the bag by 10 a.m. He'd blown through a gram all by himself in just a few days, a new personal best. For the next two hours, he watched the clock hands tick by, waiting for it to read noon so he could go on his lunch break.

Vera was the only one in the bar when he walked in. She was behind the counter with her back toward the door, pulling cash out of a black bag and stuffing it into the register, heavy metal already blasting from the jukebox.

"Hey there." He knocked twice on the bar top before he sat down at his usual stool.

"Hey you," she returned over her shoulder. Her eyebrows raised and her mouth curved into a wide smile. She seemed surprised but happy to see him.

"I haven't heard from you since that night at the parking garage," her eyes fell back to the cash register. "I was beginning to think I scared you off."

Heat rushed to his face as memories of that night flooded back—the spectacle he'd made of himself, her practically dragging his paranoid body through the streets and up the stairs, the fear churning in his gut as he climbed the ladder. All of it seemed so ridiculous now.

He also remembered how much of themselves they both shared that night. He'd said more than he'd meant to. Discovering that she had similar wounds in her past also altered how he saw her. The way she'd let him see the softer side of her had shifted something between them. The ease they'd once had was replaced with an uncomfortable closeness that felt strange to him now that they were back in their usual setting. He didn't know how to act around her.

"Uh, yeah," he changed the subject quickly. "Could I— uh—get another gram?"

"Oh, is that all I'm good for?" She pushed the register closed with her hip and turned to face him.

Shit...no.

"No, no, I just ran out this morning," he started to fiddle with his hands and bounce his knee nervously against the barstool.

"I'm kidding!" she laughed and rolled her eyes, though her gaze lingered on his face a beat longer than usual. "Don't worry, I've got your precious white pixie dust."

She pulled out a small white bag from the inside of her vest pocket and clutched it in the palm of her hand.

"How do you feel about acid?"

He darted his eyes around the room. A few regulars had wandered in behind him—a couple wearing matching Patagonias and beanies and another guy with a turtleneck and obscure metal frames, all of them with their laptops in tow. These were the work-from-home types who often brought their work out into the wild with them. The type of people who could afford to turn a dive bar into their remote office.

She asked the question so casually but didn't lower her voice even a decibel. He widened his eyes at her in confusion.

"Oh stop, no one's listening," she waved her closed fist in the air. "It's not like they can hear a thing when I've got the music up this loud."

He shrugged. "Well, I've never done acid before. What's it like?"

"Oh, you have to try it! You see incredible colors and trippy visuals like you're looking out of a kaleidoscope. You feel light and free...like you can do anything! Like nothing matters. Once you've taken enough of it, you start to hallucinate."

"Hmmm. Sounds a bit intense for me."

"It can be. But I think the best part about it is that it makes you forget about all your problems for a little while." Her eyes had a knowing look in them. "You get to just enjoy life for a minute instead of struggling through it."

This made his ears perk up. The idea of escaping his thoughts completely, even temporarily, seemed like exactly what he needed.

"How do you do it?"

"Well, it comes as a sheet with a bunch of squares on it. Since it's your first time you should really only do one, just to see how you react to it. Once you're comfortable, you can try two and you should start to see things. I wouldn't do any more than that, though. That's when you really start to lose your shit."

"Ahhh, I wouldn't want a whole sheet." He pulled another hundred-dollar bill from his pocket. "I think I'm good with just the coke for now, thanks."

"Oh, come on, please. I've been wanting to do it again for a while now and I think you'd have a ton of fun! It'll help you forget about some of the heavy stuff, ya know? We could do it after we both get off work tomorrow?"

His eyebrows raised, realizing this wasn't a sales pitch.

"You wanna do it with me?"

"Duh! That's why I'm asking, silly."

His phone lit up and buzzed against the bar as another call from Tanner came through, which he quickly declined.

"Well, I'll think about it."

She dangled the baggie from her fingertips and waved it in front of his face. "What you meant to say was, '*I'm down.*'"

"Come on, Vera," he looked around the bar to make sure no one was watching. "You know these people come into the Peach, too."

She shrugged and started to place the bag back into the pocket she'd pulled it from.

"Fine, I'll do it with you. Just give me that."

"Now, that's what I like to hear." She slid the drugs across the bar toward him and plucked the cash from his hand. "See you tomorrow!"

Rolling his eyes as she walked off to tend to another customer, he tucked the baggie away, a strange mixture of anticipation and anxiety washing over him. Vera seemed to know just what to say to get what she wanted out of him. He'd given her too much ammo she could now use in her favor.

The buzz of his phone drew his eyes downward. His gaze fell to another series of messages from Tanner that came as several short one-liners:

Yo, my parents said that you need to be out of the apartment before I get back

I didn't get why u were acting weird but now I do

U know I love u like a brother but what u did is not OK

found out thru the cops

U have until the end of the week

Just below the thread of messages was a series of photos. He swiped through the first two, and his heart fell into the pit of his stomach. They were too hard to look at. He quickly locked his phone before anyone else could see.

Now he knew. He *did* do something to her. Something awful. Something he wasn't ready to face.

His lungs shrunk inside his chest, reality closing in on him with each shallow breath. For a split second, he imagined running as far as he could—far past city limits, past state lines, somewhere where this couldn't follow him.

He bit down on the inside of his cheeks until he tasted blood and scrunched up his nose to hold in the tears that were building in his eyes. First Lucy had slipped through his fingers, and now his best friend—the only person who'd had his back since childhood—was cutting him off. And not just any friend, but someone who was practically family.

And the fact that he was getting kicked out only rubbed salt in the wound.

With tears blurring his vision, he slammed his fist down onto the counter. The other customers turned to stare, and he hung his head. Vera's mouth opened to say something from further down the bar, but Tennessee was already standing up to leave. He felt her eyes on his back as he stumbled toward the door. He pushed through the exit without looking back, the door swinging shut behind him.

Chapter 9

"Is it too late to change my mind?" Tennessee asked. He and Vera sat shoulder to shoulder on the bus, their knees touching while it pulled away from its final stop in the Richmond. They'd both just finished their shifts and caught the 33, heading to Mission Dolores Park.

"Yep! There's no turning back now!" She excitedly tapped her fingers across his kneecap like she was playing a drum set.

Uncertainty flooded his mind. How long would the drugs last? Where would they end up tonight? How deep into the darkness would they go with so few hours of daylight left? How had she convinced him to go through with this? Nothing frightened him more than the idea of surrendering control of his own mind. He didn't know what would happen when his thoughts ran wild, free from the walls he'd spent a lifetime building. Walls that were already beginning to crumble.

"What if I take too much?"

"Don't worry, I won't give you that much. You're gonna have a great time."

As the bus made its way south on its route across the edge of Golden Gate Park, Sutro Tower came in and out of view—he thought of Lucy each time he caught a glimpse of it. His heartbeat quickened and he wiped his clammy palms against his jeans.

"What if I have a bad trip?"

After everything that happened over the last week, he was in a prime position for it to go south. What would he see? What emotions would surface? Would the past continue to catch up to him?

"Well, then I'll be here to help! Dolores Park will be the perfect starting point, and we can just feel it out from there."

Vera seemed to be buzzing with energy today, even more than usual. Maybe she was nervous too but just had a different way of showing it.

"I'm worried I might think about her the whole time…" He was embarrassed saying it out loud but needed Vera to know the real source of his fear. His fingers traced the edge of the bus window.

"Oh? Is that still on your mind? Do you want to talk about it? I'm here to listen if you do."

He didn't. He wanted to avoid thinking about it at all costs. The mere mention of her name sent him spiraling.

"No, that's okay. I just—I just don't know…" his voice trailed off. He didn't have the words to describe what he was worried about. Part of him wanted to pull the cord, stop the bus, walk away from whatever adventure was waiting for them on the other side.

"But, you know," the tone in her voice shifted. "I'm also here if you want to forget about it, too." Her fingers traced their way down from his bicep to his forearm.

He turned from the window and met her gaze. She bit the side of her lip. A fluttering feeling came to his stomach—a mixture of confusion and excitement. He was speechless. Was Vera flirting with him? He didn't even know she liked men—let alone liked him.

"Whoops," she retracted her hand. "Silly me, trying to rush things."

He nodded and looked back to the window, his mind racing with new questions. In the two years they'd known each other, she'd never shown any kind of interest in him before. His thoughts raced as he tried to decode her expression—the slight head tilt, the lingering touch. The possibility she might want him sent a shock through his system, thrilling and terrifying—one more element of uncertainty to add to a day already filled with it. Was this why she'd asked to hang out with him outside of the bar? What did she really want? Was it just a momentary impulse, or had she been hiding her feelings all along? What would this mean for their friendship?

He stole another glance at her profile as she gazed out the opposite window, wondering if she could sense all that she'd unleashed within him with one simple touch.

"Are you nervous for your first time?"

"Mmhm," he hummed. As if it wasn't obvious.

"Don't be nervous! Like I said, I'll be right here to make sure nothing goes wrong. Just try to stay positive."

This did little to ease his tension. He'd developed a coke habit because staying positive wasn't possible for him. It was a way for him to numb when everything he was carrying got too heavy, allowing him to feel nothing at all. The idea that a good trip was dependent on staying positive only terrified him more.

The bus lurched down the hill, leaving the fog-shrouded Richmond behind. As they descended into the Castro, neutral homes gave way to buildings splashed with bright pastels that popped against the clouds of the gray afternoon. A preview of what the LSD might soon do to his perception.

Nearing their stop, Vera grabbed her tote bag and dug through it. She pulled out a small silver square and began to unfold it. It was a piece of aluminum foil, flattened and creased. Inside was a sheet of paper about the size of an index card, divided into perforated squares. Vera tore off two squares from the bottom right corner.

"Stick out your tongue."

"Right now? We're doing it right now?" He looked around the bus. "There are other people here."

"Yep!" She licked her middle finger and used it to pick up one of the perforated tabs from the foil. "Doesn't matter. We're getting off here."

"But I'm not—I'm not ready!"

It was her perfect moment to strike. His jaw hung just open enough for her to slip her finger in and drop the tab. Instead of landing in the center of his tongue, it fell to the side.

"What the fuck!"

"Sorry! I could tell you were about to bail on me! You had the same look on your face that you had that night in the parking garage."

"Oh god, it's on my gums," he started to panic. "Is that okay? It doesn't feel right."

"Yes, that's fine. It all gets ingested the same way. Stop freaking out."

He moved the square around in his mouth, feeling it with curiosity as he tried to get the paper back to the center. It felt strange, like cardboard. But other than the paper itself, it didn't taste like anything. As the bus slowed, she took a second square from the foil, placed it on her tongue, then folded the aluminum back up and returned the rest to her bag.

He didn't have any time to process what he'd been thrown into, nor did he have time to be upset. The moment the bus doors opened, she grabbed his hand and pulled him up.

A cool breeze hit his face as they reached the sidewalk. The paper in his mouth grew wet and mushy. This meant the drug was dissolving, already starting to seep into his bloodstream. Going home now meant he'd have to face whatever demons that emerged during his trip alone.

He stayed silent, suppressing his feelings. He reminded himself to stay positive. That was the key to avoiding a bad trip and getting his thoughts to cooperate with the new chemicals in his system.

"How long does it usually take to kick in?" He continued to move the tab around his mouth.

"Oh, I dunno. Half-hour? Maybe an hour? Trust me, you'll know when it hits."

This did little to reassure him. Desperate for distraction, he focused on their surroundings. The Castro—a historic gay neighborhood proud of its identity—provided plenty of options for this. Rainbow flags billowed from streetlamps, shop windows displayed mannequins in leathers and studs standing next to mountains of sex toys, and posters of drag queens in bright makeup promoted weekend shows. Dance music poured from every restaurant and bar they passed. Everything here seemed alive and carefree. So unlike him.

"Are you feeling it yet?" he asked after two blocks, his attention snapping back to the substance dissolving in his mouth.

Vera shook her head. "Just give it a minute to do its thing."

He nodded uneasily, walking at her side.

"Do you spit out the paper once it gets all mushy?"

"No! Don't do that. Once it's broken down into a little spit ball, swallow it."

He grimaced. "Why?"

"In case there's any left on the paper. You don't want it to go to waste."

The paper was already past that point. It had dissolved into a soggy, pulpy mass that sat heavily on his tongue. He pressed it against the roof of his mouth, feeling its texture fully—like wet newspaper, fibrous and disintegrating. His throat tightened as he forced himself to swallow. The mushy ball scraped down his esophagus all the way into his stomach. He ran his tongue over his teeth, trying to remove the persistent sensation that something unnatural had just passed through him.

"How do you know when it starts?"

"Oh, the build-up is the best part! Everything suddenly gets brighter, colors are more vivid, and you'll start smiling for no re—"

She was interrupted by the sound of shattering glass. It was a sound he knew well—a sound he heard often growing up, one that struck fear into his core.

He had no idea where it was coming from—but it didn't matter. In an instant, he'd ducked down and curled onto his knees on the sidewalk—a position he moved into with a precision that could only come as a result of muscle memory. With a curved spine and eyes screwed shut beneath the protective cage of his arms, the world became nothing but darkness and the sounds of shattering glass.

Like a terrified child all over again—he was powerless, out of control. No way to stop it except to hide. Muscles tensing harder with each passing moment. Eyes squeezed tighter. Head tucked deeper into his body. The crashing seemed endless.

"Dude, it's just a garbage truck," Vera's voice cut through the chaos. "What's your problem?"

Oh fuck.

Reality returned in stages: first, his cautiously parting eyelids, then his hands dropped from his head. He became lightheaded as he unfolded himself and stood back up. The shattering sound slowed, then eventually stopped.

"Look," she pointed behind him.

Turning, he saw a municipal garbage truck, its mechanical arms lowering an emptied public trash can on the corner.

Color flushed to his face as he brushed the gravel off his knees and straightened out his clothes. Thankfully, his jacket hid the sweat stains that had formed under his armpits.

Vera's face turned up as she tried not to laugh. "Why did you do that?"

Whether or not she meant it, he felt judgment in her tone.

"Whatever," he muttered, pushing past her. "Doesn't matter."

Avoiding her gaze, Tennessee rushed across the street as the crosswalk sign counted down the last few seconds of safety. Somewhere beneath his humiliation, he knew that Vera would understand—possibly better than most, given what he knew of her childhood. But he couldn't go there. Not right now. Not when he needed to do everything in his power to stay positive.

About thirty seconds later, Vera caught up to him. She was out of breath, chest rising and falling rapidly. Something about her face seemed different—her eyes wider, more alert, a slight flush across her cheeks that hadn't been there before.

"It's starting."

"What is?"

"I'm starting to drop in," she smiled back at him. "The colors on the rainbow crosswalk back there lit up as I was running across the street."

He looked back at the crosswalk. The colors seemed normal. Predictably bright, just as they were the last time he'd seen them. "I don't feel anything yet."

"You will," she grabbed his hand. There was something about this subtle touch of her hands that soothed his anxiety, making it easier for him to forget the looming thoughts he was so desperately trying to push down.

She held his hand all the way down 18th Street to Dolores Park. They settled under the palm trees at the center. It was a rather dreary day—the city trapped under gray clouds that weren't quite low enough to be considered fog.

On sunny days, Dolores Park would be overflowing with

people day-drinking and enjoying the views. Today, it was mostly empty. A few dog-walkers skirted the edges of the green. Tennessee and Vera had the park all to themselves, with an unobstructed view of the skyline.

He avoided looking over his shoulder, knowing Sutro Tower stood behind them on the hill. He wouldn't give his mind anything else to fester on.

"Are you feeling it yet?" She sat with her arms around her knees.

"No, nothing yet."

"I think it's fully hitting me now."

He looked over at her. She had a dreamy look on her face, lips parted in quiet wonder. Her eyes had transformed—pupils dilated into black pools, against a green halo. She seemed to be looking through the skyline rather than at it, her gaze fixed on something invisible to him. Her fingers absently traced patterns on her knee, moving to rhythms only she could hear.

"How do you know?"

"I couldn't explain it even if I wanted to," she laughed as if his question was ridiculous. "You won't get it until you feel it for yourself."

"Just try."

"Fine, fine." She focused all her energy in searching for the right words. "It's almost like... It's as if someone enhanced the vibrancy of every color and added depth to every shadow. And that everything the sun touches comes alive and starts to glow. Sorta like I went from living in the real world to a new one; a living breathing world that moves in the same way that I do. A world where everything is beautiful. There's no pain or suffering. Everything is as it should be."

He nodded and gave a slight eyeroll. What bullshit.

"You were right about one thing: I do not get it."

"You will!" she scooted closer to him.

"I actually don't believe you."

"It hits everyone at different times." She walked her middle and index fingers down his arm.

He felt nothing. The world remained stubbornly ordinary. Colors stayed flat, shadows static. His pain and suffering remained, unfortunately, intact.

If anything, he felt even more numb than usual. The shame and embarrassment from the garbage truck incident still tugged at him beneath the surface. Perhaps his habit of dissociating had created walls that were too high for even LSD to scale. Maybe his mind had become so skilled at suppressing emotion that it automatically neutralized any and all feelings—even the good ones. The trip was likely a bust before it ever began.

Within minutes, Vera plunged deep into her trip. She rose from the grass with euphoric grace, arms floating weightlessly. Her hips swayed in a way that he'd never seen her move before. Between the palm trees she danced, uninhibited, fingers stretched to touch both tree trunks simultaneously. She howled to the sky, her face transformed by a primal grin—pure freedom and joy radiating from her every movement.

It was an odd thing for Tennessee to watch. He'd never seen Vera act like this. She didn't care who was watching and didn't care what he thought about her little show. Could the drugs really be bringing all this out of her? Would he be acting like that if they ever hit him?

As she continued her ecstatic dance, circling him like a playful spirit, envy twisted in his chest. He craved even a fragment of her experience. He'd never allowed himself to be carefree like that. His entire life was spent clutching tightly to doubts and fears. To release them, even briefly, seemed impossible.

He remained anchored beneath gray clouds, tethered to this harsh reality while she soared somewhere far away from it. What he wouldn't give for just one moment of escape— one second of freedom from the prison he'd always known.

"Are you feeling it now?" she tossed her head back in his direction.

"Nope. Not a damn thing."

Maybe he was broken. Maybe his brain just wasn't like other people's. Maybe his wires didn't cross the right way, and the chemicals couldn't get to where they needed to go. Maybe he didn't produce enough serotonin and the receptors in his brain were unable to produce the desired effects.

She plopped herself next to him again, wide-eyed and short of breath. This time, both her leg and her arm were touching him.

"It'll start soon." She reached down and interlaced his fingers with hers. "It hits everyone differently."

Her hands were soft and gentle, warmth radiating from her palms. Smooth skin everywhere except where her cuticles peeled back around the nail beds. Looking up into her face, he noticed her eyes were a deep green. While her pupils were dilated and only a sliver of color remained, the green was too vibrant for him not to see. A comforting, lush green like a meadow of tall, soft grass.

Within those eyes, she saw him—the version of him hidden behind all the insecurities and broken pieces. She'd seen his flaws—his fear of heights, his trauma responses, his broken childhood—and was still here, holding his hand. There was an entirely new world within those eyes—one that assured him that he didn't need to change. That he was perfectly fine just as he was. Her eyes said all of this to him, without her lips uttering a single word.

He remained locked on them, drawn into their deep green depths. She stared back just as intently, as though seeing something in him she'd never noticed before, either. The moment hung between them—time slowing to a crawl. As they held each other's gaze, her pupils gradually expanded, the vivid green slowly retreating to thin rings of color.

This movement in her eyes made his stomach churn.

Was it the acid? Was he hungry? Butterflies? He looked down at her mouth and was overcome with the sudden urge to kiss her soft pink lips.

He succumbed to the urge before he'd even realized it, already reaching over to take her face in his hands. He leaned toward her, then paused as a flicker of doubt crossed his mind. Would this change everything between them? But as her face moved closer toward him, that hesitation dissolved like the tab on his tongue. As his fingertips made contact with her skin, any color that remained in her eyes fled and her chest released the last breath left in her lungs. His senses sharpened as he leaned closer, her face filling his vision. Goosebumps rippled across his arms, and he found himself holding his breath, suspended in the moment before their lips made contact.

Instinctively, both of their eyes closed, and their bodies took control. His hand lightly grazed her cheek and made its way to the soft part of her neck. When their lips met, the contact sent a current through him, warm and electric. The constant noise in his mind fell silent. His usual anxieties, the thoughts that ricocheted through his consciousness, faded to nothing. There was only this moment, the heat of her skin beneath his hand, the gentle pressure of her lips, and a desperate wish to stretch this single perfect moment into eternity.

For the first time in what felt like a long time, he felt whole. Lucy was unimportant. No one else besides Vera was. This was his new world, locked with his lips on hers. He didn't need anything else.

"Are you feeling it now?" She pulled away briefly.

Leaning back, he opened his eyes to see that the world had transformed. Colors blazed brighter. Vera's skin radiated with a golden light—she'd become an angel in a studded denim jacket. With a deep breath, he surveyed his surroundings: everything now in technicolor and hyper-definition.

A subtle warmth spread from his core outward to his fingertips, which suddenly felt both heavy and impossibly light at the same time. The sun broke through the clouds and a new day had begun. Even the sky was now impossibly blue. Shadows revealed hidden depths as fresh air filled his lungs, lifting his body, making it glow.

Sounds began to separate: a distant dog's bark, palm tree leaves rustling overhead. Each noise was distinct yet melodic, sharp yet harmonious.

He'd finally made it.

Chapter 10

No one ever remembers the first time they see the sky. It's been there our whole lives, right there in front of our faces. Yet, we are born with eyes that can't yet see. So this rich, marvelous blue fades into the background. Something that appears, to us, so simple—yet is the result of such a complex, scientific phenomenon. A wonder of the universe that took billions of years to make. One that gives us air to breathe and a planet to live on. Incredible, yet so often taken for granted.

"Has it always looked that way?" His voice echoed strangely in his ears.

"The sky?" Vera followed his gaze. "I guess so."

From their spot on the hill in the middle of the park, the fingers on Tennessee's left hand were interlaced with Vera's, while his other hand mindlessly stroked the grass next to his seat, as if he were petting a sleeping cat.

"It's so…blue. I've looked at it before but never really saw it, you know? Not 'til today."

Vera smirked, seeming to be amused by his demeanor. "Like I said, this stuff gives you a whole new perspective."

He nodded. "That's for damn sure. What have I been doing for the last twenty-three years? Have I just been too busy staring down at my feet to notice?"

"I dunno. Sometimes we get so caught up in the problems we've built up in our minds that we don't see the good stuff, even when it's right in front of us."

She squeezed his hand, and a wave of heat rushed up his arm.

Her words echoed in his head. How much had he missed? How much time had he wasted—worrying about problems that weren't real, blind to everything around him? If he remembered nothing else from this trip, he hoped he would remember *that* once the drugs wore off.

The sky was just the beginning of what his new eyes could see. He was now exposed to a whole new world—one of intense color, mesmerizing shapes, and objects that moved to their own beat.

He looked down at the tuft of grass in his hand.

"Whoa. Do you see that? It's breathing."

The entire bright green meadow seemed to be rolling. When one section inhaled, its blades reaching up toward him, another section exhaled and contracted. As he grazed his hands over the top of the soft, moist patches, he could even feel the rise and fall of this breath. His fingertips tingled with heightened sensitivity, picking up textures so intricate it was as if he could feel the cells that made up each blade.

"Alright, let's go." She peeled herself off the ground and tugged at his arm.

"Go where?"

"Anywhere we want. We gotta show you around while it's still light out."

As he stood up, he became lightheaded, taking a moment to regain his balance as white orbs danced across his vision. Though it had only been an hour at most since he sat down, he'd forgotten what his own body felt like on his feet. His first few steps were wobbly and unsteady, like a newborn deer learning how to walk for the first time. He became aware of small things he'd never noticed before, like how his legs carried his body weight, the way his arms swayed at his sides, and the feeling of fresh air in his lungs.

Eventually, his curious eyes began to wander. He looked up to the palm trees over their heads with their large, furry leaves all splayed out. Then across the lawn to the strange dark-eyed faces of the people close by. He looked back and forth between the vibrant sky overhead and down below to the grass that was still breathing as they made their way down the hill to the sidewalk.

Everything was the same, but somehow different.

"So," Vera scooped up his dangling arm and wrapped her elbow around it, "is it as scary as you thought it was going to be?"

He laughed deep into his belly as he remembered the fear that had overwhelmed him just hours before. Joy bubbled through him as he laughed, warmth radiating from his core to his fingertips in gentle waves. That anxious version of himself felt like a stranger now.

"It's not. Not even a little." They now were walking in unison.

"See, I told you! How do you feel?"

"I feel…" he wasn't quite sure how to put it in words. "I feel like…well, like you said, like the colors and shadows are all different…like I'm different. Like I've been blind my whole life and now I can finally see."

She smiled smugly. "So, you like it?"

"Yeah… This is the happiest I've been in a long time, actually."

Her cheeks flushed with color, and she turned away from him, a move too cute for him to resist. Stepping in front of her, he cradled her face and kissed her again, kicking up butterflies from the same place in his body that the laughter came from.

Vera pulled him along, routing their path into the unknown. She acted the same way she had the other night, excited but ominous—eager to show him whatever marvelous thing was on the other end of their journey. This time, he didn't even bother asking about their destination. The visual effects intensified with each step, and his only focus was the magic unfolding before him. Nothing mattered beyond absorbing it all and taking every ounce of beauty in.

Objects in the distance were the first to change. Their colors and shapes broke down as if he were looking through a kaleidoscope. In one moment, something was what it was, then it broke itself down into pixels that would climb on top of each other and reshape themselves into something new the longer he looked at it. A house could be a house, then become something else that was unrecognizable altogether in an instant.

His new eyes were the most powerful when it came to the objects closer to him. They could see details that his old eyes would've never noticed. He frequently stopped to admire these little pockets of beauty, like the gradient of colors that existed in a single flower or the lily pads in Vera's green eyes—the latter of which was the most distracting.

Scents seemed to have color, too; the earthy smell of soil was a deep burgundy, the fragrance of the flowers a bright, electric yellow. The sounds became something that he could see. Distant traffic merged into a wave-like rhythm, crashing and receding like an ocean made of mechanical sounds. The rustling of leaves in the trees above them sounded like whispered conversations, each tree telling secrets to the next, pulling his attention upward.

"The trees," he pulled back on Vera's hand. "Do you see all the layers?"

"Mmhm," she wrapped an arm around his back.

"Each layer of branches has its own color. Like a 3D movie before you put the glasses on."

"Our shadows have the same color layers, too," she pointed down at the ground.

Looking down at the tall, lanky figures stretching across the sidewalk, he wouldn't have recognized his shadow if it weren't connected to his feet. It wasn't just gray—it contained layers of red and blue, stacked atop each other like the colors in the trees.

Vera danced with her shadow, bumping her hip against his. Something broke loose inside him—a lifetime of rigidity crumbling in an instant. His arms began to sway, his hips found their own rhythm, and joy bubbled out of him as he watched his shadow mimic his movements. Never before had he danced with his shadow, yet here he was, delighting in something so mundane. There was a lightness surrounding this perfect moment, a feeling he'd never known was possible. Right then, under the vast sky he'd only just truly seen, he existed in unrestrained freedom.

He watched Vera's shadow reach into her bag, pull out the aluminum foil, and place a tab in her mouth.

"Want another?" she tilted the wrinkled foil toward him.

"Why not?" His arms found her waist as she placed it on his tongue.

"We gotta keep going," she folded up the foil and slipped it into the front pocket of his jeans, rather than putting it back in her bag.

"So we're going somewhere specific?"

"Mmhm," Vera stole a quick kiss before taking his hand.

"You'll see."

Tennessee trusted her completely. His need for control, vigilance, and all the barriers he'd built had dissolved like the acid on his tongue. Whether from the drug or because she'd earned his trust, he couldn't tell—but for once, it didn't matter. The voice of fear and doubt that held him back fell silent. He'd follow her anywhere.

As they continued walking, Tennessee noticed subtle shifts in his perception. The clarity he'd felt earlier began to soften around the edges. Time seemed to stretch and compress—each second seemed both never-ending and simultaneously slipping away from him far too quickly.

"You're getting quiet," Vera's voice somehow sounded both close and far away at the same time. "Where'd you go?"

"I'm right here," he said, though he wasn't entirely sure what "here" meant anymore. The boundaries between himself and everything around him had grown harder to discern. Colors began to blend and the world and all the objects in it started to meld together in a blurry mass. When he blinked, trails of light lingered behind his eyelids. The shadows that had been so fascinating before now seemed to pulse with a life of their own. His thoughts came in fragments.

He squeezed Vera's hand tighter—she was his anchor in this sea of beautiful chaos.

From that point on, the trip became a blur.

Gold light beamed off every object the sun touched. Colors deepened and shadows stretched far from the items they represented. Though nothing, not even the shadows, kept their form for long. Objects broke down at an even faster pace, often before he could get a good look at them. Anything that moved came and went in frames, like passing pages in a flip book, moving both fast and slow. Surfaces and edges blended together. He noticed this especially when he looked down at his hand. He couldn't tell where his own skin ended and where Vera's began. Even as his visual world became unrecognizable, he felt euphoric. There was a lightness in his chest and an airiness under his heels. It was like his whole body was floating.

He hadn't thought about Lucy even once, other than becoming aware of her absence in his mind. He hoped it would stay that way even once the day was over.

"We're almost there." Vera tugged at his hand as they made their way up a steep hill. "We have to catch the sunset from up there."

"Whatever you say."

He remembered his past self—so tied up in fear and hung up on Lucy. How ridiculous it all felt now, to have felt so lost without her. He didn't need her. He was happier now than he'd ever been with Lucy. All thanks to Vera—she was his everything. At least for now.

His shadow grew long at his side as the sun nestled down into the sea. The blue sky he'd been so enamored with began to disintegrate. In its place was a canvas of colors more beautiful than any he'd seen all day—burnt reds, deep oranges, and bright pink clouds. Further out, there were pockets of dark purples where night was already starting to take over.

Beads of sweat traced cool paths down his temples as they zigzagged up the switchbacks. Each step forced his lungs to work harder, their breath becoming ragged in the thinning air.

"Vera, how much longer?"

"Look up, silly," she pointed. "We're here."

A colossal three-pronged structure loomed before them, its skeletal frame clawing at the colors in the sky from the neighboring hill. With each blink, the tower seemed to stretch impossibly upward, defying gravity. The euphoria drained from his body, leaving only a cold, hollow dread. His stomach twisted into a tight, painful knot. At first, he didn't recognize it—but eventually, the cogs in his head began to turn as he realized where they were.

The world that had seemed so magical moments before suddenly came to a screeching halt, like a needle being dragged across a record.

Sutro Tower was dark and looming, its image bursting the bubble of joy inside him. No longer a mere structure of steel and blinking light, but it was now a three-headed demon with glowing crimson eyes that cut right through him. Gone was the carefree self that he was just beginning to know.

Reality came flooding back with crushing force. Panic clawed its way up from his gut, his breath becoming shaky. His chest constricted as if the tower itself were pressing down upon him, the weight of it now impossible to escape.

He launched himself down the hill, legs pumping with manic energy, feet barely touching the ground as terror propelled him forward. The whispers of his past mistakes now screamed in his ears, drowning out all reason. He hadn't stopped to think about who else he was running away from—warm, wonderful Vera—abandoning her without a word, alone in the approaching night.

Chapter **11**

Nightfall consumed the day's blue sky. Tennessee found his feet at the edge of a dark and raging sea with waves that crashed and beat against the cliffside. The wind lashed out in gusts across the shore, which sprinkled sand into both his and Lucy's hair. As the swell of the surf rose and crashed against the rocks, a strange sensation built in the pit of his stomach.

They sat in silence atop the weathered wooden steps, their faces growing damp in the misty air as the surf roared loudly at their feet. He sat a step above her with a fleece blanket wrapped around both of their bodies, as she wept in his arms.

This eerie feeling grew as her weight pressed against him in a way that felt far too familiar. Goosebumps rose up across his arms as the wind pushed deeper into the shore. He wasn't cold—rather, it was something about this moment.

It all felt so familiar...like they'd been here before.

"It's just fucked up," she said, the wind tossing around her hair, tears welling in her eyes as she looked far off into the distance.

"What is?" The words fell from his mouth without any real thought, as if he were repeating a line from a script. It was pure instinct, almost a muscle memory, like he'd said it dozens of times before.

Before she'd even parted her lips to respond, he could already anticipate what she was about to say.

"That this is how true love ends." She wiped her cheek with her sleeve.

He leaned away from her. His suspicion intensified with each breath, a growing feeling that something wasn't right. This wasn't the first time he'd heard her say that phrase.

He turned his head, beginning to question their surroundings. He looked out toward the ocean, down at the wet steps they sat on, and at the boulders on either side of them. A beam of white light circled over their heads from the lighthouse that stood behind them further down the cliffside. Surely, they'd been to West Cliff many times before, they'd even sat on these exact steps. But this night... this conversation...

She continued, "You know what you're getting into from the very start."

"Til death do you part," they both said in unison.

Her brows furrowed as her watery eyes turned to look over her shoulder at him.

"We've been here before, haven't we?" He was starting to put the pieces together.

"Yeah? We come here all the time," she sniffled. "What are you talking about?"

His eyes opened wide as he realized exactly where he was. As he pulled one hand away from her and touched his own torso and face, a giddy feeling came over him, like he was suddenly drunkenly lightheaded. He was in a dream and some-how, he'd managed to wake his mind without waking his body.

Then he remembered the last time he found himself in this place and a heavy feeling came to his chest. He realized just how fragile this moment—or more accurately, this memory—was. He needed to be careful with her so they could both remain here as long as possible.

His hand slid beneath the blanket and traveled up her back. As he moved upward, his fingers grazed over her ribs and spine until finally reaching her shoulder. The light grip of his hand transitioned into a squeeze—a test of firmness. He shook her shoulder softly, her upper body swaying and her head bobbing in response. Was she real enough to stay here with him? He needed to know if he could touch her in all the ways he wanted to.

"What are you doing?" Her tone sounded somewhat annoyed.

She didn't crumble into sand nor was she blown out to sea. She was stable. She was beautiful. And she was sitting here right in front of him, once again.

Tears of joy built up in his eyes. "You're here."

Both arms flung around her, he nestled his head against her back in the hollow between her shoulder blades and tightened his embrace. Her body radiated warmth, and she smelled like strawberries, just like he remembered. Listening intently, he heard the rhythm of her heartbeat that paired with the gentle rise and fall of her breath. Every part of her felt so real, even if she wasn't.

"What's gotten into you?"

He loosened his hug so he could look into her eyes, noticing how clear and blue they were, as if seeing them again for the first time.

"Lucy, we're in a dream."

"What? No, we're not. That's ridiculous."

"Yes! Can't you feel it? We've been here before! Probably dozens or maybe even hundreds of times!"

She fell silent. Perhaps she didn't believe him or maybe she didn't understand. Maybe she couldn't. Was she aware and part of this dream, like he was? Or was she an object—a prop—within this world? A fragment of his imagination without real consciousness?

He wondered what she knew of this world, but even more importantly, what she knew of the real one. And if she knew of the events that unfolded long after this memory occurred.

"What day is it?" he asked.

"Uh, May 28. Why?" The day her grandfather passed away.

He nodded, doing his best to make sense of it all. If she believed that it was May 28th and that this was the first and only time they'd ever had this conversation, then she must exist here within the confines of this memory. She was pure—untainted by more recent memories—because as far as she knew, none of that stuff had happened yet. Here, she simply played her role and recited her lines exactly as she had that day. She remained stuck in an endless loop of what once was.

It was like stepping into the past. Here, he didn't need to feel the pain of guilt or regret. He didn't have to worry about what he'd done. He could be with her again when she was still sweet and kind—before she'd turned cold.

For the first time in a long time, he could just be with her and be happy.

He breathed in deeply, filling his lungs with the salty ocean air. The night sky stretched above their heads, stars twinkling in the darkness. Moisture from the mist settled on their blanket while gritty sand pressed against the soles of his feet. With each gust of wind, her hair danced against his face, creating a gentle tickling sensation. It was all so vivid—he could hardly believe that none of it was real.

"Hello?" She now had an even more confused look on her face.

He threw the blanket from his shoulders, freeing his hands to cradle her face and turn her toward him. Closing what little distance was left between them, he laid his lips over hers and kissed her like it was the last time he'd ever be able to kiss her again. Savoring every second, he stroked her cheek with his thumb and tasted the salty tears lingering on her lips.

"What's gotten into you?" she said, pulling away. The tears in her eyes had started to dry and a soft smile lifted her cheeks.

"I just missed you, is all." He wrapped her back in his arms.

"How could you miss me when I've been with you this whole time?"

"It doesn't matter right now." It was now his eyes that started to well. He thought it best to keep the truth to himself.

"Anyways, keep going. Say what you were going to say."

"Say what?"

"Tell me you want to watch me die."

"What?" Her mouth fell open. "Why would I say that?"

"Oh, uh…" he realized he'd skipped ahead. Falling back into the script, he let the words come back to him as they had before.

"That's what real love is, Luce." He pulled her in tightly, taking his time to feel each word's impact, giving each syllable its moment on his lips. "An unconditional love like that goes through all the good and bad life has to offer."

Her expression grew somber as he spoke.

"True love isn't that bullshit from the movies. Love is pain, love is resilience, and, ultimately, it's suffering. Those who love each other most watch each other die."

The tears in his eyes started to blur his vision. He hadn't known when he said it the first time just how much these words would mean to the two of them.

Just as she had before, she looked out to the depths of the sea, taking her time to digest his words. He smiled as he waited, knowing exactly what she was about to say.

"You're right." She grabbed his hand tightly. "I want to watch you die."

His chest softened and the tears freely fell down his cheeks. That phrase must have replayed in his head a million times. But nothing compared to hearing it in her own voice. Now all he wanted was to turn back time so they could rewind and relive this moment again and again.

"Well, in that case," there was a tremble in his voice, "I hope you go first."

She looked up at him and smiled. All the love was still left in her eyes; their sparkle showed no signs of dimming. They hadn't found themselves back at her apartment nor had a beady-eyed monster taken over her body. She made no mention of his dad. They were each other's once again— going against the sands of time.

Suddenly, an alarm started going off loudly behind them. The lighthouse beam that was circling overhead had gone from white to red. The water started to thrash more fiercely against the rocks. The blare of the sound was familiar—it was the same sound that woke him up every morning. Its piercing wail cut through the night air, drowning out the sound of the waves and shattering their intimate moment. Reality began to tear at the edges of this perfect dream.

"I don't care what I have to do," he kissed her forehead. "I'm going to find my way back to you."

The alarm grew more insistent. The red light pulsed faster.

"What do you mean?" she asked, her voice barely audible over the sound.

Tennessee cupped her face between his palms, trying to memorize every little detail—the pattern of the freckles across her nose, the exact shade of blue in her eyes.

"The real Lucy changed. We both did. But here, in this moment—this is the true us. This is what I'm going to fight to get back to."

The dream began to fracture around them. He could feel his back pressing into the hardwood beneath his mattress.

"I'll find a way back to who we were."

And in an instant, she was gone. His eyes fluttered open as he was jolted awake. The dream dissolved, leaving only the ghost of their memory in its wake. His hand shot out to silence the alarm. The room around him was cold and empty—no ocean mist, no strawberry scent, no warmth of another body.

Tennessee pressed his fingers against his eyes, disappointed the dream had ended so soon. But the feeling remained, lodged deep in his chest.

"I'll find you again. I'll find a way back to who we were."

Chapter 12

The next day Tennessee felt...different.

He wasn't hungover, at least not in the familiar way he was used to feeling after a night out. No churning stomach or throbbing headache. The morning jitters were absent— no swirl of anxiety or dark cloud of shame hanging over him. His body, however, was sore and exhausted. Muscles ached in unfamiliar places, as if he'd run a marathon the previous day. For all he knew, he might have.

He had no memory of getting home. The cloudiness of his memory was made worse by the murky, low-hanging fog surrounding him as he walked down the hill from his apartment toward the bus stop. Nothing was visible beyond a block away, with fog transforming buildings and street signs into ghostly silhouettes. When he reached the bottom of the hill, a pair of piercing white headlights cut through the haze like searchlights. As a bus materialized from the mist, Tennessee urged his stiff legs to move faster.

Despite his grogginess, his mind felt remarkably light— as if someone had removed his brain overnight and cleared away all the useless junk he'd been carrying around in it.

The usual triggers that would send him spiraling—running late, an overly crowded bus, Mr. Green's nagging—all felt far less harsh now.

"Good morning," Mr. Green was already loading the cash register when Tennessee walked into the Peach. "Son, you do know you're supposed to be here at eight, right?"

Tennessee nodded. It was the same sort of comment Mr. Green said every morning—words that normally got under his skin and infected him like poison. Today, however, he felt detached from these words. A buffer existed between his actions, Mr. Green's words, and his emotional response. For once, he didn't feel the need to get defensive.

"Sorry about that. I'll try better tomorrow."

Mr. Green gave him a curious look. "You seem to be in rather good spirits this morning. Finally get a good night's rest?"

The details of last night were a blur—what time he'd fallen asleep or how he'd even made it home, he wasn't sure—but it felt like he'd slept for hours.

"Yeah, I guess you could say that."

"Well, I'm glad to hear it!"

Tennessee went about his day as usual, removing the books from the milk crates and placing them on the shelves. Nothing out of the ordinary. But it all somehow felt brand new. Like he could see a little more clearly than he did before. The smell of the used pages. The difference in the way that the matte book jackets felt compared to the glossy ones.

The small sense of satisfaction that came with pushing each book into its place.

Maybe this was what Vera was talking about. Maybe the drugs had cured whatever was broken inside him. Or maybe the LSD was still in his system. Every so often, an old thought or feeling would pop up, but it didn't feel as heavy as it had the day before. They simply arose and drifted away.

Then his mind found its way back to Lucy. Was that just a dream or was it a hallucination? It was impossible to tell whether he was still tripping or if he was asleep. Maybe it was somehow both.

Yet, it didn't have the same fleeting, blurry impression that most dreams had. It felt real. The rush of the wind on his face, the salty smell of the sea, the feeling of her warm skin on his, the touch of her lips. Each word, feeling, and detail felt just as real and firm as the weight of the books in his hands.

What made it even better was that she was her old self in this dream. There, the love they shared was still intact. She was still sweet and kind, still loved him in all his flaws. She was still his and he was hers. There, he could relive all of the good memories and just forget the bad.

He needed to find a way back to her. But he didn't know how.

With about a dozen books left in the crate at his feet, he left them in pursuit of answers in the psychology section.

He wasn't sure what he was looking for, but he knew this would be the right place to start.

First, he focused on the neuroscience books, flipping to chapters about dreams where he discovered that what he did last night was called "lucid dreaming"—which was the act of becoming aware that you're in a dream. He grabbed every book on the subject, then hit the sociology section for texts on hallucinogens from LSD to psilocybin to DMT. He took this stack of books down to the register and spent hours absorbing their contents, reading straight through lunch.

One of the books on LSD confirmed that the compound induced a dream-like state of consciousness—something he knew first-hand. He read accounts of how LSD had shaped the '60s counterculture movement, flipping through images of flower-crowned hippies in Haight-Ashbury and Golden Gate Park during the Summer of Love—which was just a mile or so away from where he sat now.

His stomach tightened as he read about MKUltra. During that history-making summer, the CIA had dosed unwitting subjects in a top-secret project to see if LSD could be used for psychological warfare. One man had leapt from a hotel window days after being drugged as part of the experiment. Tennessee swallowed hard but kept reading.

He learned a lot about dreams. The first bit of striking information he took away was that even as long as a dream might seem, they typically only lasted a few minutes. He learned about REM sleep and how that was the only time your body could dream. He read how in dreams, you rarely remember arriving somewhere—you simply appear and begin doing things.

Just like when we were suddenly at West Cliff last night.

The books about lucid dreaming grabbed his attention even more. One suggested regular "reality checks" throughout the day—questioning if your surroundings made sense. Was the sky the right color? Do you have the correct number of fingers? Are the laws of physics working properly? Eventually, the book promised, you'd carry this habit into your dreams, and when you'd notice something was off, you'd realize you were in a dream.

The sky outside the window seemed to be a familiar shade of grayish blue. He looked down at his hands. The first thing he noticed was the calluses lining the tops of his palms. The bruises had faded to a light purple but were still visible in some spots; a scab had formed over the gash across his knuckles. He curled his fingers to see nails that had been bitten down to their shortest point. He counted out ten digits, five for each hand. Everything checked out.

Another book described how clocks were a dead giveaway in the dreamworld. Time didn't exist there—numbers on clocks jumped erratically between glances. Tennessee found himself unconsciously glancing at the store's wall clock, checking it against his phone. Both read 1:37 p.m. Reality confirmed.

What grabbed him most was a short essay suggesting that dreams following psychedelic experiences could lead to profound healing. The essay argued that post-trip bliss wasn't enough on its own, but if someone examined the dreams through repeated LSD experiences, often through therapy, they could ease the tension in their mind for good.

Healing.

The word resonated within him. Maybe that's what had happened last night. Maybe that's why everything felt so much lighter today. Not just a drugged-out bliss, but something deeper—something that had reached the most delicate parts of him. Maybe this was exactly what he needed more of to heal from his past.

A blurry memory flickered in his mind. It was Vera slipping something into his jeans as they danced with their shadows—the very jeans he was wearing now. He dipped two fingers into the denim pocket to investigate, his fingertips grazing the crinkled surface of the foil and tracing its sharp folded edges.

After checking that no customers were approaching the register, he extracted the foil to inspect its contents. Carefully unfolding it revealed the sheet of acid. It was the first good look he had at it. It was a thin sheet of blotting paper, about as thick as a piece of tissue, perforated into thirty tiny squares. Four tabs were missing from the bottom row—which added up, given that the two of them had taken two on the bus and another two as they walked.

The image printed on the front looked familiar. It looked like one of the cards out of Lucy's tarot deck. It depicted the Seven of Cups: seven golden chalices floating on gray clouds against a blue sky. Each cup contained a distinct vision: a curly-haired face, a castle, jewels, a laurel crown, a hooded figure, a dragon, and a snake. In one corner stood a shadowy figure contemplating these treasures. Though he was no expert in tarot, Tennessee interpreted it positively—a person choosing their path to happiness. Perhaps he now had a similar opportunity of his own.

A sense of boyish glee took over him. This was it. This sheet in his hand was his ticket to happiness—his ticket back to her.

His eyes drifted to the wall clock. There was a little more than three hours left of his shift. He calculated the timing— how long until the effects began yesterday? At least two or three hours, possibly more. If he took a tab right now, he'd be coming up just as he was getting off work.

His fingers traced the squares in the last row. What was the worst that could happen in a bookstore, really? He might spend too long admiring the leather-bound classics? Start seeing patterns in the shelves that weren't actually there? Smile too much at customers? None of that seemed all that bad.

The decision made itself. He detached two squares from the bottom row—trying to dose himself the same as yesterday so he'd get the same effects.

"Well, here goes nothing," he whispered as he placed both tabs on his tongue, already imagining where he'd end up with Lucy later tonight in his LSD-induced dream.

Chapter 13

About forty-five minutes later, his stomach knotted and churned. At first, he blamed hunger—he had skipped lunch, after all. But then sweat beaded on his forehead, his palms grew clammy, and heat surged through his body, flushing his cheeks.

The acid hadn't made him nauseous yesterday—why now? He pressed his forehead against the cool countertop and hugged his waist, hoping the position would ease the discomfort. As he wheezed, his mouth turned salty and parched. The scent of old books—normally a comfort—suddenly flooded his senses in the worst way. Dust, paper, leather, and glue replaced all the air in the room.

"Don't throw up. Please don't throw up." He eyed the nearby trash bin just in case.

Why had he been so stupid? Taking acid at work was a terrible idea. Yesterday had been so different, so magical while they were at the park.

Several minutes went by in this position. His stomach continued to flip and turn on itself. As he ground his back teeth together, his jaw tensed and stressed his temples.

All he could do was take slow concentrated breaths and wonder how long this feeling would last. In for three seconds. Hold. Out for five. In for three. Hold. Out for five. He repeated this over and over as his heartbeat thudded against his ribs.

After some time, the tension started to release. With each exhale, something subtle shifted in his perception. The grain of the wooden countertop beneath his forehead transformed—he dragged his fingertips across the surface, feeling each raised knot in the wood as if reading braille. Muted colors began to bloom at the edges of his darkened vision—first indigo then violet, pulsing in time with his breath.

As his stomach started to unwind itself, Tennessee noticed oddly shaped specks of color dancing behind his eyelids. Dot patterns, oblong triangles, scattered stars, and squares with rounded corners bounced around his closed field of vision. They came in an array of gradient colors and neon hues that reminded him of the carpet pattern at an arcade.

Looking out over the bookstore, he noticed it looked drastically different than usual. The fluorescent lights overhead shone with increased intensity, as if he were gazing directly into the sun. The square rectangle of the lights imprinted themselves into his retinas, lingering as ghostly negatives for several seconds after he looked away. The store's pale, washed-out tones were replaced with a rainbow of colors. The hardwood floorboards and bookshelves now radiated a burnt amber glow that pulsed with warmth. The bubble letters on the hand-written posters popped—many of the words jumping right off the page. Even the dullest of book covers now seemed interesting.

So many things caught his attention. His head snapped from one side of the room to the other as new things caught his eye. Were the walls breathing? Were the lights flickering? Was there someone hiding in the shadows? What was that in the back corner? It was too much for him to take in all at once.

He was beginning to feel overwhelmed, so he anchored his gaze to his feet and clutched the counter's edge with white-knuckled intensity.

But there was movement on the ground, too. Orange ripples in the hardwood collided like the shallow waves of a tide pool. As he moved his feet, the tranquil waves traveled out, bounced off nearby objects, and found their way back. Watching this slowly soothed his overstimulated senses.

"Excuse me," a voice said above him.

His head snapped up to find a woman standing in front of him, another millennial in a Patagonia vest. He immediately was drawn to the tips of her claw-like fingers. They were cherry-red—tapping an impatient rhythm against the wooden counter. How long had she been standing there? Where did she come from?

"I'm ready to buy this book," she placed it down urgently.

Oh no.

He stared at her, hoping his body would fill the gaps that his mind couldn't fill. All he needed was a few seconds. His instincts would eventually kick in. Right? He'd done this thousands of times before. An interaction like this was something he'd be able to do in his sleep.

But no words came out. His tongue dried up and stuck to the roof of his mouth. He stared at her like a deer in headlights. Behind his frozen expression, a storm of emotions churned—fear, panic, and a strange urge to laugh at the absurdity of it all.

"You do work here, right?" she asked, the whites of her eyes seeming to bulge out of their sockets. There was a subtle aura of entitlement in her voice.

He nodded, eyes falling to the book she'd set on the counter. He couldn't make out the words on the front cover. They looked like ancient hieroglyphs from a language long forgotten.

"Well then?"

He gulped. He needed to act normal, even though he'd lost all sense of what normal was. With a shaky hand, he slowly slid the book over to his side of the register. The simple motion required his full concentration. He could feel the woman's impatience radiating off her like heat.

"Are you alright?" He sensed judgment in the croak of her voice.

She was onto him. Her beady eyes could see right through him. Surely, his own pupils must be giving him away. He scrambled to think of some worthy excuse for his weird behavior, but each potential lie vanished before it could reach his lips.

"Uhh, I don't feel good." A few droplets of spit came flying out of his mouth as if for dramatic effect.

"I see. Well, feel better." She cocked her head toward the book, a subtle nudge for him to hurry up. The black vest hanging off her shoulders turned to feathers. With each glance he took at her, the more bird-like she became.

He scooped up the book with two clumsy hands, turning the front cover open. He searched for the tiny price written in pencil on the top corner of the first page. He squinted down at it—the numbers dancing and multiplying before his eyes. It took every bit of focus and effort he had to make out Mr. Green's handwriting.

"That'll be…" he made his best guess, "two hundred dollars."

She scoffed loudly. "You mean twenty dollars?"

Her sharp tone jolted him like an electric shock, sending his eyes darting back to the price. Now there were even more zeros than before, stretching themselves across the page.

"Yes, so sorry. Twenty dollars." She could steal the book for all he cared. He just wanted this interaction to be over with.

"I need change." She uncurled her talons to reveal a crisp, green bill. Ben Franklin's face frowned at him as he took it from her.

He let out an audible exhale. She wasn't making this easy for him.

He pushed a random button on the cash register to open the drawer and pulled out a handful of assorted bills. The currency felt gritty and strange between his fingers, the faces on each one seemingly annoyed that he'd disturbed them from their slumber.

He counted them out slowly and carefully, "Five, twenty, thirty, eighty..."

"Don't try to short-change me." Her breast puffed out and her voice got louder. Her nose had transformed into a beak, threatening to poke one of his eyes out.

"Of course I'm, uh," he looked back down at the bills scattered across the counter. He'd already lost track. None of the numbers on the green papers made any sense to him. The longer she stood over him, her beak looking down over his shoulder, the harder the task became.

"Here." He slid the pile of money over toward her. "You can do it then. Just to be sure."

"Ridiculous," she squawked as she scratched up her change and flew out of the store.

He hadn't realized he'd been holding his breath until she was gone. He let out a strained exhale, relieved that conversation was over.

Now that the full length of the store was back in his view, the room had stretched itself out. The children's section at the back now seemed miles away. The miniature table and chair set there looked like a distant mirage. The staircase in the center spiraled upward impossibly, each step dissolving into the next like a never-ending stairway to heaven.

Even more colors called out to him—neon greens pulsing against royal purples, golden yellows vibrating at impossible frequencies. Books fanned their pages like exotic birds. He staggered out from behind the counter to explore, gravity shifting unpredictably beneath his feet.

The bookshelves were breathing in the same way the grass did yesterday. As one section would contract, another would expand. As he walked through the center aisles, the books on display inflated, elongating their spines and calling out to him. This universal breath moved at a slow and steady pace, one that matched the timing of his own breathing.

The shelves weren't the only thing that had come alive. The paper butterflies over the gardening section fluttered their wings as they floated across the ceiling. The old-world masks that hung in the display case above the bookshelves batted their eyes and hissed down at him. Their mouths moved as if they were talking to one another. Some had twisted, evil smiles, while others had large white eyes that protruded out of their heads. A Chinese dragon mask released puffs of smoke from its nostrils. A snake mask unhinged its jaw. A tiger mask revealed its large canines. The one with thick, twisted devil horns and goat-like ears snarled and spat its tongue out at him.

Tennessee averted his eyes, thankful the masks were trapped behind glass.

There was movement in the craft section—little origami creatures wiggling their limbs, attempting to escape from the shelf they were marooned on. A purple kangaroo practically jumped into his hand when he arrived. It bounced in his palm before he lowered it to the ground, and it hopped off into the distance. Tennessee smiled, picking up the remaining animals—an elephant, a swan, a pair of bunnies, and a crane—placing them all on the floor as well.

As he stood up, goosebumps prickled the back of his neck. It was a feeling he knew well. Someone was watching him. He turned to find himself staring into a set of piercing blue eyes behind gold-rimmed glasses—eyes that followed his every move. He'd seen them before but never truly noticed them.

Stepping back, he realized it was a poster with the cover of *The Great Gatsby* on it. The eyes belonged to Doctor T.J. Eckleburg, the billboard that witnessed Gatsby's tragic end. Tennessee identified with Gatsby—not his wealth, but his boundless love for Daisy. Tennessee would go to the same lengths to be with Lucy.

"Tennessee!" a booming voice shouted from behind him, causing him to jump.

Turning around, he saw Mr. Green standing at the front of the store, which now seemed impossibly far away. The space between them warped like he was in a funhouse, stretching and contracting in ways that went against reality.

Even at this impossible distance, Tennessee could hear Mr. Green's voice as if he were standing right next to him. "Why is there money laying out like this all over the counter?"

A lump formed in Tennessee's throat. His tongue felt swollen, useless. The silence between them expanded, becoming a response in itself.

"Anyone could have walked by and stolen it while you had your back turned!" Mr. Green's four arms waved frantically as he spoke, each movement leaving trails in the air. "Why on Earth would you just leave money out like this?"

Tennessee shrugged. He had no idea. He hadn't even realized he'd done it.

"And why is my granddaughter's origami display on the ground?" Mr. Green's voice ricocheted through the warped space between them. "Do you want them to get trampled on? She would be devastated if they were ruined!"

Tennessee bent down to pick up the creatures, watching as they seemed to resist returning to their prison back on the shelf. Each of his movements felt constrained and robotic, as if his joints had been replaced with rusty hinges.

"Well?" Mr. Green's hands were on his hips, his foot tapping a rhythm that vibrated through the floorboards.

"I—I—uh. I'm sorry," Tennessee's words were thick and clumsy. "I'll be right there."

But that was easier said than done. His shoes felt like they'd been glued to the floor, each step requiring immense effort against gravity's sudden, crushing weight. Mr. Green's gaze watched over him like a spotlight, analyzing his every movement. His paranoia intensified with every labored step. The distance between them seemed both endless and closing in too quickly. Dozens of terrifying outcomes played through his mind in a matter of seconds.

When Tennessee finally reached the counter, his quivering fingers fumbled with the cash. The numbers transformed before his eyes—morphing from digits into odd unreadable shapes then back again. Mr. Green's scrutiny felt like a physical pressure against him—every hesitation, every bead of sweat under surveillance. This transformed this simple task into an impossible performance where each misplaced bill was a sign of his own incompetence.

"This is completely unacceptable," Mr. Green's voice echoed deep into Tennessee's eardrums. "I don't want to see this type of thing happen again. Understood?"

Tennessee nodded, still avoiding eye contact.

"Very well, then." Mr. Green let out one last huff and waddled off toward the back of the store, a visible cloud of smoke coming up off the man's bald head, like he was a cartoon character.

As soon as his boss was out of sight, Tennessee felt his chest cave in. He felt his breath come in staggered bursts. He grabbed onto the counter with both hands as he tried to steady himself.

"You're okay. You're okay. You're almost done with your shift."

He looked back up toward the clock on the wall only to realize he couldn't read it. The red plastic seemed to be melting over the clock's face and dripping down the wall.

With a shaky hand, he patted down his pockets to find his phone. As he tapped the screen, the white numbers fractured and multiplied. The glowing digits hovered just beyond his reach, rotating and inverting whenever he tried to focus his vision on them. He caught glimpses of twos and zeros dancing with what might have been an eight or a nine.

Damn it. He dropped his phone onto the counter. He had no idea how much time had passed or how much longer he needed to be at work.

He sat behind the counter with his hands under his seat, trying his best to control his breath. With his eyes fixed down at the ground, he watched the tides on the wooden floor wade in and out, doing his best to avoid eye contact and dodge conversations with customers. If someone wanted to buy something, Tennessee would try to get through the interaction as quickly as possible. He took extra precautions not to screw up the transactions like he had before.

Eventually, after what felt like an eternity, one of his

coworkers showed up to relieve him, a signal that his sentence in time prison had now come to an end. As Tennessee walked outside, the world expanded around him—the crisp, misty air rushing into his lungs. He stood momentarily paralyzed by possibility, his mind racing yet simultaneously empty. He'd waited for this moment for so long, but it never crossed his mind to think about what he'd do when he got there.

The next thing he knew, he was heading across the street to the bar.

As he swung open the bottom half of the door, a wave of sound hit Tennessee like a physical force. The metal music pulsed and throbbed, each beat knocking into his body. Conversations fragmented into abstract patterns of sound, rising and falling in mesmerizing waves. The clinking of glasses sounded like bells.

"Ten!" Vera shouted as soon as he was inside. There was already an early happy hour crowd there, and now with Vera's attention, over a dozen faces turned toward him, their features distorted and snarky.

Heat rushed into his face as he gave a nervous smile and sheepishly walked over to his usual bar stool. He fixed his eyes on the laces of his shoes, which seemed to be tying and untying themselves.

"Are you alright?" Vera asked over the music. Her skin sparkled like porcelain just as it had the day before. "You ran off last night and nearly gave me a heart attack. I tried to go after you, but you were impossible to catch up with!"

"Yeah. I'm fine. Just a bad hallucination, I guess."

"Oh, those are the worst. That'll happen, though, when it gets dark. Where did you run off to?"

Tennessee shrugged. "No idea, but I woke up in my bed this morning."

Vera tilted her head to one side. "You blacked out?"

Tennessee nodded. "Yeah?"

"Hmm. Really? That's kind of odd."

"What do you mean?"

"I dunno. That's just never happened to me from acid before. I'm sure that's probably normal for some people. Anyways, what can I get ya?"

"Do you know if it's okay to drink while on acid?"

"Oh yeah, I don't see why not! I've done it plenty of times. Why do you ask?"

Tennessee lifted his head and looked straight into her bright lily pad green eyes. There was a peculiar comfort in them now. He suddenly felt less alone, less out of place.

"Oh!" She saw that his pupils were dilated. "You're on it now? While you were at work?"

"Yeah, a bookstore is probably not the most fun place to do acid. I found it in my pocket this morning. Do you want it back?"

"No, not at all! Keep it. Have a little fun!"

"Cool, well, thanks. I'll take a whiskey ginger, then."

A rush of unexplainable joy began to build in his gut, radiating outward like sunlight breaking through storm clouds. His muscles, which had been wound tight, gradually loosened. The anxiety that had gripped his chest released its hold, allowing him to take full relaxed breaths for the first time in hours. The further he distanced himself from his responsibilities, the bookstore, and his problems, the more the world started to feel good again.

"So, what are you up to tonight?" Vera asked as she made his drink.

He shrugged. "No plans."

"Wanna come with me to a show tonight? My friend's band is playing. Should be pretty fun—especially in the state you're in."

He really didn't have much else to do—sitting alone in his apartment waiting for sleep to take over sounded like a terrible way to spend his night.

"Sure, I'm down."

Vera slid the drink over to him, her face lighting up. "Great! I'm off in about an hour and we can head out."

Chapter 14

Tennessee savored the burning in his throat with each sip of whiskey and found satisfying pleasure in the way the carbonation felt in his mouth. Each drink came with an explosion of fizz that burst sweetly against his tongue. And better yet, the more he drank, the more at ease he felt. The choke hold of fear around being caught red-handed at the bookstore vanished. He was finally able to relax and take in his surroundings.

Allowing his mind and eyes to wander, he was drawn like a moth to the electric colors of the neon signs around the bar. These glowing images and words pulled themselves right off the wall. Not only could he see these colors, but he could feel them, too.

There were layers in the scents his nose could pick up as well. He could parse out everything from the soggy beer-soaked wooden floors to the dust mites behind the top shelf liquor to the Pine-Sol that failed to camouflage these other smells. He could even make out the cheap, musky cologne of the man standing behind him and could picture exactly what he looked like without turning around.

He spread both of his palms out on the bar top and swayed them from side to side. The awe and wonder he'd felt the day before was back.

"Have you ever felt something like this?" His question was directed at the musky man standing behind him.

"You talking to me, bud?" the man stepped into Tennessee's view. Beard, beer belly, baseball hat. He looked exactly how Tennessee imagined.

"Yeah!" Tennessee dropped his forearms onto the counter. "It's so cold. But like in a good way."

"Well yeah, it's metal." The guy furrowed the two thick caterpillars he had for eyebrows at him and chuckled.

"That'll be seven bucks," Vera approached them with an overflowing glass of foamy gold liquid, placing it in front of Tennessee's new friend.

As the man pulled the cash from his wallet, he said to Vera, "What's with this guy?" He made a gesture in Tennessee's direction.

She laughed in the slightly forced way that girls do sometimes when they're uncomfortable and whispered something into his ear that Tennessee couldn't hear.

"Hey! I like secrets!" Tennessee could feel his head getting heavier.

"Ahh, that makes sense. In that case, you enjoy there, pal!" The man lifted his beer toward Tennessee for a cheers.

"I will!" Tennessee lifted his own glass and clinked it against his, spilling much of his drink in the process.

Tennessee took a sip as the man walked away. "The people here are so much nicer than they are at the Peach! Much less pretentious and judgy."

"They sure are." Her voice was even more high-pitched than usual, almost as if she were talking to a toddler. "Just hang tight, okay? The night bartender just got here so I'm just wrapping up. Drink some water." She slid a clear pint glass toward him.

"Pshhh, who needs water?" As Vera walked away, he took another sip of sweet burning fizz.

The bar lights pulsed overhead as two girls about his age claimed the empty stools beside him. The ceiling seemed to lower itself inch by inch, while the walls got closer.

"Did you feel that?" he asked the girls, gripping the edge of the bar to steady himself.

"Feel what? An earthquake?" The one closest to him tilted her head. She was the same type of strawberry blonde that Lucy was. Her face was orange-tinted from fake tan. She was preppy—so unlike Lucy. She looked like she belonged in the Marina, not the Richmond. Yet behind her eyes burned the same inexplicable intensity that had first drawn him to Lucy.

"The walls. They're starting to close in on us."

She exchanged a glance with her friend sitting beside her—a silent conversation in a language of raised eyebrows and subtle smirks that Tennessee couldn't quite decipher.

"Someone's had a bit too much to drink," the other girl

said. She was a brunette who was just as preppy looking as her friend, but slightly bitchier in tone.

"No, really! You don't feel it?"

"Nope, sorry," the reddish blonde girl said, her smile thin and patronizing.

Tennessee blinked, and in that millisecond of darkness, something changed. When his eyes reopened, the world shifted. Her face flickered like a television with poor reception, static crawling across her features.

She wasn't the same stranger he'd seen just moments ago. It was Lucy's face that was now looking at him. Her nose bent out of shape and her lip split open. Blood was pouring out of the cracks in her face.

He let out a loud gasp, dropping his drink to the floor.

"So sorry, ladies," Vera came up behind him, now on the same side of the bar. "Let me just get someone to clean that up. Janice, there's some glass on the ground over here!"

The two girls next to him gathered their things and moved to a second set of open seats on the other side of the bar.

"Ready to go?" Vera asked.

"That's…that's her…" Tennessee said, still dumbstruck.

She touched his shoulder, "No, hun. It's not." Vera's face twisted into an uncomfortable grimace.

He didn't believe her. He tried to look past Vera's head to find Lucy again, but he'd lost sight of her.

"Let's go. Now." This time it wasn't a question.

"Okay," he spoke in a hushed tone as he went to stand up.

He felt the pressure building in his skull—until something snapped. As he rose from the bar stool, his feet missed the ground. The wooden floor fell away beneath his feet. Whatever he was standing on was trying to swallow him whole.

A strong shot of wind slapped him in the face and threw his hair across his face. He was blinded by specks of sand that forced their way into his eye sockets and crunched in gritty clusters in the back of his teeth. Squinting with impaired vision, the vibrant colors of the bar were now replaced by shades of gray.

Lifting his gaze to his outstretched arm, he could see a set of short, stubby fingers laced between his own. Just above them was a mess of bleach-blonde hair that was being tossed around in every direction. Vera was leading him somewhere.

To his right, off in the distance, a roaring black pit was foaming and fizzing against the night sky. Occasionally, its waves crashed against the shore. A deep breath in and the smell of salt rose from it, seeping into his sinuses. A subtle mist left droplets against his skin.

"How did we get here?" He grabbed her hand tighter, using it to keep his balance.

"HA-HA, very funny," she shouted back at him.

He bit down on the sides of his cheeks until he tasted the sharp tang of blood, metallic and warm against his tongue.

"Hurry up," she tugged at his hand. "They already started."

"Who?"

"My friend's metal band? I already told you this like three times."

"Right. You didn't say it was at the beach."

"You're fucking with me now, right? I told you as soon as we left the bar that we were going to Ocean Beach."

Through the distant gray haze, they walked toward a great ball of fire. Burning orange flames reached high up into the darkness and flicked their tongues at the stars. Surrounding the blaze was a group of dark, shadowy figures that were thrashing and jolting their bones like they were performing some satanic worshipping ceremony. He tried to convince his mind that they were just people. But despite his better judgment, their dark, contorted outlines made the group look like an army of demons emerging from the gates of hell.

Above the crowd, atop a graffiti-ridden cement structure, were more silhouettes that the pack down below was staring up at—these figures orchestrating their movements, directing the ways in which they should break and bend their necks and limbs.

As they got closer, the sound from this chaos overtook the roar of the sea. It didn't sound like music. It sounded like noise. A ritualistic howl came across the sand and beat into his eardrums, like the cries and clashing of deranged beasts. The overwhelming blast penetrated more than just his ears. These sounds clattered around inside of him, beating wildly on the inside of his chest. Perhaps this was why they were all writhing about like that—they needed to get this dreadful noise out of their bodies.

"Vera, I can't do this," he dug his heels into the sand.

"You're fine! I already told them you were coming."

"You told them?" Tennessee cocked his head to one side.

"Yeah. Now, let's go!" she yelled over the commotion.

As they got closer, he could see that there were far more people there than he thought among the embers and the shadowy figures. If he had to guess, there were at least one hundred bodies gathered around the fire. With each step toward them, dread crawled up his spine, and the knot in his stomach twisted itself back up again.

After a few more strides, they'd become part of the convulsing mass. The heat from the fire scorched his face and his skin started to sweat. Black air filled his nostrils and weighed down his lungs, forcing them to work harder.

He looked up toward the cement stage and the devil himself was the frontman of the band. Horns curled up from the back of his skull and sharp and pointy canines showed as he screamed a growl-like sound into the microphone. His sharp, black claws ripped at the strings of the jagged orange guitar in his hands.

"That's Dave, the lead singer!" Vera shouted over the clashing. "My friend Juliette is the drummer."

Tennessee craned his neck to try to get a glimpse of Juliette behind the demon that Vera had referred to as Dave. But he didn't see a girl sitting in the drummer's seat, only a mass of black hair that bobbed and swayed with a set of arms coming out from underneath that were beating the drum sticks down in violent bursts.

"How do you know these pe—" he turned back toward Vera, only to realize that she was gone. She'd been swallowed by the mob.

He looked for her in every direction, but the crush made it hard for him to focus. As the crowd flailed, so did he. Whether he wanted to or not, he'd become one with the horde.

"The time has come!" Dave howled from above them. "It's time for the wall of death!"

Before Tennessee could even process what these words meant, all the shoulders he'd been bumping up against dissipated. As if acting upon command, the crowd parted like the Red Sea, barking in anticipation, stomping their hooves and pounding at their chests as they awaited their next instruction.

Standing in the middle of the circle, Tennessee felt the stare of dozens of eyeballs. They licked their chops as though they were ready to take a bite out of him. He was a sacrifice, and they were preparing for a kill.

"On the count of three," Dave screamed into the microphone, "you're all going to run at each other and create the biggest mosh pit this beach has ever seen!"

Each direction Tennessee looked, there was someone cracking their knuckles, getting ready to pulverize his bones and peel the skin off his flesh. His shoes were heavy with sand. He was stuck, immobile in the impending pit of death.

Dave began his countdown. "One...two..."

Just as Tennessee was preparing to accept his fate, an arm emerged from the crowd, grabbing him by the hand and pulling him out just before the mass of bodies collided as Dave shouted, "Three!" Sand flew into the air as they kicked their feet and slammed their full weight into each other.

"Damn, Ten," Vera pulled him to the edge of the crowd. "You're real wild for getting in the middle of a mosh like that."

Tennessee's body trembled and he could hear his heartbeat racing in time with the drums that were now being hit at full force. Vera narrowly saved him from what surely would have been his demise.

"Anyways, these are my friends," she pointed around at a group of people. "We're all here to see Juliette."

Some nodded their heads in his direction or waved their cigarette- or beer-filled hands at him.

A blonde girl with colorful eyeliner and a watermelon-flavored vape in one hand stuck her other hand out in his direction. "Hi. I'm Amber! Vera told me so much about you."

Tennessee instinctively grabbed her hand and shook it. As she got close to talk in his ear, some of the fruity scented smoke flew in his face.

"You work at the bookstore, right? The Pink Peach? I love that place. So cute that you and Vera work right across the street from each other."

He nodded and tried to lift the side of his lips to form a smile. Something about it didn't feel right on his face. Tiny shapes began to dance across his field of vision, swirling and multiplying with each blink.

"Alright, alright," Vera butted in and redirected Tennessee's attention to another person. "And this is Jimmy."

Jimmy had long hair and was banging his head to the music but momentarily paused upon Vera's cue.

"Yo," Jimmy lifted his hand for a fist bump. "This the boyfriend you've been telling us about, Vera?"

"Boyfriend? I'm not…" Tennessee looked over at Vera to see that color had rushed into her cheeks.

Jimmy's eyes disappeared into his eye sockets, leaving dark pits in their place. "Oh, uh. Well, good to meet you, I guess." He went back to thrashing his head to the beat.

All around him, faces were decomposing. Eyes collapsed inward, noses flattened into the skin as if they'd been pushed in, mouths sealing shut. The crowd was transforming into a sea of mannequin-like beings.

"I'm sorry, I hope you don't mind that I called you that." When he turned to Vera, her mouth remained a motionless line across her face while her words somehow continued to form.

"I...uhm...I gotta go."

Before his mind could catch up to his body, his legs were running across the top of the sand toward the water. The thrashing crowd and roaring fire fell away behind him, their chaotic noise diminishing against the hypnotic whisper of the waves. He ran away from it all. Away from the swarm, away from the fire, away from Vera—and into the embrace of the sea.

Chapter 15

"Twenty bucks and an ID."

"You're kidding. Twenty dollars?" Tennessee groaned as he pulled out his wallet. "They're a bunch of nobodies."

The bouncer shrugged, his large body blocking the entrance. Long, gray strands of his beard waved in the breeze. "You coming in or not?"

"Only in San Francisco." Tennessee begrudgingly handed over the cash.

"Enjoy the show," the man said and stepped aside to let him into the venue.

He skipped the dimly lit bar and headed straight for the dingy red curtains to get to the stage area. He'd seen Lucy's band play here a few times before, but something about the venue looked different tonight—though he wasn't quite sure why.

The stage was small—barely more than a wooden platform elevated eight inches off the sticky floor. It was like a game of Tetris whenever they would play here, with Lucy and her bandmates shuffling amplifiers and guitars around like puzzle pieces, trying to fit all five of their instruments on such a cramped surface.

Spray paint and graffiti tags covered nearly every inch of the formerly orange walls. Decades of band names and stickers showed the history of the venue, having been around for more than one hundred years. The place reeked of liquor and aging hardwood. About a dozen mismatched tables were scattered across the room with seats that all faced the stage, their surfaces etched with initials and quotes from patrons long gone. Suspended above it all was a tiny, narrow balcony—which was really nothing more than a ledge with seats—where Tennessee usually sat to watch the show, separate from the crowd but with an unobstructed view of Lucy.

Everything was just as he remembered, but something about it felt different. He took a long sip of his whiskey ginger trying to put his finger on it. Then the carbonation on his tongue made him pause.

"Wait, I didn't order this." He looked down at his glass. Even though his taste buds felt the fizz of the ginger ale and the burn of whiskey, he was now somehow holding a beer. First confusion struck him, and shortly after came the realization.

"Oh, shit. Am I dreaming?" he whispered. "No... Am I?"

Hands. Check the hands.

Turning his right hand toward his face, he counted: "One, two, three, four, five, six."

A bit taken aback, he blinked and counted his fingers again.

"One, two, three, four, five, six." His hand looked normal. But he was somehow counting an extra digit.

He examined it even closer and named them this time.

"Thumb. Index. Middle. Ring. Ring. Pinky." An extra ring finger, hiding in plain sight.

"Oh my god," he smiled.

Still a bit apprehensive, he reached for his phone to check the time.

10:39.

He put it back in his pocket and waited a few moments before pulling it out again.

2:47. He was starting to feel giddy.

Just to be sure, he peeked back out of the curtain to get a second look at the bouncer. The man no longer had a long gray beard; instead, he was a different man altogether. The guy checking IDs now was a thin, yuccie-type in a beanie, his face completely bare of any facial hair.

"Okay, now where was I before I got here?"

He grasped for something, anything, in his memory. How he'd gotten here. Where he'd come from. Where he'd parked his car. But nothing came to mind. Like he just magically arrived here from…nowhere.

"Fuck yeah, I did it! I'm in a dream. I'm awake in a dream."

Now that he was lucid, he could finally see all the weird aspects of the venue that made it feel different; like the crystal chandelier that hung from the ceiling that looked like it belonged in the lobby of a fancy hotel, not an old divey music venue. The chairs around the tables were a mix of different things. Some were park benches, others were lawn chairs, a few were rocking chairs, and some big La-Z-Boy recliners. No two were the same, and none of them seemed like they belonged there. The exit sign flickered between English and what looked like Japanese.

And among all these impossibilities was the one thing he had come here for—the one person who felt more real than anything else in this dreamscape. Lucy was here somewhere. And he would get to be with her again soon.

Just as she came to mind, the lights dimmed. A familiar hush fell over the crowd—the collective intake of breath before music breaks the silence. Tennessee made his way toward the back staircase, stepping around mismatched furniture and dream-added obstacles that didn't exist in the real venue. The stairs seemed to stretch longer than he remembered, each step carrying him farther from the crowd but closer to his perfect view of her.

He reached the balcony just as the first notes echoed through the room, sliding into his usual spot—only now the seats up here looked like they belonged in the nose-bleeds section of the Giants stadium. From this vantage point, he could see everything—the stage, the crowd, but most importantly, her. The distance felt right somehow—close enough to see every detail, but still able to take in the full picture of what he'd lost.

As the drums kicked in, the room was coated with pink and purple lights. Lucy was center-stage, backlit by a bright white stage light that made her silhouette glow. She looked angelic as she drew the crowd in with a sultry guitar intro.

The whole band was massively talented, especially when you considered how young they all were. But there was this unspoken knowing among them that what little success they'd seen so far was all thanks to Lucy. She wrote all the lyrics, came up with the melodies, and taught the girls how to play their parts for every song. She would say she gave them creative freedom to change their parts as they wanted, but he knew her too well to believe that.

"I can't help it that the way I wrote it just sounds better," she once admitted to him when she was drunk. "They honestly can't get mad at me about that."

She somehow always got her way.

The front lights turned on as they moved into the first verse of the song and he could finally see more than just her outline. She had on a pair of shiny leather pants and a bright orange tube top. Glitter covered her cheeks and chest, and two clips on both sides of her head pulled her bangs off her face. The strap for her favorite guitar, the one her dad gave her, hung from her shoulder. Her fingers danced across the frets with ease, like she didn't even need to think about it at all.

By the time they reached the chorus, the crowd was practically eating out of the palm of her hand. Every eye in the room was on her. She swayed her hips and shoulders as she played. Her lips stayed close to the microphone as she sang in a muffled whisper, reminding him of how she would talk into his ear late at night. Every time the drums hit, she tossed her hair to the beat.

"A radio signal from your heart to mine," she looked up into the balcony and met his eyes. "You said you'd love me 'til you watched me die." She sent him up a wink.

He whispered the lyrics back to her in unison. He'd been with her the day she wrote this song, watching her transform their most precious memories into poetry. To the crowd, it was just another love song, but to him, every line was a piece of their story—promises they'd whispered on cliffsides, fears he'd confessed in her bedroom, the parts of himself he'd never shown anyone else. It was a love letter that only he could decode.

As much as he liked watching her play, being a spectator wasn't enough. If this was truly his dream, why stay in the audience?

"How do I get us out of here?" he said, looking around the room and taking a swig of his beer. "Ugh, Budweiser, disgusting."

He took a good look at the bottle in his hand. The amber liquid sloshed inside as he tilted it under the dim lights. This wasn't just any cheap beer—it was Budweiser, his dad's drink of choice. The one that had always been in their fridge, empty bottles collecting on the coffee table. Tennessee would never drink this stuff in real life. Even the sharp, yeasty scent was enough to trigger memories he'd spent years trying to bury.

In the blink of an eye, the beer bottle was gone, and his hand was clasped around a bucket glass filled with whiskey and ginger ale.

"Oh shit," a huge smile spread across his face. All he had to do was think about something and so it was.

Lucy continued to sing, "See yourself through my eyes—see there's no monsters inside."

He closed his eyes. He needed to think of somewhere they could go where they could be alone. Who knew how long he had before he woke up?

"The reflection is wrong, in my arms is where you belong."

His mind returned to that morning, drinking black coffee as she sat on her bedroom floor writing this song.

"A radio signal from your heart to mine."

Memories of her acoustic guitar and warm light flooding through her bay windows came rushing back. He needed to go back there.

"You said you'd love me 'til you watched me die," he said as he blinked his eyes open.

He was no longer seated in the stadium chair overlooking the stage. Instead, he was cross-legged on top of her plush pink comforter, the drink in his hand replaced with a coffee mug.

She sat on the floor, her back pressed against the footboard of her bed with her acoustic guitar across her lap. Sunlight dappled through the half-drawn blinds, creating shifting patterns across the worn wood of her guitar. She'd woken up with a rush of inspiration and had hardly touched the coffee he'd made her—now sitting cold on the nightstand.

Instead, she'd slipped from beneath the sheets, settled into her usual writing spot, as if the music couldn't wait another moment. Her hair was still messy from sleep, copper strands catching the light as she hunched over with that intense focus that made the rest of the world disappear.

This was Lucy in her purest form—before audiences, before stage lights, before glitter and flashy getups. This was the real her. And that was exactly the Lucy he wanted to be with.

There was something so pure about her creative process. Music just seemed to flow out of her—like the songs chose her rather than the other way around. Her focus narrowed to her fingers, her eyes following their movements against the frets, trying to find just the right note. A low hum came out of her pursed lips that matched the hollow sound of the chords she played. Every few minutes, she stopped and wrote down some words on a notepad only to strike them out and replace them with new ones moments later.

It made him feel pretty special to see her like this. She didn't let many people watch her play this raw and unplugged. He got to see her songs as they were being made, witness magic in the making. The evolution from fragments and phrases to full masterpieces.

"Sounds pretty," he said from behind her.

"This one's about you," she glanced back toward him with a satisfied look.

His body tensed as the script of that morning began to unfold. The same sinking feeling flooded through him— tight chest, racing pulse, the urge to run. Though his lucid mind knew this was just a dream, his past self's emotions played out in real-time, that instinctive fear of being truly seen surging back as if for the first time. He was both actor and audience now, experiencing the panic while simultaneously watching it unfold.

"What? What do you mean?" The words fell from his mouth as if he was reading lines in a play.

"I wrote a song about you," she smiled innocently. "About us, I guess."

"Oh. What about?"

"You know, Sutro Tower. That one night at West Cliff. Just our memories together. I guess just…what you mean to me." She began to blush. "Super cheesy, I know."

A lump formed in the back of his throat. His palms became clammy, and his heart started to race. A wave of anxiety came over him just as it had that day. He began to fidget. Feeling like he couldn't sit still, he stood up and started pacing around the room.

"What are you doing?"

"I just—I, uh. I can't…"

Each word and feeling felt like replaying a scene he knew by heart. His body remembered this dance—the fear, the hesitation, the hope that she might understand.

"Okay. I thought you'd like it," her voice now cold. "But just forget it, I guess."

"No, no. It's not that," he shook his head. "It's beautiful. Really. I just don't see how you could write something like that…for me."

She pulled the guitar off her lap and leaned it against her bed. "What do you mean?"

"There's a lot about me you don't know. People like you shouldn't write love songs about people like me."

She'd gotten up and blocked the path he was pacing, a look of concern on her face. "A lot I don't know about you? Like what?"

He took a big sigh. Lucy knew almost everything about him. She knew he'd never had a girlfriend before her.

She knew his family didn't have much money growing up— his mom worked long hours for minimum wage and his dad could hardly hold down a job. She even knew that his dad was now sober and that he was on medication to help manage his addiction.

She also knew that Tennessee didn't like to talk about any of that.

But there were a few things he hadn't told her. Things that he hadn't told anybody, not even Tanner.

"It's just that, in my family, love wasn't like this," he gestured toward her. "It was dark and mean. There were lots of lies and lots of really scary nights."

She led them both toward the bed where they sat down.

"I'm listening. If you want to tell me, that is."

"I just...I don't want you to see me any differently."

"I promise you, I won't."

Some part of him, the part of him that was still connected to the real world, wanted to spit in her face for saying that. He knew what she would do with this information. She'd break every bit of this promise and his heart all in one fatal swoop. He wondered what would've happened if he never told her at all.

But that's not why he was here now.

"Before my dad got sober, it was scary to be around him."

"What do you mean?"

The lump in his throat was throbbing. "He would hit us when he was fucked up. A lot."

"He hit you?" Her mouth fell open in disbelief.

He nodded.

She gasped, her hand covering her mouth. "I'm so sorry, I had no idea."

"Yeah, I didn't want to scare you."

"Your mom, too?"

"Yep." Tears started to fill in his eyes when he thought about what his mom had been through. "I'll spare you the details. But it was awful. There were times I feared for our lives."

She remained silent. It was probably hard for her to imagine growing up in that sort of environment. Her parents hardly ever raised their voices. She had no idea what it was like to fear the one person who was supposed to love and protect you.

"So yeah, love isn't like this for people like me. I've never known love to be gentle or kind. I'm not the type of guy you should be writing love songs for. I'm the type of guy your dad warned you about. I don't deserve this type of love."

His chest tightened. He remembered thinking at that moment she would probably run far away from him. That someone like her couldn't love someone like him. Someone so broken.

And, as it turned out, he'd been right. Someone like her

couldn't love someone like him. But he wanted to pretend, just for a little while, like she could.

"You're wrong." Her eyes pierced through him.

"You don't get it, Lucy." He shook his head. "I'll just destroy us."

"You won't. Because you're nothing like him. I love you with everything I have. I love you with everything that I am. From the deepest part of my soul and back. When I'm not thinking about music, I'm thinking about you. And now those thoughts have turned into this song—which I thought you'd like, by the way."

He smiled at that. He did love that song.

"You get to choose who you become. You can follow in his footsteps or choose a new path. That's for you to decide. But I know you deserve this type of love, because I'm sitting here right now, giving it to you."

He felt his heart begin to swell.

"You deserve all the love songs in the world because you're my everything. One day, I hope you see yourself the same way I see you."

She let go of him and grabbed her notebook off the floor. "I need to write that down."

He came down to meet her and scooped her face into his hands.

"Thank you." He was finally able to go off-script. "I know that *this* is the real you. My Lucy. I know you didn't mean all that stuff you said before."

"Before when?"

"It doesn't matter. What matters is you and me, right here and now." He wrapped her into his arms. "I promised you I'd come back for you, and I'll keep finding my way back to you. To us. To the way we were before."

He could practically feel the love radiating off her. The warmth was back in her eyes again, a look of pure understanding and forgiveness. She'd seen his darkest parts and chose to go on loving him anyway.

He brushed his fingers across her skin and leaned in to kiss her. As their lips intertwined, she climbed into his lap and wrapped her legs around his hips.

"I missed you."

"Shhh," she gave an unusually prolonged hush.

As his lips met hers, he realized that she wasn't wearing the vanilla Burt's Bees Chapstick she usually wore. Today, for some reason, she tasted particularly salty.

A rush of water then filled his pant leg, suddenly jolting him awake. He spat saltwater out of his mouth and gasped for air. All of his clothes were soaking wet, and sand was caked deep into his scalp. Both his shoes and socks were off his feet.

It was the early hours of the morning—the sun had yet to rise, but the sky was a pale gray that let him know it was on its way. He'd been out here most of the night and the high tide was only now waking him up.

He shivered as he stood up, scanning the shore for his

belongings. One of his shoes was a few feet behind where he'd been laying and the other one a little farther behind it—thankfully, one of them held his keys. He patted down his wet pockets where he found his wallet. The black fabric was soggy and everything inside of it stuck together, but nothing important seemed to be missing from it.

There was no sign of his phone anywhere. He got down on his hands and knees and dug up the sand in and around the imprint his body had made. After several minutes of digging, he sat down and let out a big sigh.

While he knew he should've felt worried—or at the very least, annoyed—about the loss of his phone, all he could care about right now was getting back to her.

Chapter 16

Making his way back to his apartment, he kept his eyes on the sidewalk, avoiding the discriminating stares of the early risers in the Outer Richmond—the surfers with their short boards and the runners in their athletic garb. Despite the wet clothes and layers of sand, he felt surprisingly clear-headed. No hangover, no anxiety, just a renewed purpose drumming through his veins.

The hot water of his shower brought him back to life, dissolving the grit and salt caked on his skin. The grains of sand spiraled down the drain in a cyclone, the same way the ring of blood had that night.

Her words still rang in his ears. *You're just like your father.*

But it wasn't the real Lucy who'd said that. The real Lucy was waiting for him in his dreams. The real Lucy saw the best in him; she loved him in all his flaws—she would've never said something so malicious. He threw on a fresh pair of black jeans and a t-shirt. Peeling the wet pair off his bedroom floor, he reached into the grimy pocket and unfolded the acid sheet. Thankfully, it remained undisturbed, the aluminum foil protecting it from the sea.

"I'll find you again," he whispered, carefully folding the foil back up and slipping it into his pocket. "Tonight."

As he walked into the Peach later that morning, he looked up at the clock on the wall. The red plastic was back in its proper place around the clock's face. The time was just after 8:20 a.m. Not on time, but not too terribly late, considering he didn't have his phone. Late enough that Mr. Green would be annoyed, but early enough that he might forgive him.

But the moment he stepped behind the counter, he knew something was wrong. Mr. Green's usually cheerful demeanor had been replaced with something tense and rigid. His thin metal frames sat lower on his nose than usual, and his eyes bore into Tennessee with an intensity that made him take an instinctive step backward.

"So you've decided to grace us with your presence today?" Mr. Green's voice was clipped, each syllable enunciated purposefully.

"Sorry I'm late," Tennessee offered. "The bus—"

"Late?" Mr. Green let out a humorless laugh. "You're more than just late. You didn't show up for your shift yesterday. At all."

Tennessee frowned, his brow furrowing as he processed the words.

"What? No... I was definitely here yesterday. I..." His voice trailed off as he caught a glimpse of the date on the register's digital display. He shook his head; it must be set for the wrong date.

"I called you three times. I left you several messages. And I never heard from you. Not a word."

"I lost my phone," he said weakly.

Mr. Green let out a long sigh. His expression softened, a look of concern replaced his anger. "Are you doing okay, son? This isn't like you. Sure, you're late almost every day, but I've never doubted that you'd show up. And to not even call? Frankly, I'm worried about you."

A cold tingle crept up Tennessee's spine. There was no way. There was no way he could've lost an entire day from his memory. He couldn't have been out on that beach for that long. Could he have? Mr. Green must be losing it.

"Uh, yeah? I'm fine, but I was definitely here," Tennessee insisted, though his voice lacked its initial conviction. "Maybe you're thinking of someone else on staff? Joe or Alice, maybe?"

Mr. Green studied him for a long moment, eyes narrowing until he eventually let out a sigh. "Look, Tennessee. You're a good worker when you're here, but I need to know I can count on you. You're on very thin ice."

"It won't happen again." Tennessee hoped that would be enough to make sure this conversation ended.

Mr. Green nodded his head slowly before turning toward his office. "There's a crate of new arrivals here that need shelving."

Tennessee nodded, grateful for the distraction. As he hauled the crate upstairs and into the quiet corners of the store, his mind raced. Was Mr. Green in early-stage dementia or something? Or had he really been lost in his dreamworld for that long?

He needed to talk to Vera. She'd be able to tell him what happened last night and put his mind at ease.

The morning crawled by slowly, but eventually, it was noon, and Tennessee slipped across the street to the bar. Vera was wiping down the counter in circular motions when he walked in, her platinum blonde hair twisted up in a messy bun.

"Dude!" Her face looked relieved when she spotted him. "What the fuck happened to you?"

"I was hoping you could tell me," he said, sliding onto his barstool.

"Well, first and foremost, you left your phone here."

A wave of relief washed over him. "You have my phone?"

"Sure do." She reached beneath the bar and pulled it out. "Janice said she found it on the floor the other night as she was cleaning up the glass you dropped."

"You mean last night?"

"No, that was two nights ago. You bailed on me at the beach, remember? Ran off into the ocean like a maniac." She slid the phone over to him. "I tried to go to the bookstore yesterday to give it to you, but apparently you never showed up."

"No, no. There's no way. I was at work *yesterday*. We were

at the beach *yesterday*—I woke up on Ocean Beach covered in sand *this morning*."

"You woke up at the beach this morning?" A bewildered look crossed her face.

As he powered on his phone, a flood of notifications filled the screen. Texts from Vera, missed calls from the landline at The Peach, a few angry texts from Mr. Green, even another call from Tanner. The timestamps were undeniable. He'd somehow managed to erase an entire day from his memory.

"Oh my god. Oh. My. God." The walls of the bar felt like they were closing in on him again. But this time, it had nothing to do with the drugs. His reality was collapsing.

He tried to make sense of the gap in his memory. A whole day, gone. He tried to remember anything—conversations with people, places he may have been, things he may have seen, anything. But there was nothing but darkness where those memories should be.

"You don't remember what you did? Like, not at all?"

"Is this normal? Has this ever happened when you've done acid?"

"No. That's literally never happened to me. How much did you take?"

"Only two. The same amount we took. I think?"

He pulled the aluminum foil out of his pocket and unfolded it. Counting the missing squares, he realized there wasn't just time and memory missing.

"Oh shit. I guess I took four."

"Yeah, that's a lot. You gotta slow your roll with that stuff. I'm not sure if you're reacting too well to it, honestly. Missing work and missing that much time? That can't be good for you."

He nodded. "Yeah. You're probably right."

Some part of him knew she was right. But, in truth, he didn't care about what was good for him right now. All he cared about was getting back to Lucy. Now that he had a taste of the old her, and a surefire way to get to her, he couldn't stop. Not yet.

"Anyways, well, thanks for holding onto my phone. I gotta get back to work now." He stood up and started toward the door.

"Wait." Vera reached across the bar. "This probably isn't the best time, but we should talk about the other night. About us."

"About us?" The words felt strange in his mouth. "What about us?"

Her cheeks flushed. "You know, when I called you my boyfriend. I know that was probably stupid, but when we were tripping together, you said you'd never felt this way about someone before, so I just assumed…"

Tennessee blinked. "I said that?"

The light in her eyes dimmed. "I guess you were pretty messed up. Forget it."

He nodded. A twinge of guilt rose in his stomach. "See you later."

Had he really said that to her? Had he given her the impression this was something more than it was? What even was it? He'd never stopped to give their relationship that much thought.

As he thought of the pain in Vera's eyes, the image of Lucy's face flashed in his mind. She was who mattered most to him. He pushed the feelings aside for now. He'd deal with the Vera situation later.

As he stepped back into the afternoon, he tipped his head back to check for Sutro Tower in the distance. There it stood in all its glory. On the sidewalk, he pulled out the foil and broke off two more tabs—placing them on his tongue before walking back into the Peach. It would be a little while until he felt anything.

He waited behind the counter for the acid to take hold. He knew he needed to act as normal as he could today. He'd sit on his hands once again and make it through another shift, do whatever he needed to get back to her.

About an hour went by before the acid started to kick in. The sensations were familiar now—the subtle rippling of the floorboard, the knot in his stomach, the colors deepening, the growing depth of the shadows. But even this familiarity didn't make the come up feel any less intense. The lights overhead pulsed in time with his heartbeat. Sweat beaded on his forehead as his body temperature went up.

Time became elastic. The clock on the wall seemed to slow down, until the red plastic once again melted entirely over its face. Tennessee found himself staring at it, transfixed. Drip. Drip. Drip. Drip. Down across the face and then in big globs down the shelves. Until a customer cleared their throat impatiently.

"Sorry," he mumbled, pulling his eyes away from it to focus.

Tennessee turned toward the register, but the numbers kept rearranging themselves beneath his fingers. Colors bled from the book in his hand and pooled onto the floor, while the sunlight streaming through the windows fractured into prisms that burned his eyes.

He somehow sloppily made it through the transaction before the bookstore began to breathe around him again. Each shelf exhaled dust and whispered secrets as old books fluttered their pages. Novels that had been dormant for years now seemed alive with movement, their spines flexing and contracting.

Sounds became disconnected from their sources—he could hear pages turning in empty aisles, the ring of the register even though he hadn't opened it, the creaking of the hardwood even when no one was approaching. The familiar scent of paper and dusty leather burned the back of his throat.

Tennessee squeezed his eyes shut, leaning against the closest bookshelf to ground himself. "Just get through the day. Your shift will be over soon."

When he reopened his eyes, his breath caught in his throat.

There, appearing suddenly in the middle of the aisle, stood the front door to his childhood home. Its splintered red wood was unmistakable. Its wobbly gold doorknob. Its crooked hinges. The dents where his father's boot had connected countless times. The door was firmly closed, but Tennessee could smell the Budweiser coming from the other side. His chest tightened as he heard the clacking sound of heels approaching from behind it. Someone was about to come out.

"No." He backed away. "You're not really here."

The door remained motionless, but the air around it seemed to bend, as if preparing to open. The knob turned slowly. Tennessee swore he could hear his dad's heavy footsteps and his raspy voice: *Get back in here, boy.*

"Leave me alone," Tennessee hissed, turning on his heels and running off into the maze of bookshelves. He wound down the stairs through the comic book section, past reference, around historical fiction—putting as much distance as possible between himself and the door.

He found himself in a quiet corner of the philosophy section. His breathing came in shallow gasps as he slid down against the shelf, pulling his knees to his chest. The same position he'd take when hiding in his closet as a child, waiting for the storm to pass.

He forced his breath. In for three seconds. Hold. Out for five. In for three. Hold. Out for five.

"Tennessee?" Mr. Green's voice cut through the sound of his breathing.

Tennessee's eyes snapped open to find Mr. Green standing at the end of the aisle, concern once again etched across his weathered face. For a moment, Tennessee was paralyzed, caught between the overwhelming sensory input of the trip and the need to appear normal.

"I'm just...just grabbing something down here." He pulled the nearest book off the shelf and pushed himself up to stand. The floor beneath him seemed to shift, the wood rippling like waves in a pond.

Mr. Green's eyes narrowed. "You're acting very strange, Alexander."

"I'm fine," Tennessee barked at the mention of his first name. "I told you not to call me that."

Mr. Green studied him for a long moment, his expression unreadable. "I need you back at the register."

Tennessee rose up from his seated fetal position and started the trek back to the front of the store, the short walk like navigating a labyrinth. The aisles stretched and contracted, books whispered from their shelves, and the overhead lights left burning trails across his vision. His skin prickled, hyperaware as he checked each corner, expecting to see the red door materialize in one of the aisles again. Mr. Green trailed behind him, his footsteps echoing loudly in Tennessee's ears.

By the time they reached the counter, beads of sweat were running down his chest beneath his shirt. The older man's presence felt suffocating, as if he could somehow see through Tennessee's skin to the chemicals coursing through his bloodstream.

"Are you sure you're alright?" Mr. Green's voice showed genuine concern. "You look awfully pale."

"No, I'm fine," Tennessee managed, gripping the edge of the counter to steady himself.

Mr. Green didn't look convinced, but he nodded slowly. "Alright, well, I need you to watch the front for a bit." He glanced toward the entrance, his expression shifting to something more formal. "Now, if you'll excuse me, I need to speak to Officer Jacobs here in my office about a rather unsettling matter."

Officer? Like a cop?

Tennessee lifted his head and saw that just behind Mr. Green, standing in the doorway of the bookstore, was a tall middle-aged man in a dark blue SFPD uniform.

Tennessee's eyes grew wide. The two men walked past the register and toward the back corner of the store. The officer looked down at Tennessee and shook his head as if he already knew everything. His heavy-duty boots shook the shelves as he walked by. Tennessee could hear the clanging of the shiny handcuffs in the officer's belt and felt the intensity of the gun at his hip.

Tennessee's heartbeat climbed into his throat and his head started to spin.

What unsettling matter? Could it be about him? Could it be about Lucy? He thought back to Tanner's text. Did the Coopers tell Mr. Green?

It had to be about her. There was no other reason for a cop to be in a bookstore. He was there to get information from Mr. Green. He was there to make an arrest. When they came back out, the handcuffs on the man's belt would be clasped around Tennessee's wrists.

Tears filled his eyes, blurring his vision. His lungs couldn't get enough air, each breath felt shallower and more forced.

He needed to get out of here. Run before it was too late. He needed to leave now.

Before his mind could even comprehend what he was doing, his body was already on the go. His feet were moving quickly beneath him to get him out from behind the counter. Before he made it out of the store, his vision became tunneled. And then quickly faded to black.

Chapter 17

By the time consciousness returned, it was dark outside. His vision, still tunneled, was laser focused on the sidewalk moving quickly beneath his feet.

He could feel his heart pounding in his chest, his arms and legs pumping as fast as they could go as he ran at full speed. There was an ache in his side where his ribs seemed to puncture his lungs. Sweat weighed down his greasy hair and caused his shirt to cling to his skin. He had nothing but the clothes on his back—his jacket and backpack left behind at the Peach.

Turning over his shoulder, he expected to see red and blue lights following behind him. But there were no lights or sirens tailing him as far as he could see. There was no one chasing him on foot—nothing but empty sidewalk stretched on behind him.

Cautiously, he slowed his pace, his lungs laboring to catch his breath.

His peripherals began to widen back out and more of his surroundings came into view. The bright headlights of cars passing by left paths in his vision, their taillights bleeding red smears against the darkness. The wet pavement beneath his feet reflected the streetlights back in fractures. Looking up, he saw the golden plumes of the Holy Virgin Cathedral. The round pyramid-like tops bounced like balloons in the night sky, floating above the building like they were filled with air, reaching up toward the thick fog. On the other corner, there were a few people standing on the sidewalk, their shadowy faces blurred by clouds of smoke. Above them, the bright neon sign of the tiki bar gave an eerie, electric buzz. He couldn't see their eyes but felt the scrutiny of their stares as they huddled together against the night chill. He realized he'd run nearly all the way home.

As he finally came to a full stop in front of the coffee shop, he recognized the familiar taste of cheap whiskey and cigarettes on the back of his tongue. Lifting his hands, he noticed they were trembling uncontrollably, veins pulsing visibly beneath his skin. The cold breeze cut through his sweat-soaked shirt, raising goosebumps across his skin.

The last thing he remembered was bolting out of the store, narrowly avoiding arrest. The cold air and the deep color of the night sky suggested it was now the last few hours of the day. Whatever happened between now and then was a mystery.

Out of the corner of his eye, he saw something move in the coffee shop window. He turned his head quickly, somewhat paranoid, and saw a dark figure standing just behind the glass. It was a man, and he was looking out the window directly at him.

Tennessee scanned the man up and down—the clothes he wore were stained with sweat. He looked deranged and unkempt, his dark curly hair sticking up at random angles around his head. Dark shadows sat beneath his deep-set eyes, which were bloodshot and wild, the pupils dilated so the only color visible in them was black. A thin layer of stubble covered his jaw, patchy and uneven. He had sharp cheekbones and a pair of chapped, chewed up lips.

Unease crept up Tennessee's spine as he studied the stranger. What was this guy doing alone in a closed cafe? And why did his presence feel both threatening and oddly familiar?

The man's eyes looked down at him with unsettling intensity. Had he seen those eyes before? The black pupils in a sea of white held him captive, almost like they embodied the darkness that they'd seen. Did Tennessee know this guy?

The two of them stood and stared at each other, motionless, for several passing moments. The man eventually lowered his thick brows, and a twisted, evil smile spread across his cheeks. A menacing look took over his face, as if an idea had just taken form. Tennessee then watched as the man's hand balled up into a fist.

It was only a split second after that the flashbacks started to flood in. Holes in the drywall. Broken beer bottles scattered across the floor. The anguish in her voice as she begged him to stop. Bruised knuckles. Washing the dried blood off his hands.

This stranger in the window was the one who caused all of Tennessee's pain. An entity that lurked in the shadows of Tennessee's mind—his existence denied, and his darkness repressed, emerging only when presented with a portal to the past. Though something deep within him knew he'd been running from this stranger for years, Tennessee couldn't recognize the figure staring back at him. But this man within couldn't be contained or compartmentalized any longer. His message could no longer go unheard. With unrelenting focus and merciless eyes, the stranger demanded Tennessee's attention—forcing him to face the truth.

A fire ignited inside him as the images flashed before his eyes. Hot tears began to roll down his cheeks.

But Tennessee refused. He wasn't the monster this man in the glass was trying to tell him he was. But the harder he resisted, the more memories he fought against. The more proof he had that he *was* just like his dad.

The boom, crash of glass. The sound of his mother wailing. The thump of repeated kicks.

You're just like your father. Lucy's voice spat in his face.

"I'm nothing like him!" Tennessee screamed at the window.

The stranger's wicked smile spread wider as Tennessee's fury and resentment built. The man eventually raised his fist up near his face and Tennessee copied him.

"Yes. You are. You need to remember what you did."
Tennessee watched the man's lips move, but the rumbling
came from inside his own chest.

More images came back: The river of red that came
from her broken nose. The trembling of her voice. A pair
of matching black and blue circles surrounding her blue
eyes.

"You did that."

It was then that something inside Tennessee burst, like a
pot of boiling water that was finally bubbling over the edge.
His vision went red as pure, unfiltered rage took over.

He'd done all that he could to try to forget—to run
from the man who stood before him. To suppress all that
lived deep inside him. To hide from the memories. To deny
the truth of what he'd done.

But now, he didn't want to run from this man at all. He
wanted to kill him.

Tennessee let out a blood-curdling scream that tore
from deep within his chest, the sound ripping through his
throat. He sent his fist flying toward the glass, knuckles first.
A thunderous shattering echoed down the street. His hand
punched through where the man's face had been, leaving a
jagged hole. Tennessee barely registered the pain at first—
only the warm rush of blood where his flesh had been torn
open, flowing down his wrist and forearm. The scab that
formed reopened.

The man was now gone, shattered into fragmented pieces. Tennessee was the last one standing.

As he pulled his arm from the window, he saw gashes where his fist made impact, mutilating the top of his hand. Several significant vertical cuts sliced up his skin in multiple places. The blood—thick and almost black in the dim streetlight—pulsed with his heartbeat, dripping down his elbow and splattering in dark droplets on the concrete.

Judging eyes burned intensely into the back of his neck from the people across the street. Window blinds snapped up and apartment lights turned on one by one. Curious heads peeped out from their windows. He heard a siren off in the distance, cutting through the fog and growing louder with each passing second.

His heart rate started to increase, and his vision started to tunnel once again. Before he even had a moment to think, he'd already taken off running, leaving a trail of blood in his path. His footsteps echoed down the empty street and then faded as the fog swallowed him, when darkness took over once more.

Chapter 18

When everything else was still a blur, the first thing that came back into focus was his lacerated hands. The knuckles on his right hand were swollen and the skin was split open in several spots. In one particularly deep gash near his middle knuckle, he was almost certain he could see the white of his bone beneath the torn flesh. Thankfully, it didn't seem to hurt all that much—a dull throb rather than searing pain. That numbness worried him more than any pain might have.

Moments later, more of his surroundings came into view. His fingers—sticky with blood—were wrapped around a steering wheel, rivers of red trailing down to his wrists. Dark red spots lined the upholstery of the truck, and a smeared handprint stretched across the dashboard.

Looking up, he saw a winding double yellow line stretching ahead outside the windshield. The headlights bounced up and down, illuminating an otherwise dark road that was steep and hilly. All he could make out was the momentary silhouettes of trees as he sped past them.

He let out a loud gasp as his brain finally processed what his eyes were seeing. His chest jolted forward as he realized he was driving, the shock forcing his vision back into focus. His foot was pressed hard on the gas pedal and the truck was moving at more than seventy miles per hour. The steering wheel seemed to turn on its own beneath his loose grip.

The last clear memory he had was his fist connecting with the window of the coffee shop, shattering the glass. And now, somehow, he was here, hurtling through darkness on a road he didn't recognize.

With a surge of panic, he tightened his grip on the wheel in an attempt to get back in control. The truck lurched dangerously toward the edge. A metallic shriek filled the cab as the passenger side scraped against the guardrail, sending sparks flying in the darkness. The sound made his back teeth grind together and his whole body clenched. He panicked and turned the wheel sharply away from the railing and into the opposite lane.

His heart was pounding loudly in his chest. How the hell did he get here?

The yellow line ahead made an abrupt turn—a deadly curve that appeared without warning in his high beams.

Shit.

There was no way he could navigate the turn at this speed. Bracing himself, every muscle in his body tensed as he slammed his foot down on the brakes and pulled at the wheel. The tires screeched as the truck drifted through the turn, echoing off the mountainside, leaving the smell of burning rubber in their wake.

By some miracle, the truck made it through the turn, wobbling wildly before coming to a lurching stop, the force throwing Tennessee back against the seat.

"Oh my god." His whole body was trembling. He could have easily died just now.

He kept his foot on the brake, afraid to move an inch. Adrenaline coursed through his veins. He felt jittery and restless.

How had he gotten here? Why was he driving? And where the hell was he going?

The cuts on his hands began to sting. As his eyes traveled upward, following the winding road that disappeared into mist at the top of the hill, the answer became clear.

Beyond the dark road and scattered trees, an open clearing showed where this windy road was heading. In the distance, reaching up into the dense fog, stood a massive three-pronged structure. Its red lights pulsed rhythmically, cutting through the mist like bloody eyes watching his every move.

Sutro Tower spoke in silence. No matter how far or fast he ran, he always ended up back to it. It had seen everything. It knew his truth. It couldn't be outrun.

When he glanced up into the rearview mirror, expecting to see his own eyes, he instead found the same dark, sinister eyes he'd seen in the coffee shop window—his father's eyes—staring back at him.

Chapter 19

Tennessee blinked open his eyes and realized he was still gripping the steering wheel. The sky had opened up, dumping sheets of rain across his windshield. Despite the wipers working at maximum speed, he could only see a few feet ahead of him through the downpour.

He glanced down at his hands—the same ones that had just been mutilated and dripping with blood—now completely healed without a single cut or bruise. The dashboard was completely clean, no dark spots lining the truck's interior.

Lucy was sitting half out the window, her whole body to the wind despite the downpour. Her cropped pink T-shirt was soaked through and clung to her chest. Water splattered across the inside of the dashboard and all over the upholstery. She flung both her arms up above her and shouted things he couldn't hear over the music and the whooshing of the wind.

There she was.

A strange lightness filled his chest as reality seemed to bend around him. He looked at the time on the stereo, then away from it momentarily and then back again, only to see that the numbers had changed. The sharp pain in his knuckles, the sticky wetness between his fingers—all gone as if they'd never existed. A familiar disorientation washed over him.

He smiled over at her, his heart swelling with a mix of relief and exhilaration. He'd done it yet again—he'd found his way back to her. Her hair danced in the wind, her laughter cutting through the storm. All that he'd gone through to get here had been worth it to see her like this again, wild and beautiful as ever. In this space between dreams and memory, they could be together as they were meant to be.

And now, he'd returned to one of his favorite memories—the night Sutro Tower got its meaning.

It had been raining hard that night. Not the usual drizzle that came through the city every few days in the early morning hours of winter—but a bad storm. A once-a-year type of storm that hit the Bay Area like a ton of bricks.

At this point, things were getting serious with Lucy. They'd been seeing each other for a few months now. There were no longer questions lingering about what exactly they were to each other or if either of them was seeing anyone else. Their relationship was at a turning point. It was something real, and something he couldn't live without.

He knew he was in love with her—though he hadn't yet said it out loud. He didn't know if she felt the same and he wasn't ready to find out if she didn't. He'd rather live in blissful ignorance than see this end too soon. So for the last few weeks, he carried his feelings close to his chest and did his best not to make them known.

There were a few times it almost slipped out. Like right when they woke up and her tired eyes met his or when she'd get up on her tiptoes to kiss him goodbye. Each time, he'd have to bite the sides of his cheeks to stop himself when the words nearly fell from his mouth.

But his actions weren't so easy to control. The love he was hiding caused him to do such stupid things. Like this night, for example. He knew better than to be driving in a storm like this, especially as drunk as he was. If anyone else would have come to him with this ridiculous request, he would've shut it down immediately. But he couldn't say no to her.

The rain had transformed her—her red-tinted curls darkened and stuck to her neck, water streaming down her face. Tennessee gripped the steering wheel tightly with his left hand and held her ankle with his right. The danger of what they were doing only seemed to fuel her ecstasy, her arms stretched wide, while he focused on every curve and dip in the winding road.

As the memory played out before him, the same swirl of anxious thoughts ran through his mind about what could go wrong, just as they had that night. A cop pulling them over. The truck hydroplaning off the road. Hitting a turn wrong and her whole body flying out the window. There were so many terrible possibilities. He kept his eyes laser-focused on the double yellow lines in front of him, trying his best not to swerve.

But the lucid part of him savored the rush of it all. There was a sense of adrenaline that came with the danger they'd put themselves in that night. Her energy pulsed through the cab of the truck like a current, rewiring his cautious nature. It was the two of them against the world, against logic and fear. The terror and thrill collided in his chest, creating something primal and addictive that was more powerful than any drug—a sensation so visceral it bordered on something otherworldly.

She finally pulled herself back into the truck as they pulled into the empty parking lot at the top of Twin Peaks. But before he could even put the car in park, Lucy was already outside. No jacket or umbrella. Just her, spinning in circles in the rain.

"What are you doing?" he yelled out the window. The words once again fell out of him like he was reciting lines. He didn't want to change a single thing about this memory. He wanted to relive it just as it was.

"What are *you* doing?" She stopped mid-spin. She walked over to his side of the truck and opened the door. She struggled to reach across his lap for his seat belt. "You can't leave me all alone out here."

"You make me do such stupid stuff." He shook his head, smiling, as he swatted her hand away and unbuckled himself.

She beamed as she pulled him toward the edge of the hillside. The spectacular view of downtown skyscrapers and streetlights was blocked by the thick black rain clouds, which hung heavy and menacing over the city. All he could make out now was a distant, blurry haze that lit up the dark clouds with an ethereal white glow. The wind howled around them, whipping her hair around her face. Raindrops pelted the viewing area, creating rivers that cascaded down the cement barriers. The air smelled of wet asphalt and the scent of eucalyptus from the surrounding hills. Far below, car headlights traced slow-moving paths through the streets, their beams mere orbs of yellow and white. His breath formed small clouds that were immediately torn apart by the wind.

Music was still playing from the truck as she climbed up on the cement ledge and continued to dance and spin in the downpour, a small yellow handbag swinging from her shoulder.

He stood back with his hands in his jacket pockets. Soon, his clothes were just as soaked through as hers. Rainwater found its way into the seams of his shoes and his socks grew soggier the longer he stood in the downpour. His jeans became heavy as more water seeped into the denim.

"Can you please come back down here? You've had too much to drink. You're going to fall down the hill."

"There's no such thing as too much to drink!" She continued dancing to Lorde's "Supercut," which was blasting from the truck's speakers. "Besides, *you're* afraid of heights—which means *you're* afraid of falling, not afraid of *me* falling!"

"That's not true. I'd rather fall down this hill one hundred times than watch you fall down it even once."

"Is that so?" She bent down toward him, grabbing the tops of his shoulders. "So you're saying you'd fall for me?"

"It's too late for that. I already did."

That night, the alcohol had made him forget to bite his cheeks. They both stood still. They both knew what he meant by that statement. That night, he wanted to pull the words right out of the air, put them back in his mouth, and swallow them. But now, he waited. Even with the rush of wind against his ears, the silence between them was deafening. Faint clouds from their exhales filled the space in the brisk air. Her face was stern and lifeless, as she scanned his expression.

She stepped down from the ledge, wrapping her arms around his back and wedging herself into his arms.

"I—uh—I'm sorry." More words started to spew out of him. "I know you probably don't—"

"I love you." Her eyes were wide, as water droplets fell from her lips.

Time seemed to stop as the rain continued to fall around them. The words he'd been holding back for months—the ones that kept him awake at night, that made his heart race whenever she walked into a room—now filled his chest with a warmth that defied the cold storm. Relief and joy crashed over him like waves, drowning out the doubt that had kept him silent for so long.

After a few moments, her eyebrows furrowed, and he could feel her body tense up beneath his arms. Right on cue.

"Uh...are you gonna say it back?"

"I love you, too. God, I've wanted to tell you for so long." He pushed a wet strand of hair away from her forehead.

"Oh, thank god," she let out a big exhale and relaxed under his arms.

"I've known for a few weeks. I didn't want to say it too soon and screw this whole thing up. I didn't think you felt the same."

"I've known for weeks now, too." A smile spread across her face. "Of course I feel the same. I can't believe you let me beat you to it."

This was the feeling he'd wanted to get back to. It was like a weight had been lifted off him. He no longer needed to hide his true feelings or bite his tongue. There was nothing for him to be afraid of anymore. He had everything he needed right there in his arms.

Just then, a gust of wind ripped through the night air and the rain started to come down even harder. Her eyes were glossy, and her cheeks were bright red from the handful of tequila shots she took earlier that night. Her face was warm as he grazed her cheek with his thumb, trying to retrace every part of this memory. The clouds coming from their exhales disappeared the closer he pulled her in until there was no air left between their lips. She tasted like fresh rain and agave. As her hands crawled up his chest, his heart started to beat faster. His fingers traced down her spine until they landed on her lower back, while hers eventually interlaced behind his neck. He could feel her goosebumps from under her wet shirt.

She pulled away and whispered in his ear as she looked up over his shoulder, "No matter where we are, no matter how much time has passed, just look up at the tower and know that I'll always love you."

He turned his head to look up at Sutro Tower—its red lights twinkled against the dark sky. He couldn't hold in the smile that spread across his face. His cheeks became flushed, and a wall of tears formed in front of his eyes. This was the high he was chasing.

He nodded. "I'll think of tonight every time I see it." He pulled her closer, resting his head against hers and using his wet sleeve to wipe his face.

"Me too." She tilted her head up and kissed him gently on the cheek.

She pressed her hips against his and a different kind of fire filled his body. A breathless moment passed between them as they looked into each other's eyes. It was such a small sign, but this little nudge was her way of telling him exactly what she wanted. He put his hand on the back of her neck and pulled her in to kiss her deeper, reaching his fingers up into her wet hair. Blood began to rush from his head down to his waistband.

Everything became more sensitive: the feeling of the cold rain on his skin, the pull of her hands on his neck, the heaviness of each breath on their lips. At that moment, the rest of the world fell away. She was the only thing he could see or feel. Nothing else existed and nothing else mattered. Not even the rain bothered him now.

Leaning down and reaching his arms around the back of her thighs, he lifted her body up so she could wrap her legs around him. Without ever pulling their lips off each other, he carried her back to the truck and set her down in the backseat. He quickly pulled his belt from its latch and shut the door.

Each layer of clothing was soaking wet, making it hard for him to strip down. As he was still struggling to take off his shoes, she'd already taken off her shoes, socks, bra, and jeans. All that was left on her body was her underwear and the now see-through crop top.

She started to kiss his neck as he fumbled to pull off his jacket, wet jeans, and his shirt, throwing each into the front seat as they came off. The upholstery became slippery as water from their hair dripped across the bench seat. When he was finally undressed, she grabbed his face and pulled him into her. The windows fogged as they breathed deeper into the rainy night.

It was the first time they'd made love and could actually call it what it was. This time it was more than two bodies uniting, but two souls intertwining.

Chapter 20

"Tanner kicked you out? Why would he do that? You two have been friends for years."

"I know, Mom. It's a long story," Tennessee sighed into the phone. "I don't really want to get into all that right now."

"So, what are you gonna do? Are you looking for a new place to live?"

"Yeah, I'm trying. It's just hard. Everything's really expensive." He'd spent the morning scrolling through listings on Craigslist after he'd woken up from his dream and realized Tanner would be back later today. "And any of the rooms I can afford want a deposit upfront and I don't exactly have the cash for that right now."

Tennessee paused, working up his courage. "That's actually why I called—I wanted to see if you could loan me some money, you know, for the security deposit. I'd pay you back."

A few moments of awkward silence crackled across the speaker, her breathing the only sound coming over the line.

"I'm so sorry, sweetie. Between your sister's club soccer

fees and your dad's truck needing new tires this month, we just don't have much to spare."

His teeth sunk into the soft tissue of his cheek and the taste of blood filled his mouth. Though he and his sister had the same parents, shared the same DNA, and grew up in the same house, their childhoods couldn't have been more different. She got to play fancy sports, like club soccer. She grew up in a home with two steady incomes. She got a sober, mild-mannered dad who was part of the carpool group for her soccer team.

He didn't get shit. Not now, and definitely not then.

"Well, are you okay?" his mom asked.

"Yeah. I'm fine."

"Are you sure? You know you can always come and live back at home, even if it is just for a little while. We'd all love to spend more time with you."

"I'm fine!" He was starting to regret calling her. "I'll figure it out."

"Okay." Concern was still present in her tone. "You're sure? You'd tell me if you weren't, wouldn't you?"

He looked down at his arms. The cuts gaped open, dried blood crusted around the edges while fresh red blots still seeped from the deeper gashes. There were flecks of glass embedded in his skin, catching the light as he wiggled his fingers. His knuckles were swollen and split, painted in layers of old and new injuries.

And in just a few hours, he would be homeless.

He didn't know if he was okay. He realized he didn't even know what okay felt like anymore. When did "fine" become code for barely surviving? When did waking up covered in blood become normal? There was no way to measure how far he'd gotten away from baseline.

"Mom, I'm fine."

"Okay, honey. You can just stay with Lucy for a little while as you figure everything out, right? She wouldn't mind."

For a split second, Tennessee had almost forgotten. But hearing her name hit him like a slap to the face. The sinking feeling started in his chest and spread outward. The cuts on his arms began to throb.

"Or better yet, maybe you two could just move in together! It's been well over two years since you've been together, hasn't it?"

"I—I'll figure it out." A single tear rolled down his cheek. "Don't worry about it."

"Your dad says 'hi,' by the way. Do you have a minute to talk to him?"

She was doing it again. It was her way of trying to mend things between them without ever actually talking about what happened all those years ago—as if these little nudges could somehow bridge the years of space that existed between him and his father. As if it could all be swept under the rug with enough small talk and polite conversation.

She wanted Tennessee to play along with the happy family charade she'd constructed, where his father was just a guy with a drinking problem who'd changed his ways—not the monster who'd terrorized them both for years.

So, talking to his dad? That was the last thing he wanted to do.

"No. Not right now. I, uh, I gotta go pack up my stuff and get out of the apartment."

"Okay." Her voice was now notably sad. "Well, he'd love to talk to you one of these days. Whenever you have time, that is."

"Thanks. Love you."

"I love you, too. Let me know when you've settled into a new place, will you?"

"Yeah, I will. Bye."

Even though it had been six years since his dad got sober, it still shocked him that his mom tried to pretend like nothing happened. He couldn't understand how she could forgive and forget so quickly—after everything he and his mom had been through. All it took was a few AA meetings and a doctor's appointment for her to brush everything— the cheating, the beatings, all of it—under the rug. What was even more baffling was that she somehow expected Tennessee to do the same.

After getting off the phone, he did his best to forget what little he remembered from the day before: running out on his shift which he now needed to explain to Mr. Green, punching a window and fucking up his arm, and nearly driving himself off a cliff. If that's what happened when he was somewhat coherent, he didn't want to know what happened in the moments he couldn't remember.

The cuts on his arm were bad. Some of them were deep enough that they probably needed stitches. But he couldn't go to urgent care because he'd have to explain what happened. The bandage wrap he found under the bathroom sink would have to do.

Now he had more pressing things to deal with. Tanner would be coming home later that afternoon and Tennessee needed to be gone before he was back.

He spent the late hours of the morning packing what little belongings he had, each item a reminder of how small his life had become. He put his clothes into two cardboard boxes he'd found in the recycling bin and placed the books piled up on the desk in the milk crate he'd been using as a nightstand. The largest of his possessions—the twin-size mattress—went in the bed of the truck. Everything else—the dresser he'd been using, the desk, and even the lamp—belonged to Tanner's family.

His truck would be his home for the time being. Reality hit him hard as he threw the grocery bag with his toiletries into the backseat. He had no address, no lease, no place to shower or cook a meal. He was twenty-three years old and officially homeless.

His hands started to shake as he gripped the steering wheel, preparing to drive away from his old life. The cuts on his arms burned. His throat felt tight. It all flashed back through his mind—Tanner's texts, his mom saying *her* name, the blood circling the drain. A pressure built behind his ribs like his chest might crack open.

It was all too much to handle. So, he decided he wouldn't deal with it. At least not right now. He turned the key in the ignition and cranked up the radio until the music drowned out his thoughts, his sights set on the bar.

Today, he would let the whiskey wash his problems away. He parked around the corner and found his way to his usual barstool.

Vera's bright smile rose as he walked in but fell the moment she saw his arm. Her eyes went wide as they traced the bandage running up his wounds.

"What happened to you?" She was so shocked by the sight of it that she didn't even bother with her usual pleasantries.

"Uh, I broke a lamp while I was moving out of my apartment today. Doesn't even hurt." The lie made his skin burn beneath the bandage.

"I dunno, babe. That looks pretty bad." She shook her head. "You didn't tell me you were moving."

He nodded. "Well, I wasn't exactly planning on moving. Anyways, can I get like six or seven shots of whiskey?"

"Like a big whiskey neat or do you want a strong cocktail?"

"No. Just a row of shots."

"Wow, okay. Sure," she pulled out the shot glasses from beneath the counter. "Do you want any chase?"

"Nope."

"Alright, you're really getting after it today," she chuckled as she grabbed a bottle of Jameson from the well. "So, where are you moving to?"

"I don't know yet. I guess just my truck for now."

"Wait, what? Did you and your roommate have a falling out or something?"

"You could say that. Honestly, I don't really want to talk about that right now."

"Well, then let's drink about it!" She pulled out another set of shot glasses for herself and started to fill them up.

"Alright!" It was the first time today that he'd cracked a smile.

They both lifted the first glass in their respective rows, clinked them together, then tapped them on the bar top before throwing them into the back of their throats. The whiskey burned like liquid fire, scorching a path from his tongue to his stomach. Already the sharp edges of his thoughts were starting to dull.

They did this over and over for the rest of the day—from noon well into the evening—finishing one shot after another. By the third round, Tennessee could feel his shoulders loosening, the tension he carried starting to melt away. By the fifth, he was laughing at Vera's stories about difficult customers, his words starting to slur.

When the row of glasses in front of them were all empty, she would fill them back up and they would repeat the cycle. The bar grew dimmer as afternoon faded to night. The throbbing in his arms dissipated to a distant ache, then went away entirely.

By the time her shift was over, and the nighttime bartender arrived, they'd lost track of how many they'd taken. Tennessee gripped the bar to keep from falling off of his stool. His words came out thick and clumsy. When he tried to stand, the floor seemed to tilt beneath his feet. They were both drunk—though Tennessee was far more wasted than Vera.

His plan worked. He'd successfully forgotten about, well, everything. The cuts on his arms, having to move out, his conversation with his mother, even why he'd been upset that morning—it all felt like it belonged to someone else. Some other guy's problems that had nothing to do with him.

"How about, instead of sleeping in your truck tonight, you stay at my place?" Vera said as she finished closing out her till. "I promise, I won't bite."

The thought of sleeping in his truck sounded awful.

"Abso-fucking-lutely." He slapped his hand down on the bar top. "But I kinda hope you do bite."

They staggered back to her apartment with a bottle of Jameson she'd taken from the bar. The night air was sharp against his flushed cheeks. When their lips weren't pursed around the bottle—the glass warm and slick from being passed back and forth—they were sloppily making out against parked cars. Tennessee pressed her against a Honda, his hands fumbling under her vest, trying to work his way up her shirt while she giggled against his lips.

"Stop, stop," she pushed his hand away. "Keep it in your pants 'til we're back to my place, okay?"

"Fine," the word came out like a groan.

He threw his arm over her shoulder, using her frame to keep himself upright. He had to concentrate on each step to keep from stumbling into the street. His head felt heavier the longer they walked, swaying from one side to the next, like a globe that had been thrown off its axis.

After struggling up the stairs, breathing heavily as they ascended the third flight, they eventually made it back to her apartment. It was a tiny studio with one little window that looked out over the street. Band posters covered every inch of the walls—Black Flag, The Misfits, Dead Kennedys—their angry faces glaring down at him through the dim light. The room smelled of menthol cigarettes.

Though rather small, it had everything you'd need: a kitchenette with a hot plate and a small fridge, a bed, a bathroom barely big enough to turn around in, and a nightstand that looked like it had been taken off the street. Clothes spilled out of a dresser in black heaps.

But, boy, did it beat sleeping in his truck.

As soon as she shut the door to her apartment, their bodies came together like magnets. Their mouths found each other and tied knots with their tongues. He couldn't touch enough of her skin fast enough; he wanted to feel every inch of her. She tugged at the buckle of his belt until it came loose and pulled his shirt up over his head as he pushed her vest off her shoulders and clumsily yanked on the button at the top of her skinny jeans.

Eventually, they collapsed onto the bed. Thankfully, Vera took off her pants, so he didn't have to keep embarrassingly trying to rip them off himself. She crawled on top of him with her knees on either side of his hips, grinding her pelvis against his. She kissed him in circles, going from his mouth to his neck to his chest, biting him softly in all the right places.

It felt good. It felt really good.

Their breathing got heavy. She started to moan as he touched her. As her fingers danced above his waistband, a deep sense of anticipation began to build. He wanted her so badly. It felt like he couldn't wait another second.

Just as her hand dipped into his boxers and wrapped around him, he felt the churn of the liquid inside his stomach. His mouth suddenly tasted of salt.

He tried to ignore it. It was nothing, right? He was fine. He just needed to stay right here and enjoy thi—

A sense of urgency took over. He jerked his head away from her and put his hand over his mouth. Stomach acid burned in the back of his throat. He pushed Vera off him and ran toward her bathroom just as the liquid started to escape his lips.

"Ow!" she said as her head hit the wall.

He found himself on his hands and knees with his head in the toilet. Chunks came spewing out of his mouth in uncontrollable bursts. His diaphragm contracted painfully and made him purge again and again. He colored the bottom of the toilet bowl with reddish, brown puke until there was no visible white left. Hot tears rolled down his face with each heave.

"Fucking pathetic," he cried into the toilet. All the emotions he'd been trying to avoid came pouring out of him. Neither self-pity nor self-loathing were accurate enough to describe it. He'd reached a new low.

"It's all my fault." He puked again as more tears escaped his eyes. "Lucy's gone and it's all my fault."

His stomach muscles began to ache from throwing up with such intense force.

"Lucy!" he blubbered, "I love you. Please forgive me."

His heart only wanted her. It didn't matter whether it was the real thing or just a figment of his imagination. She was the only person who could make this awful feeling go away.

Pulling his head out of the toilet, he felt around his pockets for his phone. He fumbled through his contacts and called her.

It rang a few times then went through to her voicemail."Hey, this is Lucy."

He threw up once more, hung up, then called again.

"Hey, this is Lu—"

He tried again and again until it eventually stopped ringing altogether and went straight to voicemail with each call.

"Lucy, please pick up," he cried into the phone with his face hanging over the toilet. "I need you right now. I'm sorry. I wish I could take it back—all of it. I really do."

He threw his phone down on the floor and hung his head over the toilet, continuing to sob.

A few moments later, there was a buzzing sound that filled the small bathroom. He looked down and saw Lucy's picture on the phone's screen. She was calling him back.

The last thing he remembered was swiping his finger across the screen to answer it.

After that, the rest of the night was completely gone.

Chapter **21**

In the darkness of night, two bodies blurred together and became one. His drunk eyes remained heavy and his vision foggy. But he didn't need to see, he just needed to feel.

She was warm and soft as her skin glided against his under the plush comforter. Her lips met every part of him, from his mouth to his neck to his chest. She climbed on top of him and the smell of her strawberry shampoo surrounded him, filling his lungs with memories of sun-soaked mornings and late-night drives.

"You're alive," he whispered against her collarbone, his voice breaking with relief. "I was so scared that you were..."

It was as if no time had passed between them. Their sex felt like a reunion, a way for them to catch up on lost time. Forgiveness and falling all in one. All the love they shared was still intact and was felt in every interaction of their bodies.

The saltiness of tears—his or hers, he couldn't tell—mixed with the sweetness of her breath. Her skin tasted like vanilla and forgiveness, like all the words he'd never been able to say.

"I missed you," he said softly into her ear. "I missed you so much, Lucy. I'm so sorry. I'm so, so sorry."

Chapter **22**

The rumbling of his empty stomach woke him the next morning. He tried to open his eyes, but the light was too bright and his lids too heavy. The front of his head was throbbing as if someone had smacked him across the forehead with a baseball bat. His throat felt scratchy, his mouth unbearably dry. Hair tickled against his face and neck. His arms were wrapped around a soft torso, his body nestled in an even softer bed.

Confused, groggy, and hungover, he tried to piece together the fragments of last night. The taste of bile on his tongue jogged his memory. Flashes came into his mind: the burn of the shots going down his throat, the discolored toilet bowl, the message that played over and over again as he reached her voicemail. He remembered Lucy's face glowing on the screen.

Then came the blurry recollections of skin against skin, whispered words he couldn't quite recall, the weight of a body that felt like coming home. It had been the kind of reunion sex that erased all of the pain and longing he'd been carrying in a matter of breathless minutes.

A bashful grin spread across his face as the pieces clicked into place. The familiar weight against his chest, the gentle rise and fall of breathing, the warmth of skin pressed against his—he was in Lucy's bed. This soft torso he was entangled with was her. She'd come back to him.

He tightened his arms around her, savoring the moment before she woke up. This was how it was supposed to be, her body fitting perfectly against his like two puzzle pieces. He'd never let anything come between them again.

He nuzzled his face into her hair, ready to breathe in that familiar scent he loved—the sweet, clean smell of her strawberry shampoo. But instead, his nostrils were assaulted by the harsh, stale odor of cigarette smoke and cheap whiskey. This forced his eyes open as he separated himself from the body he was wrapped around, the fantasy crumbling in an instant.

The first thing that came into focus was the empty Jameson bottle sitting on the nightstand, its green glass catching the weak morning light through the tiny window. His eyes slowly adjusted, taking in the chaos around him— torn band posters on the walls, an overflowing ashtray on the windowsill, black jeans scattered across the floor.

And there, beside him on the bed, was Vera. Her platinum blonde hair was spread across the pillow as she slept with her mouth open. The hope he'd felt just a moment before burst all at once.

"Ugh," he groaned, sitting up and putting his head in his hands. "Just another stupid dream."

He tried his hardest to remember what he and Lucy had spoken about during that phone call, but he couldn't recall a single word. The harder he concentrated, the more the memories seemed to slip away. Maybe that phone call had been a dream, too, or maybe he'd drunkenly imagined the whole thing.

It was getting harder and harder for him to separate reality from dreams. The drugs and alcohol blurred everything together into a haze where his fantasies felt as real as his waking life, and his memories couldn't be trusted.

"Good morning," Vera said groggily, blinking her eyes open. "What were you saying about a dream?"

"Oh, uh. Just a sex dream—but it was nothing."

"Oh, so, you don't remember?"

"What? What do you mean?"

"That wasn't a dream, silly." She kissed him on the cheek and pulled away the sheets—she was completely naked.

His eyes widened. Peeking down under the blanket that was still covering him, he saw he was naked, too.

"Great," he mumbled under his breath.

"Why do you seem so…surprised?" She started rummaging through one of the drawers of her dresser.

"I just…I don't remember," he grumbled, hoping she would just drop it. He got up to find his underwear and put them back on.

"So then you probably also don't remember drunk calling Lucy, do you?"

He wanted to crawl back under the covers and die. Why was Vera doing this to him? He didn't want to rehash all his drunk mistakes first thing in the morning. His fragile, hungover mind couldn't take it.

"You should be thanking me for saving you some embarrassment." She pulled a big tee over her body that fit her like a dress.

"Huh? Saving me?"

"Yeah, eventually someone called you back. But it wasn't Lucy."

"No. No, it was! I remember that part. I remember her face coming up on the screen."

"Okay, well, unless Lucy has a really deep, angry man's voice, it wasn't her."

"What? How would you know?"

"I'm the one who talked to whoever it was that called you back."

"You did?"

"Yeah, you were crying and throwing up and begging for Lucy's forgiveness or whatever," she gestured toward the bathroom. "So when they called back and you answered, I thought it best to step in and save what little dignity you had left."

"Well, who was it? What did they say?"

"I have no idea who it was." He could tell Vera was starting to get annoyed. "But it was definitely a dude. A pissed-off one. He said to stop calling and lose this number."

He sat back down on the bed and ran his fingers through his hair. "A dude? Who the fuck would be answering her phone?"

"Why do you still care so much?" Vera asked. "Why is this so hard for you to get over?"

"You wouldn't get it," Tennessee spat. "What we had was special. I couldn't possibly explain it to you."

"Do you have any idea how much bullshit I had to put up with last night because of you?"

"You offered to let me stay here," he rolled his eyes. "Remember?"

"Yeah, I did offer. And, as a result, I was the one taking care of you when you were throwing up. I was the one who stepped in to make sure you didn't embarrass yourself any more than you already had. And you know what I get for it? You called me by her name last night when we were having sex."

A sinking feeling washed over him—he didn't know if it was nausea or shame—but he knew it didn't feel good.

"Whatever, I don't fucking need this." He stood up to find the rest of his clothes. "I have enough to deal with."

"Not just once." Her eyes were serious as she stared him down. "Multiple fucking times."

He shrugged. "I don't know what to tell you. I was drunk, Vera. You're the one who gave me all those shots."

"Do you have any idea how that made me feel?" Her green eyes were staring at him intensely. "Do you even care?"

He was at a loss for words. "I don't know what you want me to say."

"You're joking, right?" she started to yell. "I'm here for you. And I've been here every step of the way—trying to get you to notice me, trying to help you see that other people care about you, too. But you make me feel like I'm invisible. And now you're not even man enough to apologize."

Heat filled his entire body. "You have no idea what I'm dealing with right now. You couldn't even possibly understand." He pointed at her sternly. "And you're mad because I called you by the wrong name? Boo fucking hoo."

Vera's expression shifted, something darker creeping into her eyes. "It wasn't just her name you said."

"What? What do you mean?"

"What did you do to her?" Her voice was quieter now, more serious. "You said 'you're alive' to me last night when you thought I was her. Like you were surprised she was breathing."

He felt the blood drain from his face. "What are you talking about?"

"Did you hurt her, Tennessee?"

"What are you talking about?" he started to raise his voice, panic creeping in. "You're just like her—always making me out to be the bad guy. Always blaming me for shit I didn't do."

"That's not an answer. What did you do to Lucy?"

"Nothing! I didn't do anything!" But even as he said it, his hands were shaking. "I loved her. I would never—"

"Get out." She backed up toward the door.

"What?"

"I said, get out. Now." Her voice was firm.

"Great, now you hate me, too." He pulled up his pants, his movements frantic. "Everyone always thinks the worst of me."

Vera watched him scramble for his clothes, her expression shifting from anger to something closer to pity. "I don't hate you, Tennessee."

He paused, one arm through his shirt sleeve.

"But I can't do this anymore," she continued, tears forming in her eyes. "You've been too busy looking over your shoulder at the past to even notice me. I was so stupid for thinking that loving you harder would somehow make you love me back."

He did everything he could to avoid looking her in the eye as he finished getting dressed, her words hitting harder than any accusation.

"Whatever then, I'll just go."

He slipped on his shoes and stormed out the door. She slammed it shut behind him.

Chapter **23**

Vera's words replayed in his mind as he walked outside into the cold morning air. She didn't understand—how could she? She hadn't been there that night with Lucy. She hadn't heard the venom in her voice.

You're just like your father.

Tennessee shook his head violently, trying to rid himself of the memory. With trembling hands, he reached into his pocket and pulled out the crumpled aluminum foil. Three tabs. Hopefully enough to quiet the noise in his head. He placed them on his tongue just before crossing the street and heading into the bookstore.

"Tennessee," Mr. Green said sharply. "I sure hope you have an explanation for yourself, young man."

"What?" The words stopped him dead in his tracks. Tennessee felt his stomach drop and his shoulders tense. He remembered the cop who'd been at the store just a few days ago.

"I'd like to know why you walked out of your shift earlier this week." He pushed his glasses up the bridge of his nose. "Or should I say, ran out. Our customers were awfully frightened by the scene you made."

"Oh, right," Tennessee exhaled, letting his shoulders drop. "It was a—uh—an emergency. Yeah, an emergency came up."

"And you couldn't take one minute to come let me know?" Mr. Green's eyes squinted down at him like he was looking right through him. "The store was left unattended. Our customers had to come back to the office to get someone to ring them up. Someone could have stolen from us, which is something I'm already concerned about. Even *if* it was an emergency, you handled this in a wildly unprofessional manner."

Tennessee bit the side of his cheek. He just couldn't catch a break this morning.

"This is your *final* warning. And please, Alexander, do try to clean yourself up a bit before you come into work. You smell like you haven't showered in days."

"I told you not to call me that!" He hadn't realized he raised his voice until the words had already come out. "My name is Tennessee!"

"Tennessee, Alexander, whatever you go by," Mr. Green waved his hand dismissively. "Go tidy yourself up in the bathroom, please."

Tennessee's face burned as he stalked to the employee bathroom in the back of the store, his jaw clenched so tight it ached. It made his skin crawl to be called by his dad's name. There were only a few people who even knew his legal name; he'd only given it to Mr. Green so that his paychecks would go through.

In the bathroom, he leaned into the sink and used his non-bandaged hand to splash water on his face. When he lifted his arms, the sour smell of his own body hit him—stale sweat, cigarettes, and whiskey seeping out of his pores. Mr. Green was right about one thing: he reeked. He peeled off his shirt and tried to wash the smell and grime from his skin with cold water and hand soap.

As he dried himself off with paper towels, he caught eyes with someone in the mirror. The reflection staring back at him didn't look quite right—the brown eyes seemed darker, emptier than he remembered. It was the same face he'd been seeing everywhere: in the coffee shop window, in his truck's rearview mirror. Were the drugs taking effect that quickly?

The more he stared at the face in the mirror, the more it seemed to change. He couldn't look away. The jaw grew heavier and more pronounced. The eyebrows thickened. The nose broadened.

Suddenly he wasn't looking at himself anymore. He was looking at his father.

"No," Tennessee whispered, his breath fogging up the glass. "I'm nothing like you."

The face in the mirror just stared back with cold judgment.

Tennessee's vision went red. His fist connected with the mirror before he even realized he was moving, the glass exploding into a spider web of cracks and razor-sharp fragments. Pain shot up his arm as the wound beneath his bandage tore open once again, warm blood seeping through the gauze and dripping onto the white porcelain sink.

He yanked his shirt back over his head and fled the bathroom, leaving a bloody mess in his wake.

◆◆◆◆

All the new books had been shelved the day before, so he grabbed a broom and began pushing the same few dust bunnies in aimless circles around the store. His hurt hand throbbed with each movement, fresh blood staining the flesh-colored bandage.

The LSD should've kicked in by now. He'd taken three tabs—more than enough to quiet the noise in his head—but the bookstore remained stubbornly ordinary. The shelves were just as dull as they always were. The fluorescent lights buzzed in the same monotonous way. Nothing seemed to be happening. What was taking so long?

He swept harder, the bristles scraping against the hardwood with each aggressive stroke. But without the buffer from the drugs, his thoughts had nothing to hide behind. No matter how hard he tried, they just wouldn't slow down or shut up.

I was so stupid for thinking that loving you harder would somehow make you love me back.

He tried to focus on the rhythm of the broom, keep his mind focused on the task at hand, but Vera's voice was inescapable.

There was no way she meant that. She barely knew him, after all—she couldn't possibly love him.

You're just like your father.

And there it was—Lucy's voice cutting through everything else, sharp and unforgiving. No matter how far he ran, how many drugs he took, those words always found him.

"Ugh." He slammed his fist against the bookshelf, the impact sending a jolt up his bleeding hand. A few books tumbled to the floor with dull thuds.

As he looked down at his bloodied hand, he thought of the eyes. The evil eyes that seemed to be taking over every mirror and window he looked at. Eyes that held no warmth, no humanity. Eyes that belonged to his father but somehow kept taking the place of his own.

You're just like your father.

The words echoed in his skull, no longer Lucy's voice but his own. His breathing became shallow, his chest tightening as if the bookstore walls were pressing in around him.

"Fuck this," he muttered.

He emptied his pockets onto the nearest shelf. The crumpled aluminum foil, his truck keys, and a baggie of white powder he didn't remember buying fell out. When did he buy that? Yesterday? This morning? The gaps in his memory were getting wider.

He didn't care anymore. He peeled two more tabs from the foil on his tongue. Then he grabbed the nearest book— some romance novel—and cracked it open and poured the cocaine out into its seam. The empty bag fell to the floor as he lowered his head until his nostril met the book's pages and he inhaled the entire line.

The powder burned through his nasal passages like fire, but he welcomed the pain. His left temple began to throb in time with his accelerating heartbeat. Heat spread across his scalp. When he tilted his head back and exhaled, his face went completely numb, and goosebumps rose across his arms.

And finally, the thoughts disappeared. For the first time in hours, his mind went blank.

Beneath the bristles of the broom, the wooden floorboards began to move again, like ripples in an orange pond. His head felt impossibly heavy, as if it were made of steel. He could feel the steady pounding in his chest, which he found oddly comforting.

This was exactly what he needed. This moment when the chemicals finally kicked in and painted the world in technicolor, when the sharp edges of reality blurred into something better. In this state, he didn't have to think about Lucy or Vera, or even his dad.

The best part of each drug was coming together— painting pretty pictures with his vision and allowing him to forget about his problems and silence the voices in his head.

Suddenly, a scream tore through the still air. The sound was at such a high pitch that it felt like it pierced through his ear and jolted out of his body through his chest. The sound triggered something primal in him—his vision went black, his body seized up, and suddenly he wasn't in the Pink Peach anymore.

He was back in his childhood home, crouched down as bottles flew through the air. The crash of breaking glass, his mother's terrified wails, his father's roaring voice—it all came flooding back.

The next few seconds were a blur. His body moved without his permission, his arm drawing back, something heavy in his hand.

The scream turned into a muffled cry. The bookstore slowly came back into focus. But something was wrong. Every face in the store was turned toward him, their expressions ranging from shock to horror.

"Did you just throw a book at my son?" It was a thirty-something-year-old woman who was standing two rows away from him. She was one of those young yuccie parents. Her arms were covered in tattoos and there were a pair of platform leather loafers on her feet.

"Why would you think that's okay?"

Her son peeked out from behind her hip, wiping his tears on the flannel tied around her waist. He couldn't have been any older than seven.

"Uh, wh—what?" Tennessee could hardly form words. "I threw something?"

"Yes!" Her eyebrows furrowed in confusion. "A book— this book!" She held up the romance novel he'd just used to snort the coke from. "Who throws a book at a crying child?"

His jaw fell open stupidly. He couldn't comprehend what she was saying.

"I'm—I'm so sorry," he stuttered, "I don't know what you're talking abo—"

"You're lucky you missed, or the police would be on their way right now!" She grabbed her son's hand and started guiding him toward the door. A few other customers put down their books and slowly started to shuffle out as well. The customers who remained in the store averted their gaze. These once-familiar faces now had deep, dark pits in place of their eyes.

"I'll be contacting the owner," she said as she exited in a huff. Tennessee's stomach sank.

This was it. This would be his final straw. Mr. Green had already given him his last warning, and now this—throwing a book at a child like some insane person—would surely be the end. If he lost this job, he'd have nothing left. No apartment, no friends, no Lucy.

His heart began hammering against his ribs. The shelves started to tilt and sway around him. The fluorescent lights overhead began strobing. How could he not remember throwing the book? How could he have reacted like that at all? Was he really that disconnected from reality?

Everyone is out to get you, a voice whispered from somewhere deep in his skull. *They all know what you are.*

His breathing turned rapid and shallow, each gasp barely filling his lungs. Sweat broke out across his palms, making them slick and useless. His thoughts felt like they came and went like the sharp twists and turns of a Rubik's Cube—one thought would start before the other one finished.

Nothing made sense anymore. He gripped the broom handle with white knuckles, using it as a crutch to keep from collapsing as waves of nausea rolled through his stomach.

You hurt that child. Just like you hurt Lucy. Just like your father hurt you.

He staggered toward the register like a drunk man, his legs barely working. When he finally reached it, he leaned his body weight onto it. Heat poured off his skin in waves. His vision began to tunnel, darkness creeping in, and his eyelids began to flutter.

The last thing he heard before consciousness left him was the voice, even clearer now: *You're exactly like him.*

His pupils rolled toward the back of his head, and he hit the counter face-first, his body going completely limp.

Chapter 24

"Say that again," he hissed.

"What the fuck are you talking about?" Vera squeaked from under his grip, her nails clawing at the gauze wrapped around his hands that were pressed tightly against her neck. Her back was pushed up against the inside of her apartment door.

He blinked hard, his surroundings coming into focus. As his senses returned, he felt something wet and warm dripping down his forearm. Suddenly the room snapped into sharp clarity—the familiar smell of cigarettes and whiskey. The gleam of the empty bottle of Jameson from the kitchen counter. The bloody waterfall down his arm. The weight of her body beneath his grip as she attempted to break free. Her pink lips were becoming pale.

"Let go of me!" She kicked at his knees.

What was he doing? Horror crashed over him in waves as reality sank in. A loud gasp escaped his throat as he quickly jerked his hands away, sending her tumbling to the floor.

He stepped back from her as she breathed in uneasy croaks. Her blood-covered hands cradled her neck softly, tending to the damage. There would likely be a bruise where his hands had been. The color slowly returned to her face with each breath she took.

The sight of her—gasping, trembling, afraid of him—was almost like looking at a stranger. This was Vera. Sweet but tough. She was someone who'd shown him kindness when no one else would. She'd sat with him on that rooftop and shared her deepest wounds. And, yet somehow, he did *this* to her. His legs felt unsteady beneath him and his chest started to cave in.

"What's wrong with you, you fucking psycho?"

"I'm—I'm so," he looked around the room unable to provide any explanation. Through the window, he could see it was dark outside. "I'm sorry. I don't know what's happening to me right now."

"You're sorry?" She stood up. Keeping her eyes locked on him, she moved around him like a boxer in a ring, as if she expected him to attack her at any moment. She grabbed a frying pan from the kitchen sink and held the handle like a baseball bat. "You could've killed me!"

"Vera, can you please tell me what happened?" His hands were shaking. "I'm really scared, and I honestly don't know what's going on. I have no idea how I got here or how much time has passed. I think I'm losing it. Pleas—"

"Are you fucking serious?" Her eyes filled with tears. "You have no idea what you just did?"

"I swear, I would never hurt you," Tennessee pleaded

with her. "I would never hurt anyone."

"You came in here accusing me of saying things I didn't say—talking about how I said you were like your dad." Her face scrunched up in confusion. "You wouldn't listen to a goddamn word I said and then pinned me against the door."

His heart sank. He had no memory of any of it—the accusations, the argument, the violence. It was as if someone else had inhabited his body. A cold sweat broke out across his forehead as he realized just how far gone he was. He was losing pieces of himself, entire chunks of time, where he became someone else entirely. Someone dangerous.

"Vera, I'm so sorry." His voice cracked, on the verge of tears. "That wasn't me. I don't know what's happening to me."

He stepped toward her and reached his arm out to touch her, but she moved back and gripped the pan even tighter. The metal vibrated in her white-knuckled grip, her arms shaking from pure adrenaline. Her hair was all over the place, strands sticking to the sweat on her forehead, and her green eyes darted between his face and his hands, watching for any sudden movement.

"Don't touch me," she screamed. Her voice held a mixture of fear and rage. "I don't know what the fuck you did to Lucy—but you sure as hell aren't putting another hand on me."

The sight of her—this fierce, fearless girl who'd climbed that rickety ladder without hesitation—now cowering from him felt like a knife twisting in his gut. She was trying so hard to look threatening, to protect herself, but he could see the terror behind her eyes, the way her chest rose and fell in rapid, shallow breaths. This was what he'd reduced her to.

"Get the fuck out of my house."

"No, please. I can't lose you, too," he begged. But in his gut, he knew the damage was already done.

"Leave. Right now. Or I'll swing this at your skull."

The finality in her voice ripped him open. He looked into her eyes one last time, searching for any trace of the girl who said she loved him earlier that morning. But she was gone. He'd destroyed the last good thing in his life with his own hands.

His head dropped. He left her apartment without saying another word, the door closing behind him with a soft click.

Chapter 25

The sun boiled his skin until it was red and blistered. He'd spent the afternoon baking in the heat and drawing figures in the pale, dusty dirt with a stick. His mouth was dry from thirst and his tongue felt like sandpaper against the roof of his mouth. Salty beads of sweat dripped down his forehead—he licked the ones that came down to his upper lip, not realizing this would only make him thirstier.

The Central Valley heat was unforgiving this time of year. It was the peak of the summer and well over 105 degrees outside. All the other parents had called their kids inside, since it was too hot to play out here. There were no trees or other shade in their front yard for him to take cover under. Tennessee had no idea how long he'd been out there, melting on the concrete steps to the entrance of their house, but it felt like it had been hours.

He desperately wanted to go back inside. Really, there was nothing stopping him—the front door was unlocked—but he didn't dare step foot in the house. It was far more dangerous in there than it was out here.

In the driveway, parked behind his dad's truck that he would eventually inherit, was yet another mysterious car. This time, it was a really nice red one—one of those sporty-looking kinds.

His little body jumped as the broken front door behind him swung open with a loud bang. He didn't dare turn around to see who'd opened it. Holding his breath, he made sure not to make any noise. He needed to be invisible. He kept his eyes glued to the drawings in the sand and shifted his body out of the way.

The clacking sound of high heels came from behind him as a woman emerged from the house. He didn't look up to see her face—all he could see of her was her clear platform heels that made a crunching sound as she stepped on the gravel that lined the walkway to their front porch steps. She didn't say a word to him. She just stepped right through his dirt drawings like he wasn't even there.

Before she'd even made it down the driveway to her car, the back of Tennessee's collar was yanked up and into the house.

"Get back in here, boy," his dad said with a cigarette hanging out of his mouth.

A knot formed in Tennessee's stomach as he was dragged back inside and then dropped abruptly onto his hands and knees.

The inside of the house was only about ten degrees cooler than it was outside. Even so, this felt like a big relief, having been out there for who knows how long. His parents hadn't yet fixed the broken swamp cooler in the kitchen, but at least the ceiling fan was helping to dry the sweat on his forehead. His skin felt hot to the touch and there were definitely areas that were badly burned. He'd need to wait for his mom to get home to figure out what to do to make them feel better.

They lived in a small house that always seemed to be in a state of disarray. They didn't have much—and most of what they did have was either old or broken. The couch was dotted with cigarette burns, many of the chairs around the table didn't match, clothes were left in piles, and the mountain of dishes in the sink only ever seemed to grow taller. Empty beer bottles and tins of chewing tobacco cluttered most of the surfaces.

"You didn't see shit, kid. Got it?" his dad slurred as he kicked Tennessee's knee with his boot.

Tennessee nodded with his eyes turned down. His dad staggered away, back down the hallway toward their bedroom, a bottle of Budweiser in each hand.

Tennessee kept replaying what had just happened. The way his dad had yanked him inside so suddenly. The way that woman had stepped right through his dirt drawings like he wasn't even there. The way his dad seemed mad at him now. What was it that he wasn't supposed to see?

The uncertainty twisted in his stomach. He didn't understand what just happened. He didn't know if speaking up would help or hurt the situation, but he needed to know what was supposed to be a secret.

His frail little voice worked up the courage to ask, "Dad? Who was that lady?"

Tennessee's father quickly turned on his heels. "What did you say?" The bottles in his hands seemed to tremble. "You think it's any of your business to ask questions about my visitors, boy?"

He immediately regretted asking. He knew he should've just stayed quiet.

"No, I just—"

"You just what? You think you can spy on me and then interrogate me like I'm some kind of criminal?" His dad's voice was getting louder with each word. "This is *my* house! I can have whoever the hell I want over, and I don't owe *you* any goddamn explanations!"

The veins in his father's neck were starting to bulge. "Are you the man of this house? Do you pay the bills around here? Do you do *anything* around here, for that matter?"

He wanted to run back outside. At that point, he didn't care about the heat, he just wanted to get away from the monster his dad was about to turn into. But he knew running would only make it worse.

"I'm sorry. Forget it," he mumbled.

Tennessee kept his eyes fixed on the floor as the drunken rampage began. He could only hope that the backlash of his question was met with mercy. Fists and boots collided with drywall and the man screamed at the top of his lungs. Tennessee learned that avoidance was the best way to deal with his dad's explosive moments. He braced himself and held his breath, puffing out his chest. He bit the inside of his cheek and dug his nails into his palms, doing his best to block it all out. He couldn't be hurt by what his dad said if he didn't listen.

No matter what the issue was, Tennessee always seemed to be the one to blame—and anything that wasn't his fault was surely his mother's. He'd heard it all—that it was his fault that they were poor, that he was the reason his mom stopped "putting out," that it was his fault that his dad's life had gone to shit and that he couldn't hold down a job. His dad would sometimes even say that he wished Tennessee had never been born at all—Tennessee often wished the same.

His father's fit of anger went on for several minutes, with glass shattering and new holes being put into the walls. All the while Tennessee did his best to disassociate, keeping his face turned down to the floor and forcing his eyes to glaze over. It was the only way he knew how to protect himself.

"Are you even fucking listening to me, you little bastard?" His dad threw one of the bottles right at Tennessee's head.

Tennessee let out a terrified shriek but ducked just in time. The bottle shattered against the wall right behind him and brown glass fell over the top of him and onto the floor.

Whatever liquid was left in the bottle splattered out like a firework and made the room smell of beer and moist snuff.

"Shut up, you fucking pussy!" His dad threw another bottle at him. Tennessee raised his arms to protect his head, but this bottle shattered on the floor right in front of him, splattering beer onto his shirt.

A shard of glass from the base of the bottle cut into the side of his shin. He could feel a scream form in the back of his throat, but he swallowed it for fear of being hit with something else. A rush of heat enveloped his leg as blood started to drip from the gash. He knew that crying would only make the situation worse. Every ounce of energy in his little body knew he needed to fight the urge.

As he resisted, the lump in his throat took over his chest. His whole body felt like it was on fire. Eventually, he got to the point where he couldn't hold it in any longer as tears started to fill his eyes. He grabbed onto his bleeding shin and began sobbing uncontrollably on the floor, knowing that more ridicule and torment were on the way.

Tennessee looked up to see if there were more bottles he needed to watch out for, but instead he was met with the degrading gaze of his father's brown eyes. They were filled with rage, judgment, and disgust, yet were also somehow completely lifeless. The eyes were dark, almost black. They were haunting and vengeful, like there was no mortal soul left behind them. They were eyes that knew pain, eyes that wanted to get revenge for the way the world had treated them. These eyes knew no empathy and never learned how to love.

To Tennessee, these were the eyes of an evil man.

His dad walked over, unbothered by the sight of Tennessee's bleeding leg. "I've seen worse. Hell, I've had worse done to me."

His father spit his chewing tobacco down at him, which landed in a wet pile on the hand that Tennessee was holding his leg with. Black, sticky grains of used chew mixed into the bloody gash.

"I always knew you were a little bitch." His dad shook his head as he turned back toward the hallway. "Your mother raised you that way."

This was Tennessee's first heartbreak. The kind of heartbreak that couldn't be repaired with words or time. The pain he felt that day would imprint in his memory for the rest of his life, no matter how hard he tried to block it out or run from it.

"Now clean this shit up before she gets home!" his dad yelled as he slammed his bedroom door shut.

Tennessee sat on the floor for some time even after the room had fallen silent. He rocked himself back and forth, letting streams of tears fall from his eyes while holding his bleeding, tobacco-covered leg.

"Wake up," he whispered to himself. "Please, please wake up."

Chapter 26

He woke up shivering and covered in sweat. There was tension in his shoulders and an ache in his jaw from clenching his teeth. He blinked his eyes open to a sky without an inch of visible blue as the fog rolled in with the wind. He'd slept fully clothed out in the open air on the mattress in the bed of his truck. Though there were pillows and blankets inside the cab, he clearly hadn't thought to grab them in his altered state.

Despite waking up here, like this—homeless, alone, sleeping in the back of his truck—a wave of relief washed over him. Anything was better than being inside that house again, helpless to his father's uncontrollable rage. The cold fog and the thin mattress felt like paradise compared to the terror he felt in that home.

This dream had been different. He was lucid but stuck—straining to move, to intervene, to do anything other than watch as the events unfolded before his eyes. Every time he tried to change what was happening or wake himself up, some invisible force held him back. He'd known it was a dream, but knowing hadn't helped. It was like being buried alive in his own memories, forced to relive every excruciating moment in detail, exactly as it was.

If this was how the dreams would be from now on, then trying to get back to Lucy this way just wasn't worth it. The drugs weren't giving him escape anymore; they were delivering him straight into a personal hell. The price had become too high. He'd sacrificed so much for moments with someone who existed only in dreams. He couldn't afford to lose what little of himself remained. It was time to get his life back on track.

He climbed out of the back of the truck to search through his things in the backseat. Pulling his puke- and alcohol-soaked shirt over his head, he replaced it with one that smelled slightly better. After some rummaging, he found his toothbrush and a water bottle, but no toothpaste. He brushed his teeth anyway and spit the water into the gutter when he was done. He used the rest of the water to douse his face and greasy hair, hoping to get the grimy, pungent smell off of him. Unwrapping the bandages on his arm, he noticed there didn't seem to be any signs of new bleeding. Regardless, he put some new coverings on just to make sure they wouldn't open back up again.

A bit scared to look at his reflection—afraid of whose eyes might stare back—he touched his face instead and noticed that his beard felt overgrown and scratchy. He'd need to find a razor and a place to shave after work today.

A gust of cool air hit his face which felt like being hit with a hard dose of reality. He had no home, no friends, and no Lucy or Vera—neither in his dreams or in reality. He had nothing left but his job and his truck.

He got into the driver's side, where he saw the sheet of acid laying open in the aluminum on the dashboard. A few more squares seemed to be missing than he could account for taking. Next to it was some crumpled up cash—some twenties and a fifty-dollar bill. He grabbed all of it and stuffed them into his pockets.

It took him a while to figure out where he was and how to get back to the Richmond. He drove aimlessly for several blocks, taking wrong turns until he finally found a street he recognized. He'd somehow ended up in a residential neighborhood he'd never been to before in the south end of the city. He was already late and needed to make it clear across town.

As he curved down Diamond Heights to get to Market Street, he could see the prongs of Sutro Tower peeking out above the trees. A scowl formed on his face and his free hand gripped tighter around the steering wheel.

It felt like he'd seen her just days ago. The smell of her hair still lingered in his sinuses. He could feel the imprint of the places she touched him. He could even taste her on his lips. But none of it was real. He hadn't seen her, let alone held her or touched her in so long. She was somehow so close, yet so far away.

"Hope she was worth it," he grumbled to himself. "You fucking idiot."

Eventually he made it to Clement Street and found a parking spot about a block and a half away from the store. As he was crossing the street, he stopped at the corner, toying with the foil in his pocket.

He couldn't go on like this—waking up in places he didn't remember being, destroying his body and mind, running away from his problems. He couldn't keep letting his life get worse and letting everyone in it slip away.

But even more importantly, he couldn't go back to where he'd been last night. The anxiety seemed to linger in his bones—the rattle of the ground from his dad's steps, the crashing of the bottles above his head, the feeling of the glass piercing through his skin. It all felt so real—like it had happened just yesterday. The thought of being trapped there again, helpless and small, made his chest tighten. He'd rather face his problems here than return to that prison.

He sighed deeply, his breath creating a cloud in the morning air. It was over. It had to be. He couldn't keep living in a fantasy. He'd start small—show up on time, keep his head down, stop doing drugs on the job, get his work done. Find some place to shower regularly. Maybe even try to piece together what was left of his life instead of running from it.

Pulling the folded-up aluminum out of his pocket, he tossed it into the trash can on the corner. He didn't even wait to watch it leave his hand. This small act felt so big, like the first step back to himself—or maybe even someone better. As he walked into the store, he lifted his head up just a bit higher, determined to get his life back on track. It was time for a fresh start.

"Good morning, Mr. Green." Tennessee smiled as he walked in the store.

Mr. Green kept his gaze down and gave only a dismissive throat-clearing sound in response, methodically counting the money before loading it into the register.

This standoffishness was unlike him. Tennessee turned over his shoulder and looked up at the clock.

"Oh god, I'm really late." Thirty-eight minutes late, to be exact. "I know I say this all the time, but this is the last time I'll be late. I really mean it."

"No, son. It's not that." Mr. Green dropped the bills in his hand onto the counter, peering over the top of his glasses with a stern look on his face. "I'm not sure how to tell you this…"

"Tell me what?" Tennessee's stomach was doing back flips. His mind ran across every possibility—the yuccie mother, Officer Jacobs, Tanner.

"Well, it's clear that you've fallen on tough times," he gestured toward Tennessee. "Your hair's a mess, you clearly haven't bathed in a while, and you've got deep bags under your eyes."

"Yeah." Tennessee felt embarrassed. "I'm kind of between places right now."

Mr. Green nodded knowingly. He paused as if he need-ed to choose his next words carefully. "I'm sorry to hear that. But that's no excuse to steal money from the register to use for drugs."

Tennessee's jaw dropped.

Mr. Green pulled off his glasses and set them on the counter. "I started to notice some of the money was a bit off at the end of the night. At first, it was only a couple of bucks which wasn't of too much concern—could be some miscalculations or friendly discounts. But I was sure to keep my eye on it.

"Eventually, I noticed that one hundred-dollar bills were gone! Officer Jacobs helped me install cameras and low and behold, the day after I had them installed, I saw you blatantly doing drugs in the middle of my store, throwing a book at a crying child, and then stealing more than two hundred dollars from the register before running off like a lunatic!"

"Sir, I really can explain," Tennessee pleaded. "I wasn't in a good place. I meant to replace the first few fifties, I swear. Everything just got so out of hand."

"Aside from the money—you threw a book at a child." Mr. Green lost any morsel of understanding left in his tone. "Who does that?"

Tennessee's face fell into his hands. He could feel a tightness in his throat forming as he held in his tears. The walls of the store felt like they were closing in on him.

"I don't know." Tennessee shook his head. "I don't even remember doing that, honestly."

"I took a chance on you, Alexander," Mr. Green's voice shook as he spoke. "You had no skills or applicable work experience whatsoever, but the Coopers spoke so highly of you. You seemed like a troubled kid who just needed some help getting on your feet. But I was wrong."

Tennessee braced for impact, holding his breath. He was already anticipating Mr. Green's next words.

"I—I'm sor…" Mr. Green worked to gain his composure. "I'm sorry, son, but I have to fire you."

The words bounced around like echoes in his mind. The aluminum foil in the trash can flashed through his thoughts—his initial resolve toward redemption, now meaningless. His chest felt hollow, his blood ran cold. The hope he'd carried through the door vanished like sand in the wind. The last thing he had left, the one piece of stability that remained in his life, was pulled out from under him.

Tennessee avoided the man's eyes, sinking into his body.

"I'm sorry I let you down." Tennessee turned on his heels and walked back out of the store.

Back out in the windy air, he couldn't hold it in any longer. The dam burst all at once. He let the hot tears roll down his face without caring who was watching, his shoulders shaking with each sob that tore open his chest. His knees gave out and he found himself leaning against the cold brick wall, gasping for air between waves of grief. He'd lost everything that meant anything to him—Lucy's love, Tanner's friendship, his home, his job, his dignity. Every single thing he'd ever cared about, gone. And it was all his fault—every fucking bit of it.

Picking himself up, he walked back up to the trashcan he'd dropped the drugs in just minutes before, his breath coming out in ragged gasps. The symbolic gesture of throwing it away now felt meaningless. He reached his arm to retrieve the sheet, and with nowhere else to go and nothing left to do, he unfolded it and placed five tabs on his tongue. The papery texture was almost comforting now—it was all he had left in a world that had abandoned him completely.

Chapter 27

How had he gotten here? How, in such a short period of time, could his life have just completely fallen apart? He had no idea if it had been months or weeks since everything started to crumble around him—too much had happened for him to really keep track of the passage of time.

With nowhere else to be and no place left to go, he began walking down Clement toward the ocean, hoping that the breeze would cause the tears to fly off his face before they ran down his cheek. As he waited for the drugs to kick in, he fixed his eyes to the laces of his shoes, feeling sorry for himself.

"Just when you think you've hit rock bottom," he pulled a limp cigarette from one of his pockets, "God pushes you through a trapped door."

He wasn't sure if he even believed in God. What kind of God would take away everything he had, leaving him with nothing and no one? What kind of God would make someone suffer like this? Or maybe there was no God and shit just happened—the luck of the draw, or lack thereof. But if it was all just chance, why was he always the one stuck with the bad hand? Had he done something to deserve this? Was there some lesson he was supposed to learn in all of this?

He exhaled a cloud of pink smoke. With it, his body felt looser. The concrete beneath his feet started to pulse. The spiral of his thoughts started to slow.

Lifting his head, colors started to shift before his eyes. The gray in the sky transformed to a soft blue that felt like the comfort of an old friend. The shadow stuck to his heels spread into three—one red, one yellow, one blue. He could feel the air moving through him as he breathed, weaving throughout his body like a maze. Somehow, he could see within himself with his inner eye—how his heart was pumping his blood, how the connective tissue held his bones together, and how each of his muscles lengthened and contracted as he moved around in the world.

The dark thoughts began to lift, and a hollow feeling took the place of the aching in his chest. Off in the distance, sunlight broke apart the clouds in magnificent rays, shining down on him as if God Himself was saying, "I'm here."

"Maybe things can still turn out alright..." Tennessee whispered.

Perhaps things weren't so bad after all. Maybe all of this—the job, the apartment, and even the girl he thought was the love of his life—didn't really matter. What if nothing mattered? Perhaps his entire existence just didn't fucking matter.

This thought brought a smile to his face.

If he didn't matter, then nothing he did mattered. All along, he'd been carrying the weight of his mistakes like an imaginary ball and chain, when he could've unshackled himself at any time. None of his pain was real, but rather an illusion he'd built up in his mind.

"None of it matters," he let out an airy exhale. "Nothing fucking matters!"

He dropped the cigarette in his hand and fell to his knees. He clutched both his hands to the center of his chest where he could feel a radiant golden ball of light forming. It was warm and felt like the love and peace he'd been searching his whole life for but never found. The light grew until it expanded to every cell in his body, radiating off of him and spreading into the world around him.

Perhaps this is what it felt like to finally let go and find peace. He would hold onto this feeling for as long as he could. As long as the love and light lived within him.

Suddenly, a sound broke through this peace and popped the feeling. It was a loud blare that sent a shock through his entire body, like a dagger puncturing him. Opening his eyes, he was still on Clement, but it looked more like an alien world than the city street he knew so well.

The sky was now green and none of the people around him had any faces, though he still felt like he was being watched. He was in the middle of a black river and there was a growling, yellow metal box in front of him that chugged and puttered as if it would collapse at any second. A puff of smoke in the shape of a snake emerged from one of its sides, swirling up and up until its tail disappeared into thin air.

"Get out of the road, you dirty hippy!" the big metal box shouted, continuing to stab him with its invisible sound daggers, each one puncturing one of his organs.

"Stop hurting me!" Tennessee yelled as he shakily pulled himself to his feet.

"Fucking move, kid." It sent out more sound jabs.

He gritted his teeth and moved closer to the glass face of the beast, when he caught a glimpse of a different monster. It was the man he'd been seeing in the mirrors—the one taking over his face.

An uncontrollable rage bubbled over inside of him like an erupting volcano. "This is all your fault!" His anger fueled him as he climbed on top of the front surface of the hot, metal contraption.

"What the fuck! Get off of my car!" it shouted back.

Tennessee was no longer afraid of the little metal box, nor was he phased by the sounds it was making. He could only focus on the ugly face in the glass. The face that kept blending his features with those of his father's until they were indistinguishable.

"She's right, you know. You're just like me." The evil face twisted up in a vile smile.

His vision went dark red, and all other sounds fell away. The blood in his veins was so hot it felt like his insides were boiling.

"I'm nothing like you!" The scream came from a deep guttural place in his body. It was an anger he couldn't consciously tap into, an anger that lay dormant deep beneath his surface until it was forced to come out. An anger that was unstoppable once it was released.

He lifted his leg and sent it down into the glass with a heavy stomp. He stomped and stomped and stomped, each lunge resulting in a satisfying crunch that only further fueled his rampage. He wouldn't stop until the face in the glass was completely destroyed.

But then there were hands—hundreds and hundreds of them—pulling his body down, tugging at his clothes, and constricting his legs and limbs.

"Let me go!" Tennessee shouted at the top of his lungs. "Let me go! Let me go!"

Despite his attempts, more and more hands appeared all over him. There were voices shouting near him that all faded into distant whispers as he kicked and thrashed and screamed until his throat was raw. He threw elbows and punches and contorted himself to try to get away, but more and more hands kept coming to restrain him.

Then they were dragging him down. Down, down, down, to what he thought was surely the depths of hell.

Chapter 28

"Lucy! Let me in!" Tennessee had managed to slip into her building behind one of her oblivious neighbors and was now beating his fist against her apartment door. There was a white plastic bracelet dangling from his wrist. The wounds on his arms were nearly healed. All that was left of them was a darkened line of skin where stitches had been clearly sewn in.

"Let's just talk it out, babe. Come on, please. I'm sorry!" He banged on the door some more, but she still didn't answer.

He put his head against the wood to see if he could hear anything on the other side—footsteps, whispers, even the hum of a TV, anything—but as far as he could tell, it was completely silent in her apartment.

From behind him, there were footsteps coming up and down the stairs. He could feel the heat of the neighbors' judging stares as they passed. He stayed there with his ear pressed against the door, too afraid to turn around to see their faceless glares.

"If you're in there, I just wanna talk. Just let me in."

The silence frightened him. Was she okay in there? Should he break down the door to check on her? What if she was hurt? A prickly sensation ran up his spine. He started to pace the landing in front of her apartment.

Where else would she be? He leaned against her door and slid down to the ground.

"God, if you're really there," he looked up to the ceiling, "just give me a sign. Tell me what to do."

From across his field of vision, he was hit with a kaleidoscope of colors. There were at least a dozen flyers hanging on the corkboard on the wall across from him—faded yellows, white notices, pale blues. But one colored poster in particular stood out among the rest.

Pink. A soft, familiar pink that made his heart swell.

He blinked hard, trying to focus. The poster seemed to shimmer at the edges, like it was breathing. While all the other flyers blurred into background noise, this one remained crisp, almost glowing against the corkboard—like he was meant to see it.

He stood up slowly, getting lightheaded in the process. He was drawn to the paper like a moth to a flame. As he got closer, the pink seemed to intensify, practically humming with energy. He reached out, his fingertips stopping just inches from it. The white walls of the building began pulsing.

When he finally focused his eyes on the large black lettering, the words rearranged themselves a few times before settling into place. It took all the energy he could muster to read what it said: *Lucy and the Diamonds. Tonight at the Montana Motel. Be there!*

His breath caught in his throat as the meaning of the words clicked into place. Lucy. Her name, right there in bold letters, as if the universe had planted it there just for him to find. It was her. It was her band. Playing tonight, when he needed her most. The timing was too perfect, too precise to just be a coincidence.

This was it. This was his sign. This was exactly where he was supposed to be. Everything had been leading him to this moment—leading him back to her.

He ripped the poster off the wall. The fluorescent lights began flashing above him, and each breath was shallower and more strained than the last. As he headed down the stairs, leaning his body weight against the handrail, he grew more lightheaded by the second. Another blackout was quickly approaching.

"I'm coming, baby," his voice echoed off the walls as consciousness began to slip away.

His vision tunneled and then faded to nothing. Somewhere in between the static, an image of his hands placing two items on a conveyor belt broke through—the cold steel of a pocketknife and the soft yellow petals of a sunflower. Her favorite.

Chapter 29

He handed the bouncer his ID and a wrinkled-up twenty-dollar bill, grabbed a whiskey ginger at the bar, and—just like in his dream—headed up the stairs to the balcony. Everything was as it was supposed to be: the dingy red curtains, the sticky floors that reeked of spilled beer, the orange walls with decades of stickers and tags on them. Stepping onto the tiny, narrow balcony felt like revisiting a memory—landing in the same spot each time, watching the same stage, and waiting for the same moment when her eyes would meet his. With swirling shapes dancing in his vision, he held the sunflowers close to his chest with pride, certain that by the end of the night, she'd be his once again.

Now it was all making sense. These weren't just dreams—they were messages, visions, prophecies sent directly to him from some higher power. Every detail had been too precise, too specific to be a coincidence. The venue layout, the balcony, the song she would sing—he'd seen it all before in his dream.

He would laugh and roll his eyes whenever Lucy would talk about things like destiny or signs sent from the universe. But now he understood just how right she was.

He could see it all so clearly. It was all supposed to happen this way. The breakup, the pain, the separation—it was all just a test. They were meant to be together. They had to fall apart so they could come back together. Every fight, every tear, every sleepless night had been leading to this moment. It was all unfolding according to a divine plan he was about to actualize.

He sat down in the same place he'd sat before, looking out over the perch above the small crowd and the even smaller stage. She was the first thing he saw when he sat down, his heart skipping a beat the moment he laid eyes on her. A stupid, toothy grin spread across his face.

Lucy stood in the center of the stage, tuning her guitar as the rest of the band finished setting up around her. She was just as beautiful as he remembered, though she seemed somehow different—more mature—now. She wore baggy pants that hugged her waist and a lacy white cropped tank top. There was silver glitter across both of her cheeks, sprinkled throughout her hair, and across her collarbones that made her sparkle under the stage lights.

She hadn't yet looked up to see that he was there. His stomach was doing backflips as he waited, willing her blue eyes to find his across the crowded room. What would he do when she finally saw him? Should he play it cool with a smile and a casual wave? Should he shout that he loved her, for the whole room to hear? Blow her a kiss? What was the right move to win back the heart of the woman you loved?

She wore a look of stress on her face—a strained smile and wide, anxious eyes. This was a look he'd seen her hide behind before, an expression that only he could decode. It was her way of concealing the anxiety building inside her while appearing composed to everyone else. Maybe she was nervous, or something had gone wrong during load-in. Maybe they were debuting a new song—perhaps another one she'd written just for him. Whatever the reason, she was masking it to ensure no one else would notice.

But even from way up here, he noticed. He was the one person in the world who truly understood her. The only person who knew her better than she knew herself. While others saw a confident musician getting ready for another show, he could see the vulnerable girl beneath the surface. He knew every micro-expression, every subtle shift in her posture, every tiny tell that revealed what she was really feeling. Her bandmates, her friends, even her family—they all saw what Lucy wanted them to see. But Tennessee saw the real her. He was the only one who could read her like a book, the only one who'd taken the time to memorize every page of her.

Then a man with dark hair came onto the stage and walked right up to her, setting up some additional pedals at her feet and running cables from them. Tennessee's chest tightened. Who the hell was this? And why was Lucy letting some stranger get so close to her during her pre-show routine? Tennessee watched in disbelief as the distressed look on her face melted away completely in his presence.

Tennessee's brow furrowed as he looked down at the two of them, trying to figure out who he was. He didn't recognize him. Could he be someone who worked at the venue? Maybe he was a friend or boyfriend of one of her bandmates. He knew they weren't making enough money to have hired someone to help them set up yet.

The two of them spoke to each other in soft, intimate words that Tennessee couldn't make out from his vantage point. There was an easy familiarity between them, the kind that only comes from countless private conversations. Something about the way she held herself—relaxed, open, trusting—told Tennessee that this wasn't a casual acquaintance. As the man moved around her, adjusting equipment, his fingers lingered on her arm, brushed against her shoulder, touched the small of her back in ways that were far too tender. She didn't pull away. She leaned into it.

Had he touched her like that before? When? How many times? She smiled that bright, genuine smile and tucked her hair behind her ear when he handed her the guitar cable. As he whispered something in her ear, her eyes sparkled with affection. It was unmistakable. It was the way she used to look at Tennessee when she was in love with him.

The sunflowers in Tennessee's hand began to wilt under his crushing grip, their bright yellow petals crumpling between his fingers. His heart hammered against his ribs.

Heat flooded his face. A bitter taste filled his mouth—metallic, like blood—as he bit open the inside of his cheek.

"What the fuck?" The words were barely an audible whisper but loaded with venom.

The stage lights dimmed slowly, quieting conversations to a murmur, all attention turning toward her. In the low, moody lighting, Tennessee watched her eyes scan the crowd. Her gaze swept methodically across the sea of faces below—left to right, front to back—until finally, inevitably, it climbed to the balcony where he sat.

When her eyes found him, the world seemed to stop. Her mouth fell open, but not with the joy and recognition he'd expected. This was the moment he'd been anticipating. Just like his dream, everyone and everything fell away. The dark room became a kaleidoscope of colors that bent and fractured behind her and a pink hue formed around her on the stage. His gut fluttered with a million butterflies and the feeling of hope returned to his body once more.

He smiled down at her, lifting the sunflowers up for her to see.

"I love you, I'm sorry," he mouthed in the silence.

A few moments passed as he waited for her to react. He expected her eyes to sparkle like they just had moments before. He expected her to send him the same loving smile she'd just given the pedalboard guy. In just a few minutes, she'd begin singing the words she wrote just for him. Any moment now, the love she'd been keeping locked up for

Tennessee would all come gushing out now that he was in front of her.

Any second now...

But her eyes never changed. She stared at him with a coldness he'd only seen from her one time before. The longer she held his gaze, the darker her blue eyes became, shifting from the soft sky blue he'd fallen in love with to something deep and arctic. She was completely unreadable. Even with everything he knew about her—and he knew everything there was to know—he couldn't penetrate the wall she'd built behind those eyes. They had become hollow, lifeless mirrors reflecting nothing back to him. It was as if she were demonstrating just how completely she could shut him out, how thoroughly she'd erased him from her heart.

And then, just like that, she released him from her stare and turned back to the man standing beside her. The transformation was instant and brutal: life flooded back into her features, warmth returned to her eyes, that radiant smile he'd been desperate to see came back. But none of it was for him. She'd come alive again, just not for Tennessee.

At that moment, the wings were clipped from all the butterflies in his stomach, and their corpses dropped into the pit of his gut. This wasn't how it was supposed to happen. The prophecy had been wrong. The girl on the stage was a total stranger—whoever *that* person was, she certainly wasn't his Lucy.

The pedalboard guy moved closer to her, leaning in to

share what looked like words of encouragement. Then that smile—that damn smile—spread across her cheeks again, the same one she'd just denied Tennessee. It felt deliberate, calculated. Like she was mocking him from the stage, letting him know with these subtle cruelties that she'd already forgotten all about him. He wanted to smack that smile right off her face.

Then he watched the pedalboard guy wrap his arm around her waist and pull her into a kiss. Tennessee blinked hard, certain his eyes were playing tricks on him—surely the drugs were making him see things that weren't really there. But when his vision cleared, they were still locked together, her hand resting on the back of his neck.

The kiss lasted only a moment, but from where Tennessee sat, it stretched into eternity. Time fractured around him. The worst possible scenario was unfolding in slow motion before his eyes—he was not living out what he'd imagined in his visions, he was back in a nightmare. His heart imploded like a star collapsing in on itself, turning into a black hole. Every fragment of hope he'd carried up those stairs, every delusion that had brought him here, evaporated in an instant.

"This can't be real." He began smacking his face. "Wake up! Goddamn it, wake up!"

Every inch of Tennessee's skin was suddenly on fire and his entire body was overtaken by anger. His hands clenched into a fist so hard that his nails cut into the palms of his hands. But his surroundings weren't budging. He was stuck in this nightmare with no way out.

The first few notes of a familiar melody came over the speakers and the lights turned back on, filling the room with a hazy purple hue. Once the show began, she avoided eye contact with him altogether, though each of her bandmates took turns looking up at him with growing concern.

She needed to know what she'd done. Just one look and she would see how badly she'd fucked up. She had to look up at him again. There was no way she couldn't feel the heat radiating off of him or the weight of his stare burning into her. But her eyes never looked up to meet his again.

Her complete disregard for his presence only fueled his rage.

She didn't fucking care. She knew he'd seen the kiss— she'd probably planned it that way. She didn't care that it destroyed him, didn't care that every note she sang was a knife twisting deeper into his back. Her lips wrapped around words that had once been sacred.

The room began to shift and warp around him. He watched as horns sprouted from the back of her head and permanent darkness swallowed her blue eyes whole.

She was no longer the Lucy he'd known—that girl was dead and buried. All that remained of her were the memories that haunted his dreams, ghostly relics of who she once was. The creature on the stage was an imposter wearing Lucy's face, living in the shell of the girl he used to love.

She didn't even look like Lucy anymore. Her nose seemed different, sharper. Her clothes were flashier, more revealing than anything *his* Lucy would have worn. The rings lining her fingers and chains around her neck were desperate attempts to make herself appear like she was worth more than she really was. Everything about her was wrong, unrecognizable.

His Lucy would never intentionally hurt him. His Lucy cared deeply, wholeheartedly. His Lucy was the one who wrote love songs that were now falling like lies from this imposter's mouth.

But this wasn't his Lucy. This was some twisted nightmare version of her—a demon wearing her face. This thing didn't love him. It *actually* wanted to watch him die, wanted him to suffer a slow, miserable death by its own hand, twisting the lyrics to their sacred song. It wanted to watch his heart shatter over and over again for its own sick amusement.

"I'd like to watch you die," he whispered to himself.

He slammed back the rest of his whiskey ginger and stood to leave, his legs feeling unsteady beneath him.

"Fuck you!" he shouted over the music, hurling the sunflowers over the ledge toward her stupid head.

He stumbled out of the venue without looking back. As he reached the cold night air, he pulled the aluminum square from his pocket as he walked back to his truck and placed three tabs on his tongue.

Chapter 30

He parked his truck diagonally between two spaces. He reached into the backseat to grab the half-bottle of tequila that was hidden below the bench. His movements felt disconnected from his body, as if he were watching himself from above. With nowhere else to turn and no one left to lean on, he went back to where it all began.

So much had changed since the first time he'd been up to the top of the parking garage. The last time he was here, he was with Vera. Whether she was a friend or something more, he wasn't really sure. But with the all-encompassing loneliness he felt right now, he sure wished she was there with him tonight.

That night, Vera made him feel like everything was alright, even in his brokenness. She was one of those people who instinctively cared without having to think twice about it. She listened to him even when he didn't have anything to say. One day, she just showed up and occupied a space in his life he didn't know was vacant.

"You really blew it," he said, looking up at the rickety metal ladder that went up to the old billboard as he swigged from the tequila bottle. The alcohol didn't burn at his throat like it usually did. It filled his mouth with a brief flare of warmth and then subsided into the cold depths of his chest.

He tried to conjure up the fear he'd felt that first day he and Vera had come here. It must still live somewhere inside him, buried beneath the numbness. He could remember it so clearly—the sweaty palms that made it hard to climb, the racing heartbeat that hammered against his ribs, the adrenaline that urged him to run. But now, standing in the same spot, breathing the same thick air, he didn't feel anything at all.

A void took over the space where these emotions used to live within him. Left with nothing but a hollow shell, he'd been scraped clean of any feeling at all. It was what he'd been chasing for so long now—an absence of his pain, avoidance of his discomfort. But he never imagined that freeing himself of this weight would take everything else with it.

There were just too many feelings that his system was overflooded, short circuiting and cutting off all connection to his heart. Had the emotional rollercoaster he'd been on increased his tolerance? Had his modest fear of heights simply been pushed aside by bigger, more terrifying fears? Or had watching that kiss—Lucy's lips pressed against another man's—been his final undoing—the last feeling he'd ever know at all?

The memory flickered like a broken film reel. He couldn't tell anymore what had actually happened and what was just another one of his fucked-up dreams or hallucinations. The kiss felt real—the way her smile had spread across her face, the casual intimacy of the stranger's arm around her waist—but so did the nightmare he had about his dad. Reality had become negotiable, truth a matter of his interpretation.

He took another pull from the bottle; the tequila now felt more like water against his tongue and stepped closer to the ladder. Still nothing. No flutter of panic, no quickening pulse, no jolt of survival instinct. Maybe he had nothing left to be afraid of. After all, what did he have left to lose? The emptiness inside him swallowed everything—his job, his home, his sanity, and everything he loved. He had nothing left.

He held the bottle in one hand and stepped one foot up onto the ladder and then the other. The rust flakes crumbled beneath his grip as he held onto the rungs, leaving orange stains on his palm. He hoisted himself up with one hand—a stunt he would've never imagined pulling before—climbing in pursuit of his next high. Even as dangerous as he knew it was, even as the ladder creaked and swayed, he still didn't feel a thing.

The higher he progressed up the thin beams, the colder the air became and the harder the wind blew. It whipped through his hair and clothes, carrying the smell of the ocean air with it. The sounds of traffic below faded to a dull hum, replaced by the whistle of wind and the groan of the aging structure. He eventually reached the top of the ladder and stood unphased on the platform, the grated metal floor vibrating slightly beneath his feet.

He remembered the way Vera swung her feet and looked over at him with a smile, her silhouette framed against this same view when it had seemed magical instead of bleak. He remembered feeling a strange sense of comfort, knowing he wasn't the only one with a troubled past. He remembered feeling a deep sadness that transformed into something else altogether, something that resembled happiness and wonder—emotions that had layered and blended like watercolors bleeding into one another. How could he have held all of those emotions at one time, when now he couldn't even get himself to conjure up any feelings at all?

The streetlights sparkled in the same way they did before, but something about them seemed dimmer and dull, like the magic had worn off. The homes seemed average and boring now. The air was thicker and tasted of regret. It was the same as it was, but he couldn't get himself to see it the same way he had before.

He sat down onto the edge of the grated platform and placed the tequila bottle in the same spot that Vera had sat that chilly mid-winter night, the glass making a hollow clink against the steel. It had to have been sometime in late January when they'd come up here together—back when the air had been sharp and clean, when he could still feel the sting of winter on his cheeks.

He pulled the last one of his cigarettes from the front pocket of his soiled shirt. The cigarette was partially crushed, the paper crinkled and torn, but he still set it between his lips and lit it with shaking fingers. Some tobacco fell out, the loose strands catching on his tongue and leaving a bitter, dirt-like taste in his mouth. The smoke felt harsh in his lungs.

If he had to guess, an entire season had come and gone since he and Vera had come here for the first time. The fog was lifted higher in the sky now than it had before. There weren't any clouds forming in his breath the way they had then. But it couldn't be summer yet, could it? He'd hardly noticed the passage of time anymore, floating through life in a haze, days blending into nights.

He pulled out his phone with fumbling fingers, the screen somehow cracked. The numbers swam before his eyes for a moment before coming into focus: July 13th.

"Oh my god," he laughed, and the sound echoed strangely in the empty air, hollow and disconnected from his body. The laughter felt foreign, like it was coming from someone else's throat.

Months had gone by. Whole weeks, possibly even months, were missing from his memory—black holes where moments of his life should be.

"Time sure flies when you're having fun," he said to the empty night, his voice cracking on the words. He laughed as he inhaled the smoke deeper. The laugh came out strangled, bitter.

The last time he was up here, he thought he'd reached his lowest point, but little did he know he had so much further to fall. If he could speak to that version of himself now—he would tell him to savor what little joy he had left.

Another chug from the bottle, the tequila burning its way down his throat like liquid fire. "If only she could see me now, in all my glory!" he called out to the sleeping city below, his words slurring together. "You really dodged a bullet, didn't ya, Luce?"

His whole body shook with laughter. The sound bounced off the metal framework around him, creating an echo chamber. His laugh became louder and more heinous the more alcohol he poured down his throat.

"I'm alone—always have been and always will be." He stood up on the platform, his legs unsteady beneath him, the tequila bottle clutched in his hand. "Oh, and not only am I alone, I also don't have a job or a place to live, either!"

"I'm a fucking loser!" The words tore from his throat raw and jagged as he screamed-laughed into the night sky. His voice echoed off the surrounding buildings. Heads started appearing in lit windows—curious faces peering out, their features indistinct but judgmental in the amber glow.

"That's right, you heard me! I said I'm a fucking pathetic loser!" He waved the bottle at them.

"This is exactly what you wanted," he snarled, and for a moment he could see her—not the real Lucy with her soft eyes and confident smile, but the version that she became. The one with horns jutting out from the back of her head and her cold, dead eyes. The demonic Lucy who fed on his misery and spoke poison into his ear.

You're just like your father.

"You just wanted to see how far I'd fall, didn't you? You fucking bitch!"

The bottle was about three-quarters of the way empty now, the remaining tequila sloshing against the glass. So he took one last elongated pull to finish it off.

"Well, you got me right where you wanted me. I've got no one else to turn to!" His voice cracked with the strain of screaming. "You opened me up just to break me down from the inside out! You made me feel something just to toss me out like the trash!"

He swung his arm back and threw the bottle down to the sidewalk below—not even flinching as he heard the glass shatter against the pavement with a sharp crack that echoed through the empty streets.

"Honestly…I wish I were dead just so I could cross your mind again." The words came out as barely more than a whisper, all the fight suddenly drained from his voice. Tears began to blur his vision—finally the cracks were starting to show—falling in hot tracks down his cold cheeks. The pain was unlike anything he'd ever felt before, as if someone had reached inside his chest and tore away the protective coating around his heart that he'd built up for nearly his entire life.

"Fuck this." The words caught in his throat, strangled by the sob that was trying to claw its way out. "I can't do this anymore. I can't..." The sentence died there, too heavy to finish.

Something in his body cracked open and all that he'd been holding back came flooding in. The grief hit him in waves—for Lucy, for the person he used to be, for Vera, Tanner and the Coopers, and Mr. Green, for all of it. His chest heaved with the effort of breathing around the agony that filled his entire body.

He flicked the cigarette off the platform with trembling fingers, watching the ember spiral down into the darkness. Then he grabbed the railing; it couldn't have been more than two inches wide.

Before he knew it, he'd climbed on top of the thin piece of metal, his body moving without conscious thought, driven by a pain so intense it demanded every ounce of his action. The wind whipped around him with new force. He could feel his breathing become shallow and ragged, his lungs struggling to pull in air. His heartbeat thundered in his ears like war drums.

Finally—finally—he found the dose of adrenaline he'd been chasing. Not the artificial high from chemicals, but the raw, primal terror of standing at the edge of everything. With the very last thing he had to lose on the line.

He knew he should be scared—his body was giving him all the warning signs. Every nerve ending screamed at him to step back, every gut instinct firing. His legs trembled beneath him, sweat mixed with tears on his face. But for some reason, beneath all the physical terror, he still didn't feel afraid. He didn't care if he fell off the railing, even now that the possibility was staring him directly in the face, close enough that he could feel it.

"It's not like anyone would notice," he laughed. "No one would give a shit." The words tasted like ash in his mouth.

The wind picked up suddenly, a violent gust that came from nowhere and shook him off balance. His body swayed, his arms windmilling desperately as gravity called him down. For a split second, the decision was out of his hands—the universe seemed to be making the choice for him. He checked his footing with frantic, scrambling movements, his shoes scraping against the metal as he fought to stay upright.

Could he really do it? Could he really jump and end it all right now? What if this had all been a dream and jumping was his only chance at waking up? The thought sent electric shocks through his nervous system—maybe death was just another doorway, another transition between states of consciousness. He didn't know what was real or not anymore. Reality had become as unstable as his footing on this narrow ledge.

He looked down past his feet and over the edge, his vision swimming with vertigo. The golden glass where the tequila bottle had shattered sparkled against the dark pavement, giving him some frame of reference for the distance below. Was he even up high enough to actually die? Would he just break his legs? Or worse, cling to life in some hospital bed for the rest of his days?

He thought of his parents, and the images came in flashes of memory. He knew his mom would be sad—he could picture her tears and the flowers she'd bring to his grave. But what about his dad? Was he even capable of feeling bad or sorry for someone else, or would Tennessee's death be just another inconvenience to navigate? Did his dad actually love him, somewhere deep down, but just didn't know how to show it? Would they blame themselves, or would they sweep this tragedy under the rug with all the rest of them— another family secret to be buried and forgotten?

He thought about Vera next. How she would probably never forgive herself, since she was the one who showed him this place and pushed him to climb up the ladder the first time. Would she wonder if she could've talked him down or changed his mind? Or had she already forgotten about him?

And finally, he thought of Lucy. Would she even shed a tear for him? Would she be glad that he was gone, say that the world was a better place without him in it? Would she even go to his funeral, or would she stay away to avoid the questions, the stares, the whispered speculation about what he'd done to her? Or would she use this as fuel for her next song—capturing the memory of him like a time capsule so he could live on forever in three-minute verses about love gone wrong?

Maybe none of them would care. Maybe their worlds would keep on turning with or without him, their lives continuing while his ended in silence. The thought was both terrifying and oddly comforting—to be so insignificant that his absence wouldn't even create a ripple.

He took a deep breath in through his nose, tasting the night air and his own fear, and let out a long, shuddering exhale. Could it be his last? The breath felt precious suddenly, like something he should savor.

He shifted his weight forward, feeling the railing cut into the soles of his feet through his shoes, and closed his eyes. The darkness behind his eyelids was absolute, peaceful. He couldn't make the choice himself—the decision was too big, too final, too heavy for him to make. Fate would have to decide. The wind, gravity, chance—something bigger than him would choose for him.

"Excuse me, sir," a voice said below his feet. Tennessee opened his eyes and looked down to see the security guard standing beneath the platform, his flashlight cutting through the darkness. He'd found him—fate had spared him.

"Hey! I'm going to have to ask you to get down," the guard yelled up at him. "Don't want you falling off that ledge."

He'd been given his answer. A massive wave of relief crashed over him. His shoulders sagged as all the tension he'd been carrying released all at once. The decision had been taken from him, and for the first time in longer than he could remember, he felt something close to gratitude. His lungs filled with air that actually seemed to reach his bloodstream, oxygen flooding his brain like a drug more powerful than anything he'd ever taken.

"Yeah, one sec," Tennessee's voice shaking. He stepped down from the railing, his legs nearly buckling as his feet touched solid metal again. The platform felt stable, real. His heartbeat steadied as he climbed down the ladder, each rung bringing him back to the world of the living.

"You alright?" the security guard asked, genuine concern in his voice.

"I don't know," Tennessee said, truthfully. The honesty felt strange in his mouth, foreign after so many lies and half-truths.

An uncomfortable look came over the man's face as he studied Tennessee's tear-streaked cheeks and bloodshot eyes. "Well, the garage is closed, so you're gonna have to go."

Tennessee nodded and stepped toward his truck.

"I don't think you should be driving," the guard said, his voice firmer now. "You don't seem like you're in the right... state of mind."

"I—I need it," Tennessee stuttered, panic creeping back into his voice. "I have nowhere else to go."

"I'm sorry, man." The guard shrugged. "Come back in the morning and pick it up when the lot reopens."

Like a cruel joke, the emptiness that had filled his body moments ago returned with vengeance. The relief evaporated as quickly as it had come, leaving him hollow again, but now with the added weight of having to continue living this life—now without even his truck. How did things just keep getting worse?

He dragged himself down to the dark stairwell, the clanging of the guard's keys on his heels, his legs barely able to carry his weight down the concrete steps. Once he was outside and the guard was out of his sight, he pulled the aluminum foil from his back pocket with shaking hands and unfolded it. He had about seven or eight squares left— his final companions in a world that had abandoned him completely.

As he looked down at them, tears fell from his eyes and onto the blotting paper, each drop carrying the weight of everything he'd lost. The tears blurred his vision, making the tiny squares swim before his eyes.

"You're all I have left." The words hung in the cold air like a confession. As he walked aimlessly into the night, the city stretched out before him, every light a reminder of lives that were moving forward, while his had come to a complete stop.

Without even perforating them, he stuck the remaining tabs on his tongue all at once, the taste of cardboard flooding his mouth. The paper dissolved against his teeth, taking with it his last connection to this world.

He didn't know if it was possible to die from an overdose on LSD. But maybe—just maybe—he could see Lucy, *his Lucy*, just one last time before everything went dark forever.

Chapter **31**

In a matter of minutes, reality completely disintegrated.

The streetlights began to flicker like the wick of a candle. The pavement beneath his feet started to ripple with each step. Car headlights stretched into long ribbons of light. Street signs rearranged their letters into words he couldn't read.

The darkness of the night sky cracked and crumbled above him, to reveal an endless bright white light. Pieces of the black sky fell like ash, dissolving before they hit the ground. He squinted and covered his eyes as reality folded in on itself.

After a moment or two, his eyes adjusted to the brightness, and he could see that the dimly lit streets of the Richmond were gone.

Instead, he found himself walking down a strange hallway. The paint from the pale-yellow walls was chipped and cracked along both sides. Below his feet was a light hardwood floor that creaked under his weight. The passage was narrow enough that he could reach out his arms and touch both walls.

"Where am I?" His voice echoed down the hallway.

The corridor went on as far as he could see. Just more yellow wall and oaky floorboards. But as he stared ahead, his perspective seemed to shift. The hallway appeared to breathe, expanding and contracting like the inside of a lung. The parallel lines of the walls bent inward and outward in slow, rhythmic waves.

Peering over his shoulder, he saw a sea of bright white behind him—the hallway faded into nothing once out of his view. Every step he'd taken disappeared shortly after it happened, swallowed by the light.

So he continued to walk forward, as this seemed to be his only choice, the sound of each footstep bouncing across the walls and echoing down the hallway.

Was he dead? Had the security guard really saved him or had he actually fallen from the parking garage? Was this another dream or a bizarrely boring hallucination?

He turned his hands over to examine them. They didn't have any scars or scabs. His fingers looked normal. The plastic bracelet he'd had on his wrist was now gone. And he had no idea how he'd gotten here or any concept of time.

The cracks along the yellow wall seemed to be spreading as he walked, but when he looked directly at them, they stopped moving. Only in his peripheral vision could he see them growing and cracking along the yellow paint like spider webs.

The longer he walked, the more familiar the hallway felt. An eerie feeling washed over him. The floorboards beneath his feet started to look worn in specific places, as if countless footsteps had traced the same path he was now walking.

"Have I been here before?" This time his voice seemed to come from both in front of him and behind him simultaneously.

Had he dreamt of this place before? He scanned his memory for anywhere he'd been that looked like this, but there was nothing there for him to grasp onto, making the familiarity all the more unsettling.

His breath shortened and the hairs on the back of his neck stood up. The corridor felt like it was getting narrower—or maybe he was getting bigger. The walls pressed in with each exhale. A pit opened up in his stomach that urged him to escape this place, to find a way out. But the hallway stretched endlessly ahead, and the bright white light at his heels threatened to swallow him.

In the distance, a door emerged on one side of the hallway. A wave of relief washed over him as he picked up his pace.

As he approached the door, he noticed it didn't seem to belong here. The door was big and red. It had a few dents where it had been kicked in and was off-center like it had come off one of its hinges. He'd seen a door much like this one get broken and busted time and time again by his father. It had a rusted gold knob, like the one that he'd turned fearfully each time he came home from school.

He reached toward the knob and held it for a moment. A wave of panic came over him. The metal was cold against his palm, and for a split second, he could smell beer and cigarettes seeping through the wood. His hand trembled as distant sounds leaked through—muffled shouting, glass shattering, a woman's cries.

He wondered what—or who—was on the other side.

He pressed his ear against the door's surface and heard a small voice: "Please stop, Dad. Please." The sound made his stomach lurch. This wasn't just any door—this was *the* door.

His body shuddered as he stepped away and continued walking. He couldn't face what was behind that door. Not yet. Maybe not ever.

Thankfully more doors began to appear on the horizon. Some doors had sounds bleeding through—laughter, arguments, music, crying. Others were completely silent. There was a classroom door with a small window revealing rows of empty desks—the history class where he did coke for the first time between textbook pages. Then there was a dark door with a delicate golden cross on it. It was the church room where his dad attended his AA meetings.

Then he got to a warm orange door with a small rectangular window. Through the glass, he could see the Cooper family's dining room. Around the dinner table sat

Tanner, both of his parents, and his younger sister, their faces glowing in the soft light. They were laughing as Mr. Cooper told an overly expressive story with his hands, and Mrs. Cooper passed around a steaming dish with veggies and a pot roast. Tennessee's mouth watered as the smell came through the door. Tanner rolled his eyes at his dad's bad jokes, but a loving smile hid beneath his black hoodie.

Next to Tanner was an empty seat. One he'd sat in hundreds of times before. This seat was more than just a chair.

Tennessee's breath caught in his throat. He didn't just lose his best friend. He lost the only family that had ever made him feel like he belonged. He'd been too damaged, too selfish, too broken to appreciate what his chosen family had given him until it was gone.

A part of him wanted to turn the handle. To pull out the chair and have a home-cooked meal with them. To pretend that he wasn't broken, just for a little while. But he couldn't.

"I'm sorry," he whispered to the door. "I'm sorry I let you down."

He pressed his palm against the glass one last time, then turned and continued down the corridor—more doors appearing as he went.

Eventually, he came to a generic white door to an apartment, only this one was covered with black and red posters with fonts that were practically illegible. It was the door to Vera's apartment.

He had no way of knowing what would be on the other side, but something in his gut was telling him that he needed to go through it.

There was a swell of anxiety as he grabbed the knob. He couldn't stay here in this endless hallway, but he also wasn't sure if he had the courage needed to leave it, either. What if this door led to somewhere else entirely?

"Alright, just do it." He turned the knob. "One...two...three."

As he pushed open the door, a rush of smoke blew into his face. He coughed out the menthol-scented air and spat until he could finally breathe, waving his hands in front of him to clear the air. His eyes watered as he stepped forward, each breath burning his lungs.

It was Vera's apartment, but the room itself wasn't quite how he remembered. The familiar scents were amplified beyond recognition—the whiskey smell so strong it made his head spin, the cigarette smoke so dense he could feel it in his lungs.

It was as if Dalí had painted Vera's apartment and he'd stepped inside the frame. The posters of punk bands were melting off the walls in shiny, demented globs. The metal fonts became even more illegible as they dripped like black tar. A giant boot with silver chains—much like the only pair of black combat boots he'd ever seen Vera wear—stood tall, taking up a whole corner of the room. It towered over him, easily eight feet high. The laces billowed out in impossible yards, creating large loops across the floor and furniture that slinked around like snakes.

Tennessee tried to step around one of the laces, but it wrapped itself around his ankle. He stumbled, catching himself against the wall, only to realize his hand had hit a surface made entirely of dark green glass—Jameson bottles.

Whiskey had taken over the entire room. The dark green glass made up the tile on the counters and every inch of the walls. Two bottles acted as pillows on her bed, the amber-colored whiskey sloshing around inside. When he approached the bathroom, he saw that the toilet bowl water had been replaced with brown whiskey. The smell was overwhelming now. Not just the scent of alcohol, but something sour and rotten—the smell of vomit. His stomach twisted in knots.

Cigarette smoke was coming up from the floor like a fog that made it hard to breathe. It grew thicker the more anxious he became, until he could barely see his own hands in front of his face.

"Vera?" he called out. "Where are you?"

There were traces of her everywhere, but there was no sign of her in the small dark room. Her bandanas hung from every surface and black denim jackets and jeans were laid out across the floor.

"There's gotta be a way out of here." He started searching through the apartment with growing desperation. He opened up the fridge to find more bottles of Jameson.

Within the depth of the icebox, he heard Vera's voice whisper something: *"You never really saw me, did you? You just liked how I made you feel."*

He slammed the fridge shut and rummaged through the kitchenette drawers, only to find empty little drug baggies.

As he moved through the space with more urgency, the apartment seemed to respond. The whiskey smell grew stronger, making him nauseous. The cigarette smoke thickened and started to choke him again.

He walked over to the tiny window and pulled back the curtain to try to let some air in.

"Oh my fucking god," he said in disbelief.

There was nothing out there. Beyond this little room was just more white light, like somehow this room was the only space to exist anywhere in this endless abyss.

Fuck. He was all alone in here. He needed to find a way out. Maybe one of the other doors in the hallway had an exit.

As he turned to head back out there, a loud rattling sound took over the room. The floor shook like an earthquake beneath his feet. Some of the glass bottles around the room fell and shattered, spraying whiskey as they did.

Through the open doorway, he could see a bus barreling down the passage of the yellow hallway at full speed, blowing in a massive gust of wind as it passed. The sound of the bus rushing by was impossibly loud in this space—its wheels screeching, its horn blasting a sound that seemed to come from inside his own skull.

Where did it come from? How did it get here? Could he take it somewhere out of this weird place? But just as quickly as it came, it was gone.

A final rush of air slammed the door closed with a bang and the room went completely dark. The silence that followed was absolute. In the darkness, Tennessee could hear his own heartbeat, his own breathing echoing in the void.

"You've been too busy looking over your shoulder back at the past to even notice me," a voice spoke in the darkness. It sounded like Vera's, but it was distorted and distant.

"Vera, are you there? Where are you?"

"I was so stupid for thinking that loving you harder would somehow make you love me back," the voice continued, each word cutting into him like broken glass.

Then he felt a pair of hands wrap around his neck and push down on his Adam's apple. They were cold, almost ghost-like.

"Vera!" he screamed, trying to pull the hands off of him. "I'm sorry! Let me go!"

He waved his arms and kicked his legs all around him, but they never made contact with anything. There was nobody there, only an invisible force pressing down on his windpipe. The hands felt solid and real—but when he clawed at them, his nails only dug into his own skin.

"I was so stupid for thinking that loving you harder would somehow make you love me back." There was an ache he could hear underneath the anger—the same pain he'd heard in her voice that morning when she told him how she felt.

"I didn't know, Vera!" Tennessee shouted, his voice cracking. "I didn't know what I was doing to you."

The hands tightened their grip. Before he knew it, he was being lifted off the ground, suspended in mid-air by whatever force had him by the neck. The whiskey smell grew stronger, more nauseating, and the smoke seemed to blow right into his face.

He'd done this exact same thing to her. He'd held her by the neck during some weird blacked-out memory glitch. She didn't deserve that. She had nothing to do with any of this. She just got caught in the crossfire of his own self-destruction.

"You've been too busy looking over your shoulder back at the past to even notice me," her voice now changed to disgust, filled with the bitterness of someone who'd given everything and received nothing in return. "I was so stupid for thinking that loving you harder would somehow make you love me back."

It was becoming harder to breathe. He could feel the blood rushing into his face and water starting to fill his eyes. He tried to claw at the hands, only to continue to scratch into the soft skin of his neck. Around him, the apartment began to collapse inward—the whiskey bottles cracking, the cigarette smoke swirling into a tornado, the posters sliding off the walls into pools of black sludge.

"You didn't deserve this," Tennessee strained, each word a struggle against the invisible grip. "You were so kind to me, and I took that for granted. I took you for granted. You were right. I was too preoccupied with my own shit to know what I had. I'm sorry I dragged you down with me."

His eyes started to close as his apology took the last bit of air left in his lungs. The apartment around him seemed to exhale with his words. The hands around his neck loosened their grip, the cold fingers slowly releasing their hold on his throat.

Then suddenly, he was dropped to the floor.

He hit the ground with a thud that reverberated through his entire body. For several moments, he could do nothing but wheeze. As his breathing slowly steadied, Vera's voice faded into an inaudible whisper, until it drifted off into the ether.

At the edge of the room where the window was, the nothingness was starting to make its way inside. It crept in slowly, having started to deteriorate the window frame, the wood turning transparent and beginning to fade. The curtain he'd pulled back was already mostly gone, dissolved into the white void.

The bottles and denim weren't far behind. He watched as the Jameson bottles along the walls began to dim, their green glass becoming see-through before vanishing entirely. Vera's clothes—her bandanas, her jackets, and even the giant boot—all dissolved into nothing.

Soon there would likely be nothing left of this place. The apartment was returning to the void. It was clearly his cue to leave.

With effort, he pulled himself up from the floor and made his way to the door.

"I really am sorry," he whispered to the disappearing room.

As he turned the handle, he expected to find himself back in the yellow hallway. Instead, as he opened the door and stepped through the doorway, he found himself in the entryway of his childhood home.

Chapter 32

"Goddamn it!" His childhood home was the last place he wanted to be.

He looked down to see his hand was now gripping the wobbly, busted knob of the red front door he knew so well. Behind him, Vera's apartment was dissolving quickly. Cigarette smoke and fading green glass were all that was left of it now.

He recognized the smell of his old home immediately—Budweiser, cigarette ash, and fear were all ground into the fabric of the carpet. Every instinct screamed at him to run.

But the floor of Vera's apartment behind him was gone now, swallowed by bright, white nothingness. There was nowhere left to go but forward, into the home that held all the memories he'd spent years trying to forget.

With heavy, apprehensive footsteps, he walked inside.

The house was just as he remembered—messy and out of sorts. But there was a stillness in the home that didn't feel right.

"Mom?" he called into the seemingly empty house, his voice echoing differently than it should have.

It was like all the energy had been sucked out of the room with a vacuum. All the objects appeared to be standing at attention, like they were holding their breath, waiting for something to happen. The stillness felt ominous, like the deceptive calm before the storm.

He pushed in chairs that were pulled out from the dining room table and stepped over scattered Goodwill toys, broken crayons, and coloring books. Fresh groceries were left on the counter. Half-empty beer bottles lined the coffee table and the floor around the recliner his dad always sat in. The sight of the bottles made the faint scars on his shin burn.

Something about seeing the home frozen like this made him feel on edge. He expected someone to come running from down the hall or through the backdoor at any moment to tend to things they'd left behind. But there was no sign of anyone. It was like time itself was standing still, trapped in a moment between calm and chaos.

"It's too damn quiet." His voice sounded small and foreign in the suspended space.

A low whistle came from the broken swamp cooler that blew a lukewarm breeze through the home, carrying with it the ghost of unbearably hot summer days. The silence made him hyper-aware of the sound of his steps. Each one was heavy and loud as the old floorboards moaned beneath his feet—the same creaks that had taught him to move like a shadow through his own home.

He made his way through the living room, past the small TV and the couch riddled with cigarette-burn holes toward the hallway. Then he heard the crunch of glass under his shoe, which made his whole body tense up. Looking down, he saw a cracked family photo that once hung on the wall, now shattered on the ground. He leaned down to pick up the white wooden picture frame.

He remembered the day they took that photo at the mall with painful clarity. His sister had been born just a few months before, which would've made Tennessee about six or seven. His mom was doing everything she could to hold their house together while juggling a newborn, being the sole breadwinner, and managing her husband's drunken rampages that only seemed to be getting worse. It was around that time that he started to feel like there wasn't any room for him in the house—like he was just another problem to manage.

His mom, doing her best, dressed him up in a red turtleneck sweater that matched the one she bought for his dad. The wool had been scratchy against his neck, but he'd known better than to complain. On the day of the photoshoot, his dad was cussing and putting up a fight the whole drive over while the baby cried in the backseat with Tennessee. He'd pressed himself against the car door, trying to become as invisible as he could.

The photographer set them up in front of a gray background. His mom sat on a little bench holding the baby up toward the camera and Tennessee sat right beside her, his small body rigid with anticipation.

"Now, Dad," the photographer said, "go ahead and put your hand right there on the little guy's shoulder."

Tennessee remembered wincing as his dad's big hand came down hard on his shoulder. He was used to only being touched by his dad if it was a punch, slap, or kick. He remembered being able to smell the beer on his hot breath as his dad panted down his neck. Tennessee sat up straighter and made sure not to move, every muscle in his little body wound tight. He didn't know what his dad might do next, but any wrong move could cause him to explode again.

"Alright, kid, smile!" the photographer said, looking into the lens. "Everybody smile like you love each other."

Smile like you love each other. The words had felt like a cruel joke even then before he really understood why.

As he looked at the photo now, he could see how hard he was forcing his little gap-toothed smile. He could see the fear behind his young, innocent eyes, the hypervigilance that had already become his default state. Even at this young age, he was already scanning for exits and calculating threats, rather than being a kid.

He could also see the desperation in his mother's eyes—not just the usual exhaustion you'd expect from a woman who'd recently had a baby—but the frantic hope that if they could look normal enough, maybe they could *be* normal. His mom always did her best to make sure they looked like a typical family. Whether she was keeping up this image for other people or as a result of her own delusion and denial, he didn't really know. But it sure pissed him off to see the lengths she went to pretending—forcing everyone to play their part in the "loving family" act.

She was probably thankful they'd taken this photo when they did. Her face healed, but she never looked quite the same afterwards.

"Fucking bullshit." His voice was filled with decades of buried rage. He threw the photo back down to the ground and stepped on it deliberately, the glass making a satisfying crunch under his heel as he continued down the hallway.

He walked past the door to his sister's room and into his own childhood bedroom. There was very little in there: a small bed with a blue blanket, a bookshelf filled with paperbacks he'd stolen from the library, a little desk where he'd struggled to do his homework before he stopped doing it altogether, and a small closet in the corner where he would hide when he felt like he needed to.

There were holes in the drywall from angry fists—some were a result of his own teenage outbursts when the rage had finally surfaced, and some were from his dad. The room felt more like a jail cell than a place that should feel sentimental. Even now, standing here as an adult, his shoulders hunched automatically, his body remembering how to shrink.

He turned around and faced his parents' room across the hall. Only a small crack of light drilled into the dark room from where the door was left ajar. He took a few apprehensive steps forward and kicked the door fully open with his foot, allowing the light to illuminate more of the room.

Their room was in a similar state as the rest of the house—clean laundry left in piles waiting to be put away, beer bottles lining dressers and nightstands, shoes thrown chaotically around the room. The space felt compressed and hostile, the walls seeming to lean inward like they were trying to contain all the ugly secrets they held.

In the middle of the room was a king-size bed. In the dim light, Tennessee saw that there were two people in the bed, but he couldn't make out their faces. Something about the scene felt wrong, intimate in a way that made his skin crawl—like he'd walked in on something he wasn't supposed to see.

"Mom? Dad?" But the two people in the bed paid him no mind, continuing their movements as if he wasn't even there.

He stepped further into the room, squinting his eyes to see better. One of the people had broad shoulders and curly brown hair that matched his own. As he got closer, the details became sickeningly clear—the two people were nude, and his father was face-down on top of a woman who definitely wasn't his mother—a stranger's body beneath his father's. Tennessee could see his dad's bare cheeks thrusting, could hear the rhythmic creaking of the bed springs.

"Oh god!" Tennessee shouted in disgust.

Just as he turned on his heels to exit the room, a loud sob pierced the silence, causing him to jump. The sound was raw, broken—a heart being shattered in real time.

"How could you!" she screamed, her voice cracking with betrayal. His mother's silhouette cast a long shadow into the room. She stood in the doorway with his baby sister on her hip, the infant's face red from crying. Just a few inches to the right of her, there was a pair of little arms hugging the door frame and innocent brown eyes that were peeking curiously into the dark room.

The little boy in the doorway was him.

"No," Tennessee whispered, his adult voice breaking as he looked at this little version of himself. His eyes began to water as he watched his own small face wrinkle up—the confusion, the fear, the terrible understanding that something was wrong without fully understanding it. "You shouldn't be here. You shouldn't have to see this."

He was too young to understand the mechanics of what was happening, but old enough to recognize betrayal when he saw it on his mom's face. He hadn't gotten the birds and the bees talk yet. He had no idea why his dad would be naked in bed with another woman but based on his mom's reaction—the way her whole body shook with rage and grief—he knew it wasn't good. He knew enough then to know that it was something he shouldn't have seen.

His mom's shouting only got louder, and his dad's grunts became audible and even more obscene. It sickened

Tennessee to his stomach that his dad didn't even care enough to stop even after he was caught—didn't cover himself, didn't show shame, didn't acknowledge the family he was destroying. The little boy at the door began to cry, creating a chorus of pain that filled the house.

Tennessee wanted to scoop up his younger self, to cover those innocent eyes, to somehow shield him from this moment that would fracture something inside him forever. But he was trapped in this memory, forced to watch his childhood die in real time.

Tennessee couldn't stand being in the middle of this mess any longer. He pushed his way through the doorway, passing through the three figures as they vanished like clouds of smoke into thin air. The sound of crying—his mother's, his sister's, his own seven-year-old sobs—echoed in his ears even as the vision of them dissolved.

He reentered the hallway and made his way back to the front of the house, his legs unsteady beneath him.

"Wake up," he said, pinching himself hard enough to leave marks. "I'm done with this dream. Wake the fuck up."

The silence lasted only a few moments.

"My children deserve better! I deserve better!" his mother screamed as she barreled into the living room, his dad following closely behind. "You need to leave. I'm serious this time!"

"Who do you think you are, you fucking bitch?" his father's words slurring together as he stumbled into the walls, knocking their family photo off its hanger. "You can't kick me out of this house. I didn't do a goddamn thing."

"You've been forcing your own son to sit outside in the heat so you could fuck some other woman!" she shoved her index finger into his chest. "He could have died out in that heat!"

Tennessee always felt weird when they talked about him like he wasn't in the room. It made him feel even more invisible than he already felt—a ghost in his own life, a witness to his own destruction, but never an active participant in it. Even now, as an adult watching this unfold, a familiar ache settled in his chest.

She turned away from his dad, throwing her hands in the air. "You're a horrible father and an even worse—"

"Shut the fuck up!" his dad interrupted her by throwing the beer in his hand at her. The bottle spun through the air, some liquid pouring out of it. Thankfully, he missed by about a foot or so. The glass bottle shattered when it hit the floor, spraying beer and bits of tobacco across the living room. The sound of breaking glass made Tennessee's entire body flinch.

"What's wrong with you? Your son is sitting right there!" Rather than pointing toward the entrance of the hallway where Tennessee now stood, she pointed toward the couch. "Hasn't he gone through enough already because of you?"

A little boy with a blank stare sat silently on the shabby orange couch. He had both of his hands tucked under his thighs, fingers digging into the fabric. The little version of him tried to be strong by showing no emotion—he didn't want to make the situation worse—but Tennessee could see the rapid rise and fall of his small chest, could see the way his jaw was clenched and the way he bit the inside of his cheeks to keep from crying. Tennessee knew just how hard it was for that little boy to watch his parents fight, knew the terror that was coursing through that tiny body.

"The little bastard's fine!" his dad shouted, gesturing dismissively at his son. "Besides, he's a little weakling who needs to toughen up, anyway."

Even decades later, the words hit Tennessee like a physical blow. That little boy didn't need to toughen up. He needed protection, love, and safety—not to be called names.

The little boy didn't move an inch. Even though every part of him wanted to cry, he knew doing so would only make things worse. His small body was tense with hypervigilance—shoulders hunched, ready to duck, eyes constantly scanning for new threats. He wanted to run off into the other room and hide in his closet like he usually would, but it was too late to run and hide. Any sudden movement would make his head the new target for one of his dad's beer bottles. He avoided eye contact at all cost, instead staring down at the floor, allowing his eyes to purposely blur out of focus.

No one was going to save him. Detaching from reality was the only way the little boy knew how to survive. What was happening in front of him was too painful to let himself experience fully. Tennessee recognized that look—it was the same one he still wore when life became too much, when he needed to disappear inside himself.

His parents' yelling intensified as Tennessee looked down at his younger self. Tennessee wanted to scoop up the little boy, to wrap him in his arms and tell him none of this was his fault. He wanted to carry him far away from this place, to give him the childhood he deserved. He wanted to tell his younger self that everything would be okay, even if he wasn't sure that was true. He knew that the little boy really needed someone—anyone—to help him right now.

"You poor kid," Tennessee whispered as he stepped toward the couch. "No wonder we've been running this whole time."

"That's it. If you're not gonna leave, we are!" His mom started to walk past his dad, toward the hallway to grab the baby from her crib.

"No, you're not," his father put his arm up, blocking her path. "You're not going anywhere!" Tennessee's dad yelled louder the more his mom tried to push her way past him. "Doesn't matter what I did, you're not leaving me, woman!"

"Move, asshole!" Then she spat into his face with all the contempt she could muster.

A look came across his father's face that Tennessee would never forget.

His dad's thick eyebrows furrowed, casting dark shadows over his deep-set eyes. His curly hair stood up at random angles around his head, wild and unkempt. The look in his eyes was evil and completely deranged. If his dad ever had a soul to begin with, any trace of it had left his body when he wiped the spit off his cheek. This was the moment Tennessee learned that people could become monsters, that our capacity for evil lived closer to the surface than anyone was willing to admit.

"Oh, you're gonna get it now, bitch." His dad cocked back his arm and turned his hand into a fist.

Tennessee knew exactly what would happen next. He'd been avoiding this memory for decades—had tried to drown it, bury it, run from it, anything he could to get away from it. His dad's fist would collide with the side of his mother's face, sending her to the floor on her hands and knees. This wasn't the first time he hit her, and it wouldn't be the last—but would certainly be the worst.

The first of these blows would be followed by five more shortly after. Eventually, his punches would turn into kicks. His father would stand over her and repeatedly bash in her eye, nose, mouth, and teeth until her face was bloody and unrecognizable. With each strike, her cries would grow louder, more desperate. She would even call out to Tennessee, asking him for help, but he was too terrified to move. He couldn't do anything to save her. Her hair would get saturated in beer as she wriggled across the floor like a wounded animal. Splatters of her blood would line the walls and his dad's shirt. The baby would start to cry from the other room and eventually the sounds of their wails would blend together like a tragic song. She would be beaten within inches of her life, all while Tennessee watched helplessly, motionless as it happened. All because of something that *his dad* did.

The little boy was paralyzed by fear, screaming in silence within. He wanted to help her but couldn't. He didn't know how to stop his dad without getting a beating of his own. There was nothing he could do but pray that his dad would stop and that this would eventually come to an end.

Now, Tennessee stood in the middle of this fight once again. Only this time, he wasn't a small, helpless little boy. Even as scrawny as he was, he was taller than his dad. This was his chance—maybe his only chance—to save his mother and himself.

Tennessee watched as the struggle continued, the moment of impact approaching almost in slow motion. Every detail became crystal clear—the way his father's fist trembled with rage, the fear in his mother's eyes, the way the little boy on the couch was holding his breath. He could hear his own heartbeat pumping loudly in his chest, drowning out all the other sounds.

This was it. He could change the outcome. He'd been brought to this place for a reason. It was now or never.

"Don't hit her!" Tennessee shouted, his voice exploding from somewhere deep in his chest as he sprang into action.

He moved quicker than he ever had in his life—stepping in between his parents fearlessly, putting his own body in his father's strike path. Every muscle in his body tensed as he threw himself forward. He couldn't let it happen again, even if he was the one who got the beating. He squeezed his eyes closed and braced for impact.

Adrenaline was coursing through his veins. A second passed, then another. Any moment his dad's fist would connect with his face. Any moment now he'd be getting the punch that was intended for his mom, and maybe—just maybe—that would be enough to change everything.

Several moments passed, but it never came.

As his heartbeat slowed and softened, he noticed that the shouting had fallen away into absolute silence. Cautiously, he opened his eyes to find that he was no longer standing in between his parents. They were gone and so was the house he was just in. The little boy, the couch, the beer bottles—all of it disappeared.

And so had...everything.

Chapter **33**

He opened his eyes to pitch-black darkness. His childhood home, as well as everyone and everything in it, had vanished into nothingness.

"Mom, are you there?" His voice was small, almost lost, in the void. The silence that answered felt infinite, stretching to the ends of both time and space.

He blinked hard a few times, trying to determine if his eyes were even open. The darkness was so complete it felt like it was pressing up against him. He brought his hands up close to his face until he could just make out the faint outline of his fingers.

"Two hands." He touched each fingertip deliberately, counting them out. "Ten digits total."

The familiar ritual should've reassured him, but something felt different. This place didn't feel real, but it didn't quite feel like a dream, either. The air felt thick in his lungs. The ground beneath his feet seemed hollow. But there was nothing else here.

"Maybe I'm asleep...and this is something...somewhere in between," his words echoed in the darkness.

He extended his arms, sweeping them slowly through the space around him, but felt nothing there. He took tentative steps forward, then to the sides, his feet searching for walls, obstacles, anything to define the boundaries of this place. But there was only emptiness stretching in every direction.

"Hello?" he shouted into the void. "Is anybody there?"

A few chilling moments passed by. Once again, only silence answered.

"I'm alone."

And then something strange happened—he noticed the crushing weight that permanently lived in his chest was no longer there. For the first time, possibly in his entire life, the loneliness didn't feel so bad.

"I'm alone," he repeated, louder now. A wave of relief washed over him. The constant noise in his head—the guilt, the rage, the desperate scramble to outrun his thoughts—all of it had finally gone quiet.

He took a deep breath in, soaking up the feeling.

"Finally," he whispered.

"Finally!" this time shouting, his voice echoing back from everywhere and nowhere all at once.

Finally, he could stop running. Finally, all the chatter that nagged at him from the chambers of his mind had fallen silent. The war in his head was over. He'd escaped. All the pain, all the mistakes, all that haunted him—was gone.

Life itself had become the dream. A long, grueling nightmare that he could finally wake up from. It had only been a matter of moments, but already the memories of his life were starting to feel blurry. He felt their edges starting to dim as his old self began to fade away.

Then, from deep within the silence, something broke through. A sound so faint he almost wasn't sure it was really there.

Tennessee froze, his breath catching in his throat. He strained to listen, his pulse quickening. "Is that real or am I imagining it?"

The sound came again, clearer now—a voice, definitely a voice. A woman's voice. But there was something wrong with it. It was amplified and muffled like it was coming out of a blown-out speaker. He couldn't quite hear what she was saying—but he could tell that she seemed to be repeating the same phrase over and over again.

"Hello?" he shouted again, walking in the direction he thought the voice was coming from. "Who's out there? What are you saying?"

Her voice grew louder and became clearer the farther he walked into the darkness. Tennessee's heart began to race. He knew that voice. He knew it even better than he knew his own. Even distorted by the strange space of this void, he would recognize it anywhere.

"Lucy? Is that you?"

The sound of her voice made his chest lighten. Maybe this was his chance. Maybe in this place between dreams, this place somewhere in the middle of life and death, between memory and reality, they could be reunited one last time.

"Lucy!" he called out, breaking into a run toward her voice. "I'm here! I'm coming!"

But as he got closer, he realized what she was saying. Repeating over and over, like a broken record stuck on the worst possible song.

"You're just like your father," her voice said.

The words hit him like a gut punch, nearly bringing him to his knees. He slowed his pace. With each repetition, the hope in his heart crumbled little by little.

"Lucy! Where are you?"

But she didn't answer. She just kept repeating those five words, over and over. Each repetition laced with pain and betrayal, said with the same coldness he couldn't erase from his mind, no matter how hard he tried.

"You're just like your father. You're just like your father. You're just like your father."

"I'm nothing like him!" Tennessee shouted into the void, the recent image of his helpless childhood self flashing into his mind. "You know that, Lucy! You know that!"

Then he heard a second voice. It started out just as faintly as Lucy's did, only this time it was a man's voice. It sounded familiar, like it was someone he knew. It was growing louder, getting angrier.

Two shapes appeared in the distance like a mirage—tiny, barely visible in the darkness. Tennessee began to run toward them, now desperate to get to Lucy and figure out who this other person was that was raising his voice at her.

"I'm coming, Lucy!" he shouted, sweat forming on his brow.

Both of their voices grew louder as he closed the distance. The reddish tint of her hair became more vivid, her features sharpening into focus the closer he got to her.

Just at her heels, a disheveled man with dark features towered over her small frame. His body language was aggressive—waving his arms, puffing his chest out, pointing his fingers in her face. Each movement was meant to intimidate, to make her feel small.

"Who the hell is that?" The question came out in a huff. Tennessee watched the man posture toward her, the way Lucy shrank away from him. Something was very wrong. He had to get there and stop whatever was happening.

As she walked away, he grabbed her shoulder and forcibly turned her back to face him. "You can't leave, don't be ridiculous," the man's voice carried through the void.

"Get your hands off her!" Tennessee shouted, but neither of them seemed to hear him.

Tennessee squinted through the darkness. As he got closer, the details of this man became clearer. The man's build...the way he moved...the curly hair that stood up in every direction...

It couldn't be…could it?

He ran with everything he had, his heart hammering against his ribs as their voices grew clearer. Something terrible was happening—he could hear it in Lucy's tone, see it in the way she kept trying to back away. He needed to get to her.

"I can't do this anymore, Tenny," Lucy said, her voice breaking. Even as she tried to get away from him, the man matched each of her steps. "If you're not going to get help, then I can't do this anymore."

"Lucy, stop! You have no idea what you're talking about. I'm fine," the manic man said as he grabbed her wrist. He had a crazy look in his eyes. "You can't leave, don't be ridiculous."

"You don't even see it, do you?" her voice cracked as she held back her tears. "You're losing it…arguing with your reflection, breaking things, starting fights out of nowhere. And if I ever try to bring any of that stuff up later, it's like you don't even remember it. You act like it never happened at all!"

"No, I know what you're trying to get at," the man's voice was distant and deranged. "Don't you dare go there."

"I'm scared! I'm scared for you, and I'm scared *of* you!" Lucy managed to pull her hand away from his grasp. "My mom sees this stuff all the time at the hospital—the blackouts, the rage that comes out of nowhere. The kind of trauma you went through breaks people. She says you're showing all the signs of PTSD, and if you don't get help—"

He grabbed her by the shoulders, shaking her as he spoke. "You're scared of me? Are you seriously telling me you're scared of me?"

"See! This is what I mean!" She slapped her palms against his chest. "You're acting fucking crazy. It's like you can't even hear a word I'm saying!"

"No, no, no," Tennessee said, stopping in his tracks. "This isn't real. I would never—I don't—"

But even as he spoke, fragments of memory began clawing their way out of the pit he tried to bury them in. The holes in his bedroom wall. The shattered picture frame. The blood he'd washed off his hands that circled the drain in the sink. The gashes on his knuckles that he couldn't explain.

"That's not me," he said louder, as if speaking at a higher volume could make it true. "I'm nothing like that—I'm nothing like *him*. I would never hurt her."

Then the man started to rattle her body around even more violently. "Don't call me crazy! I'm not fucking crazy! I don't need any help!"

"Stop!" Tennessee shouted at his other self. "Stop it, asshole!"

But the recognition was undeniable now. Every gesture, every expression of rage, every cruel word—it was all him. This was what he'd been running from. This was the truth his mind had buried so deep that he had almost no recollection of it.

The scene continued to unfold before him with horri-fying clarity. "Say I'm not crazy. Say you aren't going any-where!" his other self said, shaking her over and over again.

"Knock it off!" He yelled at himself. But his pleas dissolved into the void. The man couldn't hear him, trapped in his own rage.

Lucy's resistance finally crumbled. "Please, stop, Tenny! I won't leave, I swear. Just let me go," she begged.

The change in his other self was immediate—like the flip of a light switch—so fast it almost seemed sinister. The energy drained from him, replaced by cold satisfaction. "I knew you wouldn't," he said with a menacing smile. He then leaned down to kiss her cheek before releasing her and turning to walk away.

Once he finally left her alone, Lucy now stood in her own rage. Only her fury wasn't unruly or dramatic. It was quiet, brooding. Like it had been building for a long time. Despite her best efforts to swallow it down, she'd reached a boiling point.

He knew what was coming next. It was the one piece of this memory that stuck with him. The words that had been haunting him since the moment they were said. It was the one thing he was fighting tooth and nail to be untrue, but he was seeing now firsthand just how right she actually was.

"You're just like your father," she said under her breath.

The words were barely audible, but they stopped his other self dead in his tracks. Tennessee felt his stomach drop as he watched the man's shoulders tense.

Lucy's tone was one Tennessee had never heard from her before. It was cold and unloving, like he'd shaken all the joy and compassion out of her. It was clear she'd been pushed past her limit.

"What the fuck did you say?" The man turned slowly. His voice sounded deadly.

"I said, you're just like your father!" she screamed into his face.

In an instant, his eyes went black, and his upper lip curled up. He stood strangely still. "Take that the fuck back."

"No! It's true. Don't you see how you're acting?" she said, waving her hands in the air. "You're no better than him. And you'll become the same monster he was if you don't get help."

"Say that one more time." The words came out like a growl.

"You're going to become a monster, just like your dad," she whispered flatly, a single tear rolling down her cheek. Her body was trembling beneath his stare.

Tennessee watched the thick brows furrow on his face from across the void, casting dark shadows over his deep-set eyes. The look in his eyes was evil, as if his soul had left his body. His jaw clenched and he showed his teeth like a wild animal.

"No, no, no!" Tennessee shouted at himself. He could see it so clearly now. "You're only going to prove her right!"

His other self's face darkened to a dangerous red. His fingers formed a fist with deliberate, terrifying slowness. Tennessee could practically taste the violence in the air. He had seconds—maybe less—to prevent what was about to unfold.

"Wait, wai—!" His legs were pumping as fast as they could carry him. "Don't do it!" Yet no matter how loud he shouted, they still couldn't hear him, and his legs couldn't get him there fast enough.

Then with an impossibly loud crack, Tennessee's body exploded in pain as he slammed face-first into an invisible wall of glass at full speed. A rush of heat came to the center of his face, his nose crunching against the barrier. He staggered backward, his vision blurring after the impact.

"What the—" Blood poured from his nose in hot streams.

As his vision refocused, from the other side of the glass, he could see that his other self had cocked his arm back. Lucy's face had gone white with terror, her hands raised defensively as she shrank in anticipation.

"No, no, no!" Tennessee yelled, pressing his bloody palms against the invisible wall. "Stop! Whatever you do, just fucking stop!"

But his pleas were useless. There was no way for him to change the past now. All he could do was press against the glass and watch himself destroy the only person who had ever truly loved him.

The first strike hit her eye and brow bone with a sickening thump, a terrible shriek leaving her body upon impact. The blow sent her stumbling backwards. She brought a trembling hand up to her face, holding the skin on one of her eyebrows where a gash had opened up. She held her other arm up, trying to shield herself.

"No!" Tennessee screamed, his voice breaking as he slammed his whole body against the glass. "Get the fuck away from her!"

"Tenny, stop! This isn't you," she cried out in pain. She was shaking now, her whole body crouched as if she was trying to disappear into herself. "Don't you see it? You're doing exactly what your dad did. You don't want to be like him, remember?"

"Listen to her! This isn't you!" Tennessee screamed at himself, pounding his fists against the glass until his knuckles split open. "Look what you're doing to her! Look at her!"

But his other self was beyond reasoning with. "Stop saying that!" His face was twisted into a vile scowl, spit flying from his lips down toward her. "I'm nothing like him! I'm nothing like him, you hear me!"

Lucy's eyes went wide as she realized there was no reasoning with him—realizing that the man she loved wasn't there in the room with her anymore. Someone else had taken over his body, someone unrecognizable. She whimpered like a wounded animal with nowhere left to run.

"Please," she whispered, barely audible. "Please, Tenny. I'm sorry. I take it back."

"Too late for that now," he snarled. "You can't just take it back. You meant every fucking word. You're the only person on the planet who knows about that part of me—the only person who knows the truth about my family."

"No!" Tennessee screamed into the glass, his heart shattering as he watched the love of his life reduced to this trembling, broken thing. "She's trying to apologize! Just leave her alone!"

"Please, I'm sorry," she said desperately, now sobbing uncontrollably.

"You threw my biggest secret back in my face!" he screamed down at her ruthlessly.

And with those words, something snapped inside him completely. His whole body began to shake with fury, hands trembling as rage consumed every fiber of his being. He was beyond reasoning, beyond mercy, beyond anything remotely human. His former self was drunk with anger.

There seemed to be nothing that would stop him. He followed exactly in his father's footsteps, his knuckles splitting open against her face as he struck her over and over. The sound of bone against flesh filled the void, punctuated by her weakening cries, until her gorgeous face was unrecognizable—swollen, bloodied, and broken.

"STOP, YOU FUCKING MONSTER!" Tennessee roared, his vocal cords ripping in his throat. He pounded his fists against the glass until blood ran down his arms in rivers. "SHE'S INNOCENT! SHE DOESN'T DESERVE THIS!"

This was what he'd been running from—the truth buried beneath layers of chemicals and pathological denial. All the drugs, all the alcohol, all the desperate attempts to erase this moment weren't enough. The truth finally had caught up to him, waiting for him in the darkness.

"Please, Tenny!" Lucy's voice was barely human now as she reached up with shaking hands toward the man towering over her. "Please stop."

"YOU'RE DESTROYING EVERYTHING!" Tennessee wailed, throwing his entire body against the barrier. "EVERYTHING GOOD IN YOUR LIFE IS GONE BECAUSE OF THIS! JUST STOP!" He kicked and punched at the wall with manic desperation. The crack of his own hands breaking barely registered—nothing mattered except getting to her, saving her from himself.

The sight of her—eyes swollen shut, nose crooked and streaming blood, lips split open, and trembling—made Tennessee's stomach lurch. The woman he'd loved more than life itself, reduced to a broken, bleeding shell at his own hands.

"Don't you ever fucking say that about me!" his other self snarled, wagging a bloody finger in her destroyed face. "I'm nothing like my dad!"

The delusion—the complete disconnect from reality—made Tennessee snap. His chest burned with a white-hot rage toward himself.

"YOU'RE EXACTLY LIKE HIM!" he screamed, hurling himself against the glass with such force that his shoulder popped. "YOU'RE WORSE THAN HIM, YOU PATHETIC PIECE OF SHIT!"

After several kicks, elbows, and body slams into the wall, he finally heard the glass crack, and a spider web of fractures spread across its surface. This sent him into a frenzy where he pushed even harder, using everything he had to break down the barrier.

"I'm coming," he managed to say while ramming the glass with his shoulder. Eventually, it gave just a little bit more and created a small opening. He kept going—slamming his entire body weight into it. He didn't care if his shoulder popped out of its socket. He would break every bone in his body if he had to. "I'll save you!"

Eventually, there was a hole big enough for him to get through. The shards of glass ripped through his clothes and pierced the skin of his face, forearms, and shins. Blood poured from his wounds as he squeezed through the jagged opening. But the pain meant nothing. All that mattered was reaching her.

"STOP! STOP!" he screamed as he tumbled through. "YOU HAVE NO IDEA WHAT YOU'RE LOSING! YOU'RE DESTROYING EVERYTHING!"

He looked up to see he was too late. Lucy and the past version of himself were gone. He couldn't save her from him—he couldn't take back the past. He was alone again in the darkness. Only now, it was far from peaceful. Something inside of his chest imploded, collapsing in on itself, as he fell to his knees.

"How?" he sobbed into his bloody hands. "How did I let this happen? How could I have done this to her?"

Blood seemed to be pouring out of every part of him. Tears fell in steady streams from his eyes. An uncontrollable wave of emotion took over as years of carefully constructed walls crumbled all at once, leaving him raw and exposed.

"There's no denying it anymore," he whispered into the void, his voice quiet and hollow. "I did that. And there's nothing I can do to take it back."

For so long he'd played the victim. He told himself that the world and everyone in it were the problem. A curated lie to help himself feel better—a method of self-preservation—to prevent him from seeing clearly. But now, the truth was undeniable. He was the problem. He was the cause of his own misfortune. He'd been feeding himself lies and delusions. But the only person he could blame for his broken heart was himself.

"It was all my fault," Tennessee choked out. "It was always my fault."

He'd become the monster from his nightmares— the very evil he'd spent his entire life condemning. Every promise he'd made to himself, every vow to be different, had been for nothing. He was supposed to break the cycle, be the dam that stopped the violence, but instead he made the current stronger.

"She was right," he said, his shoulders shaking. "I'm just like him. Actually...I'm so much worse...I should've known better."

Tennessee felt sick to his stomach. "How could you do this? How could you do this to someone you love? Someone who loved you! She was trying to help you! And this is how you repay her?"

The words poured out in desperate gasps. "I'm sorry! I didn't mean to! I would never hurt her on purpose!"

What was left of his sanity was fracturing, unleashing a fever of conflicting voices that had been talking over each other inside his mind for years. They poured out in overlapping narratives of rage, guilt, and self-loathing—all screaming at once.

"She should have left you!" he said as he slammed his broken hand into the glass. "She should have never been with you in the first place. You were never good enough for her!"

"What's wrong with me?" he screamed, his voice echoing in the emptiness. "What kind of monster does this? I wish I could take it back. I need to take it back! I need to apologize and make it right somehow." He slammed his forehead into the glass.

"You deserve to have the same thing to happen to you!" he said in disgust. "You should get the same beating you gave her!"

His hands became weapons against himself, attempting to deliver the same pain he'd inflicted on her. He beat his face with wild, unhinged fury—spit and blood flying as he tried to literally beat the monster out of himself.

"It should have been me, not her," he wept between strikes. "Someone needs to hurt me the way I hurt her."

He beat his face until his cheek and arm were sore. When that didn't seem to be hard enough, he started to slam his head into the glass wall repeatedly—again and again until his eyebrow split open and blood streamed into his vision.

"Just kill yourself," he whispered through bloody lips, his voice growing weak. "I don't deserve to be here. Someone like me is better off dead."

He no longer needed to run away. The only escape he wanted now was death.

Blood was pouring out of his forehead and nose like a waterfall. The knuckles in both of his hands were broken. His mouth filled with blood as a few of his front teeth started to come loose.

"I never deserved you," he whispered to the darkness, to her memory, to the ghost of what they'd been. "I'm so sorry, Lucy. I wish I could tell you... I'm a fucking monster. You were right."

"You're a fucking monster," he repeated, spitting blood and another tooth onto the ground.

After countless blows, his vision blurred, and his body tilted sideways. His legs gave out beneath him, and he collapsed, consciousness fading as darkness claimed him—a darkness deeper and more final than any he'd known before.

Chapter **34**

The smell of stale beer and lemon-scented cleaner washed over him as he opened the lower half of the Dutch door to get into the bar, Christmas lights hanging across its frame. A handful of regulars were already enjoying their afternoon beers. He pulled his hood up over his head to hide his swollen cheeks and black eyes. He rolled his sleeves down and put his hands in his pockets to try to cover the gashes on his knuckles and arms.

Conversations died as he shuffled through the dingy bar. A woman in a bright orange Patagonia close to the door stared and then immediately averted her gaze when he made eye contact with her. Two men playing cards on the bar top paused mid-game. Even with his hood up, the damage was impossible to hide completely—his split lip, the way he favored his left side as he limped across the wooden floors. As hard as he tried to go unnoticed, the weight of their stares followed him all the way across the room to his usual bar stool farthest from the door.

Vera wasn't paying attention when he walked in, helping another customer at the other end of the bar. As he waited for her to come over, he held his gaze down, staring at the metal bar top, carefully preparing the words he was about to say to her. His heart hammered against his ribs as he rehearsed different versions of his apology, each one feeling more inadequate than the last. He had high hopes for turning a new leaf with Vera now that he'd seen the truth and understood where he went wrong. This was his chance—maybe his only chance—to salvage something good from the wreckage that had become his life. If he could just make her understand, if he could show her he was capable of change, maybe he wouldn't have to face the world completely alone.

After a few minutes, she noticed him and walked over.

"Hey! What can I get for yo—" she stopped speaking as soon as she realized who he was, her smile vanishing. Her eyes scanned his face, seeing the full extent of his injuries. She stepped back instinctively, putting distance between them, her hand reaching for something in her back pocket he couldn't see. "Wow, you look fucked up."

For a moment he lost his breath. All the words he'd been practicing in his head just moments ago scattered as he looked at her. He felt his stomach fill with butterflies as his nerves took over.

Her reaction confirmed what he'd been trying to deny— he must look even worse than he initially thought. The neon lights above the bar felt harsh and exposing, highlighting every bruise, every cut, every sign of how far he'd fallen since she'd last seen him. He could see himself reflected in her eyes: a broken man with missing teeth and beaten cheeks, barely recognizable as the person who used to sit in this stool.

"I'm okay," he said, "I just came to—"

"No, you can't be here," Vera said sternly. Her face was twisted into a look of disgust. "I'm not selling here anymore. And I'm especially not selling to you."

"That's not why I'm here. I just wanted to say—"

"I don't care why you're here," she cut him off. "And I'm not going to help you with whatever situation you got yourself into. You can take your bashed up face and get the fuck out of my bar. I'm not gonna fix your problems anymore."

Tennessee's stomach dropped. He'd never seen Vera treat anyone like this before. She didn't even speak to strangers this harshly. This standoffishness was so unlike her. The woman who'd supported him in facing his fear, who'd vulnerably shared her deepest wounds with him on a rooftop, who'd said that she loved him, was gone. Now she was looking at him like he was a stranger. Worse—like he was a threat.

"Please, just hear me out. I just want to say I'm sorry. You were there for me when I was at my lowest, when I had nobody else to turn to. You were so kind to me when you didn't have to be. And I fucked up—majorly fucked up. You didn't deserve to be treated that way."

"No shit. I don't fucking care," she started to raise her voice. "It's too goddamn late. You've done too much damage for me to forgive you now."

"No, you're right. I messed up really bad. But just listen," he stammered. "You were right about everything. I took you for granted and was too busy dealing with my own shit to know what I had...to know what we had."

"What we had?" Vera's face turned up into a scowl. "What the fuck are you talking about? I was practically invisible to you. Between crying over Lucy and whining about how hard your sad little life was, you barely even noticed I was there."

Tennessee flinched as if she'd slapped him. Heat rushed to his face as the words hit him deeply—each one true, each one a knife being twisted.

"I know, I'm sorry. But Vera...I love you," he said, reaching his bloody hand over the bar toward her. "I'm sorry I was too caught up in the past to realize it. I want to love you the same way you love me."

"Don't try to pull that shit on me now after you almost crushed my windpipe," she scoffed.

The words made his stomach sink. A flash of memory came to his mind—her terrified face, his hands around her throat. He swallowed hard, pushing the image away.

As she continued to raise her voice, Tennessee could feel the stares burning into his back. The bar fell completely silent, conversations dying down to a murmur. Even the jukebox seemed quieter. Everyone stopped what they were doing and turned to listen to what was going on between them. The weight of their judgment pressed down on him.

"You clearly don't know what love is. Even when it falls right in your lap, you don't know what to do with it."

No, that wasn't true. He did know what love was—the way his chest ached when he thought of Lucy, the way he would have moved mountains for her. That *had* to be love. It had to be. If it wasn't love, then what the hell had he destroyed his life for? His chest tightened as panic crept in. The problem wasn't that he didn't understand love; the problem was that love made him crazy, it drove him to do things he never meant to do.

But he knew he could be different now that he knew the truth. And he could be different for Vera.

"You're right, but I'm gonna be better," Tennessee was laying his heart out, his voice taking on a desperate edge. "I've been doing a lot of…reflecting. I now see just how wrong I was. I know you can't believe me right now, but I want to try to make it right. And I want to treat you better. Can we please just start over? I think we really have a shot at being something if we just tried again. Please."

"Someone must've really hit you hard, huh?" Vera shook her head with something that looked almost like pity. "In what world would you think you could walk into this bar after all this time asking for a second chance—especially after what you did to me?"

"I'm sorry. Please," Tennessee begged, his hands starting to shake. "Just give me one more chance."

"Get the fuck out my bar." Vera had a blank look on her face.

"Vera, please. Just try to hear what I'm saying," he begged, his voice cracking.

"Is there a problem over here?" A deep voice said from the other end of the bar. It was a large, husky man in a construction vest who Tennessee had seen here several times before. "You need us to help you get this guy outta here, Vera?" The guy motioned to the group of three men sitting beside him.

Vera raised an eyebrow and cocked her head toward Tennessee with a look that said *time to go*. The silent communication between them made Tennessee's heart drop. This bar—a place that once felt like a home away from home—now another place where he was an outsider.

"Okay, I'll go," Tennessee said defeatedly as he got up from his seat, his legs feeling weak beneath him. "I just hope you know I meant every word of what I said. I really do love you."

"Don't ever come back here." Vera shook her head.

With those last words, Tennessee left with his head hanging low. All the eyes in the bar watched him as he made his way out the door like a dog with its tail between its legs.

Chapter 35

He found himself moving quickly up a set of stairs, his shoes stomping loudly as he ran at full speed. Each step echoed through the narrow stairwell as he used the handrail to whip himself around the sharp corners of each new flight.

After making it up all five floors, he finally reached the door to Lucy's apartment. "Lucy, baby," Tennessee panted as he pounded on the door with his fist. Dark red droplets splattered against the white paint with each impact—he barely registered that the gashes on his knuckles started bleeding again.

"Open up, it's me. I have something to tell you. Please, it's important."

Eventually, he heard some rustling behind the door. Footsteps, maybe some whispers. Tennessee pressed his ear against the wood, straining to make sense of the sounds on the other side.

Then the door cracked open just wide enough to reveal a single eye.

"Lucy, sweetheart! I'm so glad you're home," he said, relief washing over him. But the eye in the small opening wasn't blue—it was dark brown. His smile fell, realizing it wasn't Lucy behind the door. Then fragments of memory and recognition clicked into place. It was the dark-haired guy who'd set up her pedals that night at her show—the one who'd kissed her on stage.

"Can I help you with something, man?" the pedalboard guy said on the other side of the door in an annoyed tone. He kept the door mostly closed, his body blocking the entrance.

"Oh, it's you." Tennessee's jaw tightened. "Well, *man*, you can help me find Lucy. Is she home?"

"Depends." The stranger's voice dropped lower—a pathetic attempt to seem more intimidating. "If you're the psycho ex she told me about, she wants nothing to do with you, bro."

"Yeah, *bro*?" Tennessee said, mocking him. "I'd like to hear that from her."

Who did this asshole think he was? There was no way Lucy was actually into someone so...ordinary. He was clearly a Marina bro—one of those fratty types that Lucy made fun of. He was just so unbelievably cliché and mediocre...

"Look, dude, just get out of here," the man said, his eyes scanning Tennessee's battered face. "Looks like you've already gotten your ass kicked once today. You trying to make it twice?"

Tennessee started to laugh, the sound echoing strangely in his ears. "There's no way she'd be with someone like you. This has to be a dream."

He held up his hands, counting his fingers methodically. "One, two, three, four, five, six..." He paused, blinking hard. "Six fingers. Yeah, okay." He looked around the hallway, squinting in the overhead lights. "And how did I even get here?" The question genuinely puzzled him. "I don't remember how I got here... I don't remember..."

He pulled out his phone, glanced at the time, then put it away and checked it again. The numbers had changed completely.

"Oh, this is definitely a dream," he said with satisfaction. "Which means you're just...what, a projection or something?"

The guy's brows furrowed in confusion. "Dude, what the hell are you—"

Tennessee used his distraction to shove his entire body weight against the door, bursting into the apartment and sending the pedalboard guy back a few feet.

"What the fuck?" the man yelled as he gained back his footing, and he puffed out his chest. He was larger than Tennessee remembered—at least as tall as Tennessee and maybe twenty pounds heavier.

"You can't just barge in here like this." The pedalboard guy took an intimidating step toward him.

Tennessee doubled over with laughter, stepping casually toward the kitchen. "Oh, this is rich. My subconscious really went all out with you." He wiped tears from his eyes. "The whole protective boyfriend thing, the macho-man act—it's like a bad movie."

"What the fuck are you talking about?"

"Look, dream-guy, this has nothing to do with you," Tennessee spoke as if talking to a child. "I have some things I need to fix here so everything can go back to normal. I'll clear up this whole mess, then I'll wake up, you'll disappear, and Lucy and I can get back to our real life. Our life together. Make sense?"

"She was right about you. You've completely lost it." The man blocked Tennessee's path toward the bedroom. "You're not talking to her. You need to leave."

With the man's face just inches from his own, Tennessee could smell cheap body spray and morning breath—details that struck him as oddly vivid.

"Ha!" Tennessee laughed in his face. "That's exactly what someone like you would say. Very convincing, but I see right through it. Don't worry—once I fix things with Lucy, you won't be here anymore."

"She doesn't want to hear it." The man was getting more agitated. "You need to leave. Now. Before I make you leave."

An evil grin twisted across Tennessee's face. "I'm going to talk to her. There's nothing you can do to stop me."

"I can and I will." The man pushed his hand into Tennessee's chest and shoved him, causing him to stumble backward.

"Look, I'm not afraid of you." Tennessee steadied himself quickly. "This isn't your fight. This isn't your dream. Just get out of the way so I can do what I need to do. And that way, no one has to get hurt."

"Try me, bitch," the man said, stepping toward him again. "You're not laying another finger on my girlfriend."

A few more chuckles escaped Tennessee's mouth. "She's my girlfriend, not yours."

"Excuse me?" Lucy said, emerging from the bedroom, her voice sharp and cold. "I most certainly am not."

"Babe," Tennessee's face lit up at the sight of her. "You look amazing, you're all healed."

Her face was restored to its former beauty. Her nose was a slightly different shape, but there was no other evidence of his attack anywhere on her body or face. All her bruises and gashes were gone. She looked as radiant as she always had been, even in her oversized pajamas.

"Say that again, bro," the man puffed his chest out even more. "Say that again and see what fucking happens."

"What are you doing here?" Lucy asked Tennessee, disgust creeping into her voice. "I told you I never wanted to see you again. And now, almost a year later, you're here bleeding all over my floor. You need to go." Her tone was ice-cold.

"A year? It hasn't been that long, has it?" Tennessee quickly brushed this off, remembering that time works differently in dreams. "Well, I just need to tell yo—" He stepped toward her.

"She said, get the fuck out." The man stepped into Tennessee's path, his face once again just inches away from Tennessee's. "She doesn't care what you have to say. She doesn't want to hear it."

Things were escalating quickly, but Tennessee's smile never wavered. He was amused by the show being put on by this dream character. But he knew this was all just noise—obstacles to clear before he could set everything right and wake up back in his old life.

Tennessee knew he didn't have much time here. He needed to act now if he was going to fix things before he woke up. If he was ever going to make it right, he needed to get this guy out of his way so he and Lucy could have a moment alone together.

His fingers traced the familiar outline in his back pocket—the knife was there, waiting to be used. Tennessee pulled it out and flicked it open with a single movement, the blade catching the sunlight streaming through her bay windows.

"Look, I don't want to use this," Tennessee said with an almost apologetic smile. "Like I said, I just wanna talk, apologize, get some things off my chest. Then I'll wake up and it'll be like this whole thing never happened."

Lucy's eyes went wide, looking up to the man next to her. "Emmett, don't go near him," she whispered, backing away toward the bedroom. "You don't know what he's capable of."

"Emmett? That's your name?" Once again, this detail struck him as oddly specific. "Huh. My subconscious really committed to this one." Why would his mind create a name for this guy now?

"Now you're threatening us? You're fucking insane." Emmett's face flushed red as his jaw clenched. Though he was putting on a brave front for Lucy, Tennessee could see the fear creeping into his eyes.

"Oh no, it's not a threat," Tennessee said matter-of-factly, gesturing casually with the pocketknife. "I need you gone, now. As soon as you get out of the way, the sooner Lucy and I can have our conversation, get back together, and then get on with our lives."

"There's no way I'm leaving you alone with her!" Emmett lunged toward him, putting out both arms like he was about to try to grab the knife from Tennessee's hand.

Without hesitation, Tennessee swung the knife in a wide arc, slicing through Emmett's shirt and across his chest. The movement felt automatic, like swatting a fly.

"He just stabbed me! He stabbed me!" Emmett staggered backward, clutching his chest with a look of pure disbelief.

A red stain quickly bloomed through his light blue muscle tank. Blood gushed from the gash and splattered in fat droplets onto the white kitchen tiles. All the color drained from Emmett's face as he grabbed the counter for support, his legs shaking.

Lucy let out a gut-wrenching scream, her hands flying to cover her mouth. "Tenny, how could you?"

"Don't worry," Tennessee said calmly. "It'll all be over soon. You won't even remember this part."

As Tennessee stepped toward him again, Emmett's survival instincts kicked in. Clutching his wound with one hand, he swung wildly at Tennessee with the other, his fist connecting with Tennessee's jaw. Tennessee stumbled but barely seemed to register the blow.

"Stay back!" Emmett gasped, trying to put the kitchen island between them. Blood seeped through his fingers as he pressed them against the cut on his chest. "Lucy, call 911!"

But Tennessee moved with purpose, circling around the island. When Emmett tried to move toward the door, Tennessee caught him and plunged the knife deep into his neck. When he pulled it back out, the silver blade was painted completely red.

Emmett's hands flew to his throat as he crumpled to the floor. A horrible gurgling sound escaped him—he could no longer speak after his vocal cords had been punctured. He began coughing up blood uncontrollably and started to choke as air failed to make it to his lungs.

"This can't be happening! This can't actually be happening!" Lucy started to shout frantically as she ran around the kitchen, seeming to be looking for something.

But Tennessee couldn't give Lucy the attention she deserved or deliver a proper apology with this guy hanging around. He needed to get rid of this obstacle once and for all so he could finally get her alone.

He stepped over Emmett, positioning himself with both feet on either side of his body. Emmet stared up at him with wide eyes, blood from his mouth spattered onto Tennessee's jeans.

"No hard feelings," Tennessee said conversationally, crouching down as if they were just having a friendly chat. "I just needed to get her alone for a minute and you were getting in the way. Man to man, you can understand that, right? You won't feel a thing, I promise."

Emmett's eyes became glassy, his life draining away as Tennessee raised the knife over his head. He let out a loud croak which was the closest sound he could make to a scream.

Tennessee drove the blade into Emmett's chest repeatedly, each thrust methodical and purposeful, each blow spreading more blood across Lucy's white kitchen and onto Tennessee's clothes. Emmett coughed up more blood and his groans became more strained each time he was stabbed. Eventually, the noises stopped altogether, and his eyes glazed over. His body fell still, and a pool of blood formed on the floor around him.

"Perfect." Tennessee stood up and wiped his hands on his jeans. "Now that that's taken care of…"

With a smile, he turned to find Lucy. "Now, Lucy, my darling, let's have that chat."

He looked around the room to see that Lucy was nowhere to be found. He could hear her voice somewhere in the apartment, but it sounded muffled and distant.

"Luce?" Tennessee called out, setting the bloody knife down on the kitchen island. "Sorry you had to see that. Let's just talk and I can explain everything."

He followed the sound of her voice, which led him to the bathroom door. Pressing his ear against the wood, he could make out her whispered words.

"Mhm. His name is Alexander Tennessee Walker, but he goes by his middle name." She seemed to be on the phone. "Apartment 505, please hurry," her voice cracked as she cried. She sounded absolutely terrified.

Tennessee jiggled the handle—it was locked. "Lucy, he's fine. None of this is real anyway," he said, knocking on the door. "Just come talk to me, it'll all be okay."

"Oh god, he found me," she whispered. "Please send someone here, quick."

"Come on!" Tennessee pounded on the door harder. "I need to do this before I wake up!"

"Please, Tenny," she begged. "I know somewhere deep down you still care. Just please try to remember that. You don't have to hurt me."

"What?" Her statement angered him. "You got it all wrong, I'm not here to hurt you! I never stopped loving you! I'm here to get you back!"

She fell silent. He could hear a muffled voice speaking to her through the phone.

"Lucy! Just let me in." He shook the door handle even harder.

"Please, just go," she shouted through tears.

"Not until we talk it out," Tennessee said as he rammed his shoulder into the door. "If you won't come out, I'm coming in."

After three or four hard thuds with his shoulder, the door cracked enough for him to fit his arm through the opening and unlock it from the inside. The splintered wood scraped against his skin as he forced his way in.

Once he swung the door open, he found her sitting against the far wall with her knees pulled to her chest, a cell phone pressed to her ear. Tears streamed down both cheeks, remnants of black mascara ran in dark smudges down her face just like it used to when she would cry in the shower. Even with this fearful look in her eyes, he still thought she was the most beautiful girl he'd ever seen.

"Oh my god, he broke the door down," she squeaked into the phone.

She pressed herself harder against the wall as he stepped toward her, trying to make herself disappear. He crouched down so he was at eye level and reached out to caress her cheek with a gentle touch.

"Don't touch me," she growled.

"Like I said, I just wanna talk," Tennessee said with a smile.

"Ma'am, are you still there?" the voice over the phone said. "Officers are now just four minutes out."

"Yes, I'm here," she peeped.

"Lucy, we don't have time for this!" Tennessee's patience was wearing thin. This was all taking too long—he needed to deliver his apology and set things right before he woke up. "I just need to get something off my chest and then we can both wake up from this awful nightmare that has gone on for far too long."

Tennessee ripped the phone from her hand and threw it against the wall, shattering the screen. Before she could react, he grabbed her by the shoulders and pinned her against the wall.

The moment his hands made contact, she began screaming and flailing to get out from under his grasp. "Don't fucking touch me!"

"Lucy, I need you to know that I'm sorry," he began saying, almost like he'd rehearsed it.

She kicked and thrashed, trying to get herself free, but he pressed her down harder with each attempt to escape. His grip tightened, fingers digging into her shoulders. He refused to let go until he said what he needed to say.

"Just listen to me!" He shook her violently, her head snapping back and forth.

"Help! Help!" she screamed at the top of her lungs. "Someone help me!"

Her cries only made him more frantic. He needed her to hear him, to understand that he wasn't there to hurt her. "Please, just let me say this! Then we can go back to how it was. Just you and me, like it's supposed to be."

"No!" she cried. "You're fucking crazy!"

Something snapped inside him. She wasn't listening—she was ruining everything. His hands moved to her throat, pressing her harder against the cold tile wall.

"I'm sorry, okay? I should have never hurt you like I did. You're my world, my everything. And life hasn't been the same without you."

Her eyes bulged as his thumbs found her windpipe. She clawed desperately at his hands, her nails drawing blood from his knuckles

"I love you so much," he continued, his voice breaking with emotion. "I was so stupid to treat you the way I did. I would never want to hurt you." He leaned forward to plant a gentle kiss on her cheek.

"Tenny, please," she gasped. Her bare feet kicked frantically beneath her.

"Let me finish." His thumbs pushed down on her even harder. "You were right—I need to get help. If I don't, I'll become just like...just like my dad, like you said. It's been really hard for me to admit that." Tears began streaming down his face. "But I want you by my side as I get the help I need. I know our love is strong enough to get me through it."

Her struggles were weakening now. "You need...to let me...go," she whispered with her final breath.

"I can't let you go, Lucy," he sobbed, maintaining his grip. "I haven't been able to stop thinking about you. I've been miserable without you."

The color drained from her face and her eyes rolled back, showing only white. Her hands fell limply to her sides. Her body went heavy under his grip.

"Wait, no. Shit," Tennessee said, releasing her. Her head fell forward. "I wasn't done! You need to wake up!"

He grabbed her face, tapping her cheeks frantically. "Come on, Lucy, wake up! This is just a dream, remember?"

Red and blue lights flooded the apartment through the windows, painting the walls in alternating colors. The sounds of sirens grew louder, cutting through his panic.

He closed his eyes tight, pulling her lifeless body against his chest. "Wake up, Tennessee. Wake up!" he commanded himself desperately.

When he opened his eyes, her lips had started to turn blue. He released her, and her body crumpled to the bathroom floor.

Frantically, he began pinching his arms and slapping himself across the face, trying anything to jolt himself awake. "This isn't real. None of this is real. Wake up!"

Tennessee heard multiple pairs of bulky combat boots begin making their way up the stairs of the complex. Deep voices shouted commands as the police breached the apartment.

"We have a body in the kitchen!" one officer called out.

"And a weapon!" another responded.

Tennessee stumbled to the sink, his legs barely supporting him. He splashed cold water on his face and looked up at his reflection in the mirror. The face staring back was no longer his. The cold, dead eyes he'd been avoiding in mirrors. The dangerous capacity for violence. The same monster he'd spent his entire life running from—now there in the reflection.

"The suspect is in the bathroom," one officer said into their radio.

"Wake up, wake up, Tennessee," he whispered to the reflection, water dripping from his chin. "You've got to wake up."

Acknowledgments

They say it takes a village to raise a child. They should say the same for writing books. In the eight years it took me to finish this project, so many people have been a part of this journey that have impacted both me and this story. There isn't enough space in this section to capture just how grateful I am for each of the people listed here.

Thank you to my mom and my sister—to whom this book is dedicated. Since the beginning, you've always believed in me. You told me I could do it, even in moments when I felt utterly defeated by this project. Thank you for holding the vision when my arms were tired.

Thank you to Nicole Arata, who read the very first draft and has been rooting for me ever since. Thank you to Ashley Montoya for being my go-to beta reader and for answering my incessant questions about how to make it better. Thank you to Anthony Uribe for recommending Bird by Bird by Anne Lamott—it helped me get this book over the finish line. Thank you to Alyssa Mendoza for championing me through every small and large accomplishment along the way. Thank you to Rey Silva for being the Samantha to my

Carrie. Thank you to Natalie Deorio and Brandon Molica for the endless positivity and support.

Thank you to Justin for letting me ask you a million questions and for bringing me back to reality when I needed it. Thank you for always being proud of me, even when I had nothing to show for it. Oh, and thanks for taking me to my first metal show.

Thank you to Lindy Mockovak for letting me join you in building our wonderful writing community and making writing feel less lonely. And thank you to all the writing club members who've sat alongside me on this journey as we co-created something great.

Thank you to my former virtual writing group—Libby, Kristina, MJ, Kelly, and Lana—for letting me join you in the early Sunday mornings and for beta reading. Thank you for sharing advice and the magic of self-publishing—this wouldn't be here without you showing me it was possible.

Thank you to Jeff Lyons and Alyssa Matesic for early coaching on the characters and developmental edits that helped me unravel this idea into an actual story.

Thank you to my therapist, Laura Whyte. You've been with me through the harder, personal parts of this process. Because of you I could let go of the shit that didn't matter and choose myself.

Thank you to every additional beta reader who gave me feedback to make this book better: Caitlin Aiello, Tim Ma, Meganne Ward, Mavish Khan, and the likely handful of others I drunkenly shared it with in 2022 but whose names I forgot now.

I'd also like to thank everyone who helped me in the process of getting this book published. Thank you to my editor Halley Sutton, my cover designer Luísa Dias, my book formatter Lebanon Raingam, my audiobook narrator and editor Derek Urichich, and sound designer for the prologue Caleb Hodgson.

And finally, thank you to all those who read this book. Whether you've picked up this copy as an ARC reader, bought your own, are listening to it, or have borrowed it from the library—thank you! Thank you for giving this story a life that lives beyond the confines of my computer. You give my words meaning and I can't wait to see what you do with them.

About the Author

Jess Munday's writing explores the quiet moments that shape us and the complexities of self-perception, with a bit of sparkle for the world around us. Originally from Merced, California, she now lives in San Francisco with her dog, Biscuit. She's a firm believer that a good brunch with the right people can fix almost anything. This is her debut novel.

Connect with her at
jessmunday.substack.com
or follow her on Instagram
@jessmunday_writes

Made in the USA
Monee, IL
14 January 2026